THE BODY'S MEMORY

D1483888

THE BODY'S MEMORY

JEAN STEWART

ST. MARTIN'S PRESS ◆ NEW YORK

The author gratefully acknowledges these publishers for permission to reprint the following:

"Don't It Make My Brown Eyes Blue," composer Richard Leigh. Copyright © 1976, 1977 United Artists Music Co., Inc. All rights assigned to SBK Catalogue Partnership. All rights administered by SBKU Catalog. International copyright secured. Made in U.S.A. All Rights Reserved.

"Let the Good Times Roll," by Leonard Lee. Copyright © 1956 Atlantic Music Corporation. Copyright © renewed 1984 Atlantic Music Corporation. All Rights Reserved.

The poem "Incidental" was first published in *Women's Studies Quarterly* XII:4 (1984).

The poem "Passing" was first published in *The Disability Rag* (May/June 1986).

The author gratefully acknowledges permission to reprint a passage from *Household Words* by Joan Silber, which appears on page 210 of this book. Copyright © 1976, 1980 by Joan Silber. All rights reserved. Reprinted by permission of Viking Penguin, a division of Penguin Books, U.S.A., Inc.

"I Heard It Through the Grapevine," written by Norman Whitfield and Barrett Strong. Copyright © August 1966 by Stone Agate Music. Reprinted by permission of Jobete Music Co., Inc. All rights reserved.

Portions of this work first appeared in slightly different form in *With Wings: An Anthology of Literature By and About Women with Disabilities* (Feminist Press, 1987), and in *The Disability Rag* (September/October 1986).

Design by Glen M. Edelstein

Library of Congress Cataloging-in-Publication Data
Stewart, Jean.
The body's memory / Jean Stewart.
p.   cm.
ISBN 0-312-02875-X (hc)
ISBN 0-312-09253-9 (pbk.)
I. Title.
PS3569.T4648B64   1989
813'.54—dc19   89-4115

First Edition: June 1989
First Paperback Edition: July 1993

10   9   8   7   6   5   4   3   2   1

for Meredith Eisberg (1954–1988),
feisty and rude,
a formidable warrior

ACKNOWLEDGMENTS

I wish to thank my literary agent and friend Frances Goldin for her persistent, noisy faith in me and in the book through long periods of drought and distraction. I also thank my editor George Witte, whose intelligent readership, tolerant spirit, and deft diplomacy were extremely helpful. Gifted free-lance photographer Peter Frey deserves special thanks.

I'm deeply grateful to the MacDowell Colony, the Virginia Center for the Creative Arts, and Vassar College Library for the priceless gift of quiet work space.

A hardy band of readers/critics put in long hours poring through manuscripts and offering incisive commentary combined with generous support: Robert Guter; Rosaire Appel; Mary Johnson; Nancy Mattox; Paul Johnson; and Bob Hershon. Thanks also to Carol Emshwiller, Burt Hatlen, Debbie and Joe LoSurdo, Theresa Brettschneider, John Crawford, Miriam Beerman, Carol Barnette, Marque and Marc Miringoff, and Ruth Levine.

I particularly want to thank my sisters and brothers in the disability rights movement, whose passion has helped me to burn off layer after layer of unexamined, "unlived life." If "courage" is to be found in the pages of this book, it is *their* courage, not mine. Special respect and admiration are reserved for my colleagues/friends in ADAPT (American Disabled for Attendant Programs Today), for the folks at the *Disability Rag*, and for Merry Eisberg, to whom this book is dedicated.

Finally, my deepest thanks to Bob Miller, whose fierce, gentle, separable parts of a whole: voice, and the political/moral passion that informs it.

It is a privilege at last to be able to acknowledge formally two other primary debts. Pianist Konrad Wolff and flutist/orchestral conductor Gerald Quinlan, two great mentors and friends, first gave me music and thereby gave my language song, a pulse. I also thank all the musician and composer friends who've kept my life and work anchored in music, and hauled it back when it strayed.

I'm deeply grateful to the MacDowell Colony and the Virginia Center for the Creative Arts for their priceless gift of uninterrupted work time and quietude. Special thanks to fellow MacDowell Colonist Lynn Rogan. My heartfelt appreciation, too, to the library staff of Vassar College for providing a work environment that became, at times, my second home. Especially impressive were music librarian Sarah Ransom and the reference librarians, whose generous research assistance went well beyond the call of professionalism. Also helpful with research were attorney Mickey Steiman and Dr. Andrew Chernack; cellist Abby Newton; Dave Murray (Dave's Professional Wheelchair Service); Nancy Mattox; and Brent Raven.

Photographer friends Bruce Davidson and Peter Frey deserve special thanks for their graciously given time, energy, and marvelous skills; Tony King and David Blumenkranz were also most generous.

Of my hardy little band of readers/critics who over the years put in thankless hours poring through manuscripts and offering incisive commentary combined with generous support, the following must be mentioned: Robert Guter; Rosaire Appel (special thanks for that ungrateful horse!); Mary Johnson; Nancy Mattox; Paul Johnson; and Bob Hershon. Two informal writers' workshops, brainchildren of Burt Hatlen and Carol Emshwiller, provided valuable dialogue, the latter in fact serving as a forum for readings from the earliest draft of this book. I thank the instigators and members of both groups.

THE BODY'S MEMORY

Life that is unlived, rejected, lost, life that we can die of.

For our sadnesses . . . are the moments when something new has entered us; our feelings grow mute in shy embarrassment, everything in us withdraws, a silence arises, and the new experience, which no one knows, stands in the midst of it all and says nothing.

It seems to me that almost all our sadnesses are moments of tension, which we feel as paralysis because we no longer hear our astonished emotions living. Because we are alone with the unfamiliar presence that has entered us; because everything we trust and are used to is for a moment taken from us; because we stand in the midst of a transition where we cannot remain standing. That is why the sadness passes: the new presence inside us, the presence that has entered our heart, has gone into its innermost chamber and is no longer even there,—is already in our bloodstream. And we don't know what it was. We could easily be made to believe that nothing happened, and yet we have changed, as a house that a guest has entered changes. We can't say who has come, perhaps we will never know . . . [It is] the seemingly uneventful and motionless moment when our future steps into us . . .

So you mustn't be frightened . . . if a sadness rises in front of you and, . . . like light and cloud-shadows, moves over your hands and over everything you do. You must realize that something is happening to you, that life has not forgotten you, that it holds you in its hand and will not let you fall.

—RAINER MARIA RILKE

To be human is to be a conversation.

—MARTIN HEIDEGGER

There comes a time when only anger is love.

—DENISE LEVERTOV

*P*ETER SAYS I SHOULD write everything down.
He says it will save me.

Of course, he was drunk at the time. We were at O'Reilly's, drinking bourbon. Quiet wintry night in Greenwood, Long Island. Empty streets, empty pubs. Old man Hank Williams on the jukebox.

Peter has never seen me crack, so I don't know how he knows what will save me, but I trust his instincts.

As I recall, he tended to be in Europe whenever my life caved in. It seems we're often out of sync; I see him only once every few months. That's how it is with Peter and me: the oldest of friends, we feel no urgency to keep in touch. There'll always be a Peter, I suppose I've told myself for most of the years I've known him. We might as well have twenty years of marriage

3

behind us, we sometimes laugh, shaking our heads at the casual way we take each other for granted.

But he wasn't in Europe when they first discovered this tumor, in 1975. He was right there at my bedside, he came to see me every day. And eighteen months later he was there again, hugging me, crying, telling me there are worse things than having half the muscle in your hip cut out. I'd walk again, it would just take time, that's all.

Peter cries easily. All the blue goes out of his blue-gray eyes.

This time he's not assuring me of any such thing. Crybaby notwithstanding, Peter is a grown-up in his expectations. The best kind of grown-up: one who lets you forget it, doesn't rub your nose in all the dues he's paid along the way. Like my other soul mate, Ellen, Peter is a survivor. And like Ellen, Peter learned as an adult how to do what most adults never learn to do, and kids can't teach them: how to play. Learned it from scratch, each of them, having emerged in one miraculous piece from a childhood that didn't acknowledge play.

But I'm getting ahead of myself. When I called him yesterday to tell him that the tumor had recurred, that I was waiting for a bed at Liberty Memorial, that this time I may lose my hip joint, possibly my leg, he didn't say, Everything will be all right, Kate. He said, "Where are you now?"

I was home, staring across the living room at Sam on the sofa, his pink cat-pads twitching in sleep. *He's dreaming of running away.* I felt as if I were speaking from the bottom of a well. Later Peter told me that it wasn't so much my words as the sound of my voice that had alarmed him. He suggested we go out for a drink; we ended up at O'Reilly's.

I'd forgotten how wonderful is bourbon. I like to fill my cheeks with it and hold it there until the fire forces me to swallow. I try to maneuver it into every crevice—under my tongue, around my gums, on the roof of my mouth. I wish I could bathe

in it, wish bourbon were a man who would lie with me, surround me, fill me up with bourbon fire. Obliterate the world.

I hadn't seen Peter in several months, as usual. Our last get-
together was prompted by his stern upbraiding: "We've got to
get you out of this gimp mentality," he'd said. By that time I
couldn't walk without a cane, and the muscle stress pain in my
leg was constant. Those unlucky friends whom I most trusted
bore the brunt of my despair, I'm afraid. My self-prescribed
antidote that night met with Peter's approval: a trip to Nathan's
Amusement Park, where we rode all the fastest, scariest rides.
Strolling through the penny arcade, we watched the crowds
part before us—me with my cane and Peter with his wooden-
legged limp—like the Red Sea.

Toward the end of the evening I managed to persuade him to
accompany me on the ferris wheel, which he thinks is wimpy.
Our ride nearly over, we were just cresting the top for the last
time when the motor jammed. We spent the next two hours
dancing (well, sort of) in our cart, drinking bourbon from Peter's hip flask, looking out over Long Island toward New York.
We recited poetry: his, mine, Shakespeare's. "'Oh pardon me, thou
bleeding piece of earth,'" Peter bellowed, "'that I was meek and gentle
with these butchers . . .'" And we sang. "'Down on the picket line, . . .'"
we shrieked; "'Kisses sweeter than wine,'" we crooned. The people
in carts on either side of us stared, envious.

Peter looked good last night, looked to be in full focus. (I on
the other hand looked puffy, smeared. Kept staring at myself in
the mirror behind the bar. My eyes were the worst of it: small
and red, like a rabbit's. The bourbon only made them worse.
Everything about me looks spineless and quivering these days.
Hunched shoulders, pale lips.) His hairline seems to have receded another inch or so; he wears what's left in a graying pony
tail. "My fans like it," he says. Fact is, Peter's fans—I'm president of the club—wouldn't mind if he shaved his head and

5

glued flypaper there instead, as he threatens to do every time a mosquito abuses his dome. So long as funky country blues keep on rolling out of Peter's brilliant guitar, he can do no wrong.

Dim light and Hank Williams flattered his features last night; he looked more finely etched than I recalled. I liked the delicate lines at the corners of his eyes. I liked his broad, sturdy back. When he swung down off the stool to check out the jukebox and stood with his back to me, his head bobbing country-western rhythms, I suddenly remembered our first lovemaking, five years ago. It was an oddly experimental phase in our relationship: we became lovers for a month or so until we both decided, quietly and without regret, to drop the experiment. A friendly back, I recall. A decent, honest back. I remember being sprawled under his sweaty kisses, telling him to slow down, when suddenly he sat up and turned that friendly back to me and, sitting on the edge of the bed, took off his wooden legs. To be more comfortable, he said.

Earlier that night he'd repeated the story he'd already told me—though never with such feeling, in such detail—of the limbs he'd been born with, the first ten years of hospitals, one after another decision by his parents to try to change surgically what in those days could not be changed, to give him something to walk on. *Wood,* his doctors had finally concluded, in the middle of one last effort at "corrective" surgery. *He'll never walk on bones.* So they'd cut off his little-boy legs above the knees and gave him wooden ones. His mother agreed to keep paying the tutor who came to the house, because her son refused to go to school. He was too ashamed of the funny-looking feet sticking out of his pants, even though the feet wore shoes that looked like all the other kids' shoes. But all the other kids didn't have great hinged joints protruding through their pants legs whenever they sat down.

Peter, remember that night, why didn't you turn off the light?

Peter returned to his stool, and Crystal Gayle sang out, *"Don't*

6

it make my brown eyes blue," and I looked at his lovely clear gray-blue eyes and thought of them brimming over in the hospital last year. "You look good," I said, and then we sat in silence; I caught his eyes in the mirror and knew he was wishing he could say, So do you.

He said, "You look scared."

He wanted me to talk, of course. He wanted answers to questions he was afraid to ask. So we went over the essential fact: that they obviously hadn't "got it all" last year when they removed my tumor for the second time, even though they thought they were being extra careful. Who knew? I guess they did their best.

Peter hates the pervasive "they." "Who the hell are *they*, anyway!" he exploded last night, wincing. (His stumps must have been chafing. He once told me the chafing is worst when he's agitated.) He calls it "the language of medical crisis," this refusal to refer to doctors by anything but third person plural. "It's *us* and *them*," he snorted at his bourbon. "Though actually, it makes perfect sense."

(There's another language, too, the language of cancer. To *get it all*. To *take out muscle*. And the hideously descriptive term for removal of legs, high up at the hip: *hindquartering*, they call it.)

Peter's frustration is mine: we both want hard medical facts. In this case they don't seem to exist. The doctors don't know how extensive is my tumor; they think it's resting on—but don't know if it's penetrated—bone. Don't know much until they open me up. (To *open up* a patient. To *go in there*.)

In the hospital last year, Peter brought me reams of carefully culled, Xeroxed technical papers on tumors, their causes, types, treatments. I waited until I was discharged and then combed through them, curled on the living room sofa in Peter's New York apartment, where I'd gone to convalesce.

We ordered another round. (Peter ordered a double.) "Here's to Medicine," he said, raising his glass. Finally I spoke the ques-

7

tion that was burning a hole in my brain. Peter had lived without his legs for thirty years; would he go through that *now*, if he had to, knowing what he knows?

He was a child at the time, for chrissake! What did *he* know? They didn't even tell him what they'd done to him for three days, and the phantom pains sure felt like real legs . . . When they spoke of "the decision to amputate," he was so doped up he thought they meant *in the future.*

"You know how I found out? The morphine wore off, that's how, and my head cleared a little, just enough to notice how funny my legs felt, and I reached down. It was a mistake, they thought they'd told me, they didn't realize I'd misunderstood—"

He was shouting. He stopped and looked away, toward the window: snow, big wandering flakes. Silent jukebox, bartender standing very still, his back to us, head bent over a handful of checks as if trying to figure something out.

"At least," Peter added, "you can prepare yourself for whatever happens."

How strange I felt! Even now, a day later, playing back that remarkable conversation, I feel lightheaded, elated, like a child about to step out onto ice so thin she knows it will crack, and all she cares about is getting as far as she can before ice gives way to water. It's true: I can prepare myself.

Fact is, I've already started out across that ice. No stopping now, no turning back.

Once when I was ten, my uncles took my cousin and me ice fishing on Lake Placid. Maggie and I, dawdling, drawing pictures on the snow-covered ice, fell farther and farther behind the men. We were playing tag, ignoring someone's shouted warnings, when I stepped on the edge of a fishing hole and went through. What I remember is diving down to find the bottom, to see what it was like. I didn't even try to stay afloat, I dove down. Maggie of course screamed for help and then hauled me out herself, and within seconds my uncles arrived and carried me back to the house.

I try to visualize that snowsuited little girl diving down through February water toward a bottom too far off for her fierce kicks. How does such a person prepare for the loss of a leg? How do wild things learn domesticity?

"I used to climb mountains," I told Peter, "ride horseback, snowshoe through woods . . . Good thing I've done all that already." It was a sort of token farewell speech to two-legged agility, the only self-indulgence I intend to permit myself. As soon as the words were out I was impatient to call our meeting to order.

So I asked him how to prepare myself.

I must try to record everything he said next. Must memorize the words.

He said, "You don't have to become a docile nitwit just because you're disabled. Look at me. I've sung to people in twelve countries. Alone. No band, no road manager to lug my stuff around for me. I could have ended up in a sheltered workshop. Do you think I've let my style be cramped?"

Hasn't he? Who knows what his style might have been. Anyway, just because Peter (or Ellen) does it doesn't mean it's possible.

"I live," he said, "a pretty freewheeling life—"

But how large are his expectations?

He said I've got to shift priorities, that's all. Think of all the things I've never gotten around to doing because there were always so many distractions and choices. All the reading, the letters to friends—

But won't I feel trapped by these things? As soon as I perceive them as my only options, won't I hate them?

"Do you realize," he said, "how little time people spend *thinking?* It's always easier to hang out with friends. It's easier to *do* things than to think. After a while people forget what it was they

9

would have thought if they'd taken the time, and they end up being afraid of their own minds. You have the chance to be a different sort of person, one who thinks. You're a writer, don't forget. Be glad you're not losing your brain."

Wisdom. He said I have the chance to become wise.

I asked him if he is wise. He said he doesn't claim to be. Not everyone recognizes the choice. His spirit was clipped at an early age; he says it's only now, thirty years later, that he's beginning to understand these things. He's spent most of his life mistaking quantity for quality: women, travel, booze . . .

We were quiet then. As we prepared to leave he said, "Think of it as an exciting new adventure, an opportunity to learn." He seemed to be talking to himself. Turning to face me, one coat sleeve dangling, he said, "Tell you what you do. Write everything down. No matter how bad things get, write everything down.

"You're strong, you know," he said.

We'll see.

February 9, 1978

A PREHOSPITAL JOURNAL, then. To be kept separate from all other writings, from all other parts of my life. This, after all, will be something altogether new, I think.

Blizzarded in, I listen to Clara Haskil playing Scarlatti. Why have I not played this recording for so many years? Faithful companion, there for me when I come back to it; we pick up where we left off. Rippling, lean piano. My room is at last well-ordered, calm and spare. I love its wide brown-painted floorboards. I love the seashells, carefully arranged and rearranged on my bookshelf until they look right.

I've been trying to recapture the contented goldenglow I used to feel inside my snug house during snowstorms. It's not working, I drift into a last-six-days-on-earth mentality, immobilized by terror, though at other times I coast evenly along. Nighttime is the worst, the most assaultive: What will be found when I'm sliced open, how much more of my beloved only body will be carved out this time? And afterward? What will be the quality of my life?

Friends are kind and loving, they try to shelter me. But cancer is, well, cancer. Like its own cells, the word keeps on working, delivering one stunned realization after another at odd, innocent moments.

I lean on the windowsill in my dark room, Scarlatti for company, watching snow in the streetlight. The night air is thick with it, fierce whirling sheets. Soon I'll be watching this from another bed. I'll be alone, looking out the window. I'll be in great pain.

Silence. I lie back under my five blankets. Abruptly quiet and warm, I doze, grazing meadows, running down a beach until, without warning, a team of surgeons enters the room and I become the invisible observer: still body on the table, masks, round overhead light, scalpels cutting muscle, blood, oscillating saw cutting bone.

It seems to me now that all my life has been a training ground, seasoning and tempering me for the Real Thing to come. Now the Real Thing is here, and I feel no readier to face it than a ten year old. I clutch at my friends and let go of them, clutch and let go. They all tell me I'm strong; I listen and nod assent as if they were describing someone else.

Somehow I will salvage this horror, make it work for me, turn it to my favor. Somehow I'll come through, and when it's over I'll be not only whole, but larger.

WAITING FOR A BED AT LIBERTY MEMORIAL

It won't be so bad
a little vacation
I won't have to grade
student papers for a while
I'll get lots of attention
friends will bring gifts
nice tsatskes for my room
cream cheese bagels and *The*
Times not just on Sunday morning but
every single day
I'll read only novels
stories and
Studs Terkel
not one academic
journal and if I have
to use a wheelchair
for a month or so till I'm healed
I'll hitch up the rear end
some fancy pinstriping
mag tires
pair of foam rubber
dice I'll wear black leather
people will want to take
pictures All thanks to
the preppy little whitecoated
man with the Kennedy jaw
who goes sailing a lot
who says my tumor
is back

February 11, 1978

T
HEY'VE CALLED ME. I'm going in tomorrow.
One small suitcase is packed. My classes at the university will be covered by colleagues for a while. Beth and Jeremy, who live down the street, will water the plants and feed Sam. Ellen will drive me to the hospital.

Peter is right. I must get it down. As soon as I'm able, in the hospital. A reason to live through it. What else is there?

Listen, Kate: when you break, examine the pieces. Let nothing go by. Transform the nightmare, make poetry of the dark.

Montale: *"Bring me the sunflower, crazed with the love of light!"*

14

*F*EBRUARY YES. WHAT day is it? Surgery was on a Monday, and this is the start of my third day since surgery, this is Thursday then? Thursday the sixteenth? A high crystalline Demerol-haze morning, sunshine out there I think. I've washed up in the blue basin with strawberry soap, Ellen gave it to me. Wild strawberries in a hospital room. Stronger even than the odd chemical smell of my starched sheets . . . I'm surrounded by plants, jade and Spathiphyllum and Beth's red red rose and daisies and tulips—a greenhouse, they put me in a greenhouse to heal me . . . Music, Dvorak . . . I'm working on my third cup of coffee, coaxed out of the sweet Ecuadorian aide with the purple handwoven vest.

They've cranked up the bed, I'm sitting upright. They did as I asked and put my typewriter on the little wheeling tray table and rolled it in front of me. Heavy limbs. Typing an effort.

Heavy eyelids, coffee notwithstanding. The nurses were startled at my request.

He says it went well. He told my friends that, didn't he, my surgeon? He came into the waiting room and told them all that it went well, and they all hugged, even the ones who don't know each other . . . He told me the same thing, didn't he, yes, looming over my bed out of the gray cotton batting . . . Where did he come from, appearing like that over my bed, what did he say, let's see, that it went well, he said that. He said he felt sure he got it all this time. He said he had not removed as much muscle and bone as he'd thought he might have to. Didn't he say the tumor had appeared to be well contained? Sleepy. Didn't he say he thought I'd still be able to walk? No interference with my motor ability, he said. What is his name. Doctor Dickson.

And my leg is still here, sleepily attached to my body. I can feel it, a sleepy log wrapped in cotton and adhesive, that doesn't feel the hand resting on it. Of course I signed a release that specifically prohibited removal of limbs, so he'd be in big trouble if that log were not nestled here against my body . . . Didn't he say it would be two separate operations—first they'd wake me, let my leg heal a little, and then sometime later they'd chop it off if they had to? Have I made this up? Doctor Earle the second-opinion surgeon said to watch out for these guys; some cancer surgeons, he said, only care about statistics, the knife-happy ones . . . He worried about me, did Doctor Earle. He was my surgeon last year and now he's moved to Maryland and I had to find someone new, because I wanted to be close to home, close to my friends, but I did fly to Maryland for my second opinion. He worried that I might end up one-legged. Unnecessarily one-legged. When I finally found Doctor Dickson they spoke at great length on the phone, and Doctor Earle told me, "I think he's okay, I think you can trust him."

Sleepy. The room they put me in before surgery was a night-

16

mare, a four-bed "semiprivate," three loud TVs blaring three different shows and constant throngs of visitors, the room so thick with them the nurses couldn't get in and out. So they staked me for the extra expense, did my beloved friends, and had me moved to this quiet little "budget" private room. It has a dresser with a mirror, a little stuffed chair, one straight-backed chair, two bedside tables. It is very small, with one very large window.

They hugged each other, my friends. Sleepy. They love me beyond my comprehension.

Late night. Hard to sleep, flat on my back. Can't roll over, can't lie on my side, too painful to move except when I must, to get the bedpan under me.

17

MOONLIGHT VAGUELY LIGHTING her room. End of third day, pain starting to burn off the fog. The pain is a dull steady roar, like a thousand-foot waterfall heard at a distance, like a forest fire, bone-deep, thunderous, at the center of her body. Postsurgical pain: the body wakes, remembers violence. How long is the body's memory? *I look as if I've been run over by a truck.* She has not yet seen the wound itself, only the edges not hidden by bandages. *I am mutilated.* Awful reddish-purple bruises surround the cut, her entire right buttock is yellow and caved in. The wound is a monstrous twelve inches long . . . *How long is the body's memory? If there were no cut, no bruise, no crater where they took out muscle tissue, if all the evidence could be whisked away and the line of her hip restored to its old, sweet curve, would she not still carry that memory in her bones, carry it forever, the act so savage that no amount of anesthesia could have*

prevented her knowledge? A whisper, a rustling in the blood, the informa-
tion leaking into her dreams: knives, snipping of muscle, sawing of
bone . . .

REMEMBERING MARK

The brown eyes of my astronomer
lover (different hospital, last year)
glowed brighter than the brightest star
tracked by his fine-tuned instruments.
The little wrinkles
at the corners—did he look at his stars
like that?
His stars didn't look
back at him as I looked back
at him.
(How did his wife
look back at him?)
At my bed-
side his brown eyes devoured
me. His brown beard
was soft as clouds, when the nurses
were gone he'd bend and kiss me
and my body would fall away
from its wound, away from temperature
and blood pressure and breakfast
tray, would fall into his skyful
of stars. His long hands
were the first that ever found
me, their touch went straight to the nucleus
of every cell.

His hands didn't yet know
I'd been run over by a truck.
When I'd ask him, Mark, do you want
to see it,
he'd say no.

He was afraid, wasn't he.
That I would look mutilated,
unlovely, that he would
recoil, that I would see
him recoil, that I would recoil
from his recoiling. That guilt
and loathing would turn him
from me.
He would not look at it
for a month. When he did he
said, cheerful:
What's so bad about that.

By then the last
bits of scab and stitches
were gone. It was
after all only six inches,
half its present
length.

Demerol, let me not maunder,
remembering Mark.
This poem is full of webs.
Let me drift in and out
of your haze   a drowsy
kitten   Fold me in your arms
as you would a battered
child
Fold me in your arms
as he did
Demerol
sing
to me   fold me
in your arms

21

Saturday

A PARADE OF DOCTORS has been in today, in addition to my surgeon. Doctor Buchheister is young and boringly glamorous in his sweater vests and open-necked shirts. I imagine myself chiding him: *You know, you should wear your hospital coat more often, you might look a little more like a doctor and less like a Greek god.* It would be fun to embarrass him, he's terribly serious and self-important. When he changes the dressing, he thrusts a pillow between my legs to hide my pubic hair, fastidiously discarding the dirty bandages in the wastebasket. An intern, I suppose. He never answers my questions.

Doctor Rabinowitz is next, a large, loud man in his forties. It's his style, he seems unable to help himself. He means well enough but is, all in all, only slightly less ridiculous than Doctor Buchheister. Doctor Rabinowitz breezes in and immediately wisecracks about my typing: "Well well, what do you think you're doing!" (Me: "Being interrupted by you.")

He advances to my bedside and peers at the page in the type-writer. "*Saturday,*" he reads aloud. "A university prof keeping a diary? That's kid stuff!"

In the hospital last year, a doctor walking crisply past my room glanced in my open door, continued on his way, stopped a few feet down the hall, spun about, retraced his steps, and stared at me in disbelief. "I've never seen a patient typing!" he crowed to the entire ward. For one split second I thought he was referring not to me but to some small creature he'd spotted in my room, briskly typing. A mole, perhaps, or a cockroach.

Rabinowitz burdens his voice with such sarcasm that I know he's merely puzzled. "I'm a writer," I say, trying to match his tone, not bothering to add that I'm not yet a professor, I don't have tenure. Finally, forgetting the game of wits, wagging a finger at him: "You know"—pausing for effect—"you're a *very* obnoxious man."

"I'm terribly obnoxious," he says instantly. "I'm awful."

From this moment on he is changed, explaining in his best professional manner why so much pain, why the allergic reaction, and so on. Pushing aside the little bedside table bearing my tape recorder, he examines the wound. When he leaves, the table is left where he pushed it, beyond my reach, littered with dirty bandages.

Enter Doctor Barnwell. The most human, the kindest and most thoughtful of my quartet of doctors, he always listens to my questions or complaints, always answers me directly. A very likeable man, he has a clear, intelligent face. I ask him about the allergic reaction, and he speculates that my skin is reacting ei-ther to the type of tape used in the dressing or to the solution used on the wound, or possibly to a combination of both. He inspects the wound area closely, making no attempt to hide my pubic hair. A man in his middle forties, he is, I suppose,

23

"beyond all that." Perhaps only the youngest, or least experienced, are embarrassed by a female patient's nudity. He ponders, trying to recall what brand of tape had initially been used. "Don't scratch it," he says shortly when I tell him that at night the itching's almost unbearable. He promises a medication that will lessen the itch but will, unfortunately, kind of knock me out, too. I'm being presented with options, and a warning. Admittedly, it's not much of a choice, but I find myself appreciating his implicit respect.

A decent, sensible man, Doctor Barnwell sometimes sits in the blue upholstered chair and talks to me. He is the only doctor assigned to me who gives the impression of ease, with me, with himself.

*H*ER SURGEON, DOCTOR DICKSON, comes by every evening, sometimes in the middle of grand rounds (white hospital coat), sometimes directly from OR (surgical "blues"). Always he looks very tired, prematurely aged, with lines in a face that should not yet have lines. A good face, its tired look arouses Kate. His manner with her remains stiff, although daily another crack or two opens in what started as cold professionalism. She wonders if he too sometimes finds this surgeon-patient business a provocative intimacy. How can he help it, when he sits a few feet from women's beds and looks at them, stretched before him in their nightgowns? Yesterday he walked in as Kate was brushing out her hair and blurted, "Rapunzel, Rapunzel." He even smiled, reluctantly, watching the yellow curls, until Kate pointed out that Rapunzel had long hair. "Picky, picky," he replied.

The day before, he had come in as Peter, seated in the corner, was playing his guitar. Kate had been sprawled in bed, Martha and Ernie (her favorite students) at her side, all three listeners rapt. The intruder, her surgeon had glanced from one to another, not moving from the doorway. Kate had acknowledged his entrance with a nod, turning back to the music. "Finish the song, Peter," she'd commanded. The doctor had kept his silence, his face inscrutable. Later, alone with her, bending over her to change the dressing, he'd said only, "He's a good musician."

Positively expansive behavior, she reflects wryly, recalling his manner a month ago, when first she'd come to him. The examination had been careful and efficient, his answers to her questions abrupt. Yes, there did appear to be a "tissue mass" in the area of the old scar. Yes, this type of tumor has a high recurrence rate and a tendency toward greater aggressiveness with each recurrence. Yes, it appeared to be resting on her pelvic bone and may in fact have penetrated bone, possibly part of the hip joint. No, it should not be referred to as "cancer"; different cell type, he'd said shortly, declining to adopt Doctor Earle's interpretation. "Let's call a spade a spade," he'd hissed when she'd repeated what Doctor Earle had said—that in view of the tumor's obvious aggressiveness it should probably now be regarded as a low-grade sarcoma. Doctor Earle, it would appear, was a foolish man, childishly insisting that a spade was a crane, or a backhoe, when in fact, as Doctor Dickson could have told him from the start, a spade was only a spade.

Privately Kate consulted her internal reality index and decided that this spade was cancer, let them call it what they would. Removal of muscle, bone, hip joint? Cobalt, chemotherapy? Her head was clotted with their words, their promised nightmares. Surely the choice of diagnosis was no more than a semantic exercise when the chamber of horrors outlined for her coincided so precisely with the set of "options" available to "real"

26

cancer patients. Better to have realistic expectations, she told herself, than to suffer later the shock of betrayal, the fall from innocence. Better to adopt the language that would most harshly prepare her for what was to come.

At the same time Kate knew that Doctor Dickson's refusal to call her illness cancer was not the usual doctorly paternalism. She could not envision that spare, well-groomed, hard-voiced man protecting a patient from an ugly truth, could not in fact envision him protecting anyone from anything, so brittle did he seem to her in those days before the theater of their relationship was reduced to a hospital room and her own dramatic role to that of a vulnerable (in his terms) young woman in a red night-gown. Already she knew him well enough to recognize his chilly empiricist's devotion to the integrity of scientific language; to him, cancer was a cell type, whereas Doctor Earle seemed to espouse a more functional approach. In the end, Kate's muddled efforts to define the two camps mattered little, of course; their recommendations were the same.

Kate also knew, with the innate wisdom of the patient, that her decision to regard herself as cancerous must be kept from her doctor. Nothing would have enraged him more than the knowledge that his patient was adopting a set of assumptions not his own—indeed, in conflict with his own. Her illness, after all, was his property; she had consigned not only her body but her knowledge about her body to his despotic care. Nor did she resent his sovereignty; she cared only that he give her full information on which she could base her own amateur, highly charged conclusions. She recognized their naivete and strove to make them as informed as her culturally acquired, mythology-ridden notions of cancer would allow. At the same time, she trusted herself and her conclusions far more than she trusted the Keepers of the Facts, who did not, after all, live in her body.

But full information had seemed, in those presurgical days, difficult to come by. The canny Doctor Dickson had apparently

27

understood that the more hard facts he supplied her, the better equipped she would be to form her own contrary assumptions, based on which she would undoubtedly later judge his work. He'd found her manner quirky and her energetic pursuit of his medical expertise unbecoming. "Why don't you leave the driving to me," he'd rasped once, in answer to her questions about this hip fusion procedure (they always called their cuttings "procedures")—what was it, why did he recommend it, when might he perform it, would she be able to walk afterward? (A hip fusion, she gleaned, was a melding of the bones of the hip joint, rendering the joint permanently frozen. Hip fusions, he'd said, were often prescribed for people who'd had polio or other orthopedic disorders; in the absence of functional muscle, the fused hip provides a built-in support similar to a leg brace.) Kate had flinched at his outburst. Shocked and frightened, she withdrew her questions; he was, after all, the man whose blade would soon cut her open. He must not be antagonized.

Kate is musing on the progress of their relationship, recalling with satisfaction yesterday's fleeting shy smile, when in he walks, wearing his surgical blues. The look on his face is of ineffable weariness; all day long he has stood over a table, cutting and stitching human bodies. His eyes, usually blue, look colorless to her. (*How many bodies?* Most were children, she guesses; he is by reputation one of the finest children's orthopedic surgeons in the country.) Colorless and rather sad. (*Had one of them died?* She would of course have no way of knowing if the last body his hands had touched, before hers, had been dead.)

"How's it going?" He advances to her bed. His hair is a fine

28

silver-brown. His hands are small. She has never seen him laugh.

"No complaints." She smiles. She wants to please him—as she wants always to please everyone—to make him smile, smooth the furrows from his brow. Wants him to like her.

He'd said to her yesterday, awkwardly patting her arm: "You're a good patient." He meant, You're cheerful, you don't make life any harder than it already is. (Or he meant, You keep your place. She decided not to guess what he meant.) It was his highest praise, she knew.

He smiles. (That was easy.) "How's the allergy?"

"Not as bad as yesterday."

He walks around the bed to her right side and examines the edges of the wound. It's a hideous sight; the allergy caused violent red pustules to erupt which bleed when she scratches them. Gently he lifts the dressing, looks under it, removes it. She peers down at her hip. Each time she looks, it is as if she's seeing it for the first time. *This is what you did to me.* She fantasizes a blood-drenched battlefield, littered with bodies. Two soldiers of opposing armies are hunched over the wound one has inflicted on the other. There is no thought of blame, only the imperative: *Help this body to heal.*

Wait. Soon he'll go, Kate, and then you can look at it and weep.

She looks instead at his hands, peeling back the tape. Impeccable. He does not bite his fingernails.

He is her most intimate lover. He's seen her stripped not only of her clothes but of her skin as well, he's handled parts of her that no one else has touched. Kate shivers, staring at his wedding band, at the little hairs, trying to visualize these two rather graceful small hands lifting the flap of her skin—twelve inches!—like a skirt, exposing her as she lay on a table, unconscious, for all the rest to see.

Soft wetness. Blood drained off by suction, no hiding behind that. Her surgeon can see it all: muscle tissue, bone . . . He can see her tumor. Rubber

29

gloves. Heavy, vomit-green, dishwasher-proof—No, no, they wear fine, thin rubber gloves, surgeons do, thin as skin and transparent to their clean hands . . . He can see her tumor, the dark secret nub of it buried in her flesh, beating like a heart, when he touches it, it jiggles like a chunk of gristle packed in jelly, no, it is soft, it oozes, when he touches it, it closes around his fingers and sucks him in. When he touches it, her body explodes, pieces fly about the room, spattering the walls. Isn't it, after all, the moment she has waited for all her life—the sacrificial altar, the touching of her tumor, the cutting-out? Cut it out, sever it, let it float away down rivers of blood, dark beloved tumor, flesh of her flesh, black flowering orchid.

At other times the tumor is not real to her at all; she does not believe in it. The wound, the gouging-out, was arbitrarily inflicted by human hands, man hands. Even the cobalt treatments, weeks later, will have the feel of arbitrary "necessities," the work of men who like her, who touch her body ever so gently, who speak to her with respect.

Ellen—Kate's other best friend, with Peter—reports that Lucy, her five-year-old niece, thinks Kate's tumor is "made up."

Ellen is sitting, as she speaks, in the blue upholstered chair which is tilted back against the wall, her long legs propped up on Kate's bed, hands clasped behind her bushy Afro. Ellen has a way of appropriating space, Kate thinks admiringly; the moment she steps into the room it rearranges itself, becomes *hers*. If she were anyone else, this kind of imperialism-by-personality might pose problems, but she's Ellen, Kate's oldest friend from college days. Fact is, Kate *gives* her the room.

Lucy's met Kate, in fact they've spent considerable time around each other, Ellen having logged a good many hours of child care—much of it in Kate's company—throughout Lucy's short life, while her mother worked. (Lucy's father is dead.)

"Who made it up?" Ellen wanted to know.

Lucy said it was the doctors.

"But why? Why would the doctors do that?"

Lucy shrugged. "Because they *like* her," she said in her another-dumb-grown-up-question tone of voice.

"But," Ellen persisted, "why would doctors make up something like that just because they like her?"

"So they can *operate*," Lucy said, portentously closing off the conversation. She was playing with her favorite doll, whose glassy left eye she had just carefully removed.

"Not the doll *I* gave her!" Kate shrieks as Ellen recounts the dialogue.

They exchange looks. A beat. "She *operated*," they say in unison, and they roar, until a passing nurse tells them to pipe down.

Sunday

THE WOMEN! NOT AN American in the lot: Anne is German, Eleanor's from the north of Scotland, Mamie is Panamanian, Mrs. Condista is Filipino, Melba is Puerto Rican.

Just met Henrietta a while ago: tall coffee-with-cream-colored thirty year old (she told me) with perhaps the most musical speech of them all. Don't yet know where she comes from, as we only spoke for a few minutes while she mopped my floor in her blue housekeeper's dress. She spoke of her fear of getting old and lonely; she's looking for a husband, but all the men she meets at parties—the ones she finds attractive, who seem interested in her—are married, and all the unmarried young men are so arrogant, they seem to care only about themselves, their looks, their clothes.

"You don't have to be lonely just because you're single," I

blurt, the words sounding blithely presumptuous the moment they're out of my mouth. Henrietta looks doubtful; she's about to expound further when another housekeeper in the hall summons her to a meeting.

She's just come back. A fine, big woman, very shapely, full-featured, a cello for a voice. She's from Barbados, been here seven years. She goes back regularly for visits, especially now that her aging father is dying of cancer. She came to the States to find work, says everyone leaves the West Indies these days— even though it's beautiful, there are no jobs.

Mamie says the same thing of Panama. An old-fashioned populist, Mamie runs the gamut in her politics from rank anticommunism ("One chicken per family!" she deplores, shaking her head. She is very dark-skinned and very fat. "No matter you got ten, fifteen people you family, one chicken all you get in Cuba!") to a solid working-class identity, of the rich-get-richer—poor-get-poorer variety. "I love my country," she says, "but the Panama government let everything rot. They promise to give jobs to the poor people but they don't do nothing!" She plumps my pillows ferociously as she speaks.

Sweet Eleanor the Scotswoman—a nurse's aide, I think— wears a funny little Victorian-style cap, a round, flattened, lacy, ribboned thing that reminds me of those old faded dimity curtains preserved from my grandmother's childhood. She speaks fondly of her homeland: "It's still quite primitive up there," she says. "Not like the south of Scotland. There aren't many places left in the world that are still *primitive*," she says.

But Anne the German, diminutive blond Amazon, is the star of the show. This sexy little bully apparently dominates the entire staff, including the doctors, who seem alternately attracted, bemused, and terrified. Her combination of savvy, high energy, and sense of mission add up to a formidable force; I imagine she frequently enrages the doctors with her casual appropriation of their powers, for her medical expertise appears to equal theirs,

33

at least where commonplace problems are concerned, and she does not hesitate to act on her own impulses when she believes the best interests of the patient are at stake. Thus it was Anne who, when the rather offhand and haphazard efforts of my various attending physicians failed to clear up my blazing allergy, took matters into her own hands. She made no attempt to hide her scorn for my ineffectual doctors. Even the kindly Doctor Barnwell had clearly lapsed in judgment, having prescribed a healing ointment which he applied daily, smearing each new layer over the crusted accretion of previous days. Sputtering and clucking, Anne removed the dressing and surveyed the damage. "This is a *mess!*" she exclaimed, shaking her head. She disappeared and returned a moment later with a bottle of acetone, with which she proceeded to douse the mucky battlefield, avoiding of course the wound itself. She was gentle and efficient, and I found myself trusting her instincts implicitly, though I suspect her actions were in flagrant violation of hospital protocol.

When she was done, she stood back and admired her handiwork, tilting her head as if I were a just-completed canvas. It did indeed look miraculously better already; with sunlight pouring in and a delicate breeze from my open window tickling the bedclothes, she decided to leave the wound exposed and let Mother Nature heal the allergy. "It will be all right now," she pronounced, drawing aside my loose hospital gown. She made me promise to let the air get at it as much as possible and then she vanished, my tender, tyrannical little fairy godmother.

Passionately committed to her work, at once driven and seductive, Anne has about her some mysterious quality which she calls her "femininity." She is endowed with great personal power, of the room-transforming sort; like a sunflower in a field of twitching gray weeds, she compels attention, sets the rest of us in motion. Those piercing blue eyes, her primary instrument of power, make the most trivial exchange somehow draining. They are almost impossible to meet.

Not surprisingly, Anne is also vain and egocentric. I catch her indulging in little inward smiles of self-congratulation at her own flamboyant bursts of theater. When not preening herself on her intelligence, competence, good taste, multiplicity of friends, and so on, she is abusing the staff for its stupidity and general lack of culture. "These people!" she spits, head jerking backward. "I have nothing in common with them. They are not curious about the world, they go to work and come home, go to work, come home, they don't read, they don't listen to music. They don't *know* me," she says with satisfaction. "I don't talk about my life with them. I am a *very private person!*"

She stops in the midst of a whirlwind of room-straightening to fix me with her shocking blue eyes. "But *you!*"—her sense of drama is faultless!—"*You* are *different!*" It is her third favorite theme, and she lingers over it fondly: "I can tell by your eyes that you are *wise*, you have *substance, depth. . . .*"

I have not yet caught my breath from this last peculiar veering of her mind when she launches into an impassioned discourse on the subject of Anne: Her Life And Loves, punctuated by much finger-wagging (as in naughty-naughty) and arm-waving. She seems to want to stress her energetic interest in men, and yet she's spending more and more time in my room, performing for me. Her behavior around me is provocative, even flaunting; twice when I was seated in the low blue chair opposite my bed, waiting for her to finish fussing with my linen and pillows, she climbed up onto the bed on all fours, ostensibly to change cassettes—she's mad about Bach—and paused there, her back to me, her short nurse's uniform ridden all the way up around her lovely bottom. She held her pose for whole minutes while chatting about Bach and pondering which tape would suit her present mood.

35

She wears me out, does Anne. I engage in long inward debates as to her real character. Is she nothing more than an exceptionally talented hustler? Does her contempt for the staff direct itself specifically at non-Aryan races? Is she—as one of the housekeeping staff confided in a whisper—"whacko"? Does she have a crush on me? Is it possible that she really is, as she would have me believe, a dedicated and brilliant woman who knows her own worth and is caught in a humdrum job that's clearly beneath her?

Certainly she's entertaining. But nurses are not supposed to wear out their patients.

Sunday night

Anne washed my hair today.

I was talking with Ellen when in she charged, armed with towels and a plastic pan. "I am going to wash your hair," she announced. Ellen's jaw dropped; she'd been interrupted mid-sentence. "Do you have shampoo? Lift your head. Do you want your friend to stay or go?"

Meekly I directed her to the shampoo, lifted my head, and said my friend could stay. Within seconds she had cranked my bed down flat and propped her funny little pan under my neck. Ellen was speechless, intrigued. She watched as I was stripped to the waist and a pitcher was filled with hot water. Before she could open her mouth to offer assistance, she'd been commandeered to refill the pitcher.

When Anne started pouring hot water over my head, lathering my hair, kneading my scalp with her brisk, gentle hands, I nearly swooned. What voluptuous pleasure! I closed my eyes and drifted into silence, garnering sensations, trying to memorize her hands, hair swirling round my face like seaweed, water's caressive warmth. Profoundly deep joy, profound calm, so shocking to my anxious, coiled body that I fairly exploded with rapture, each cell lost in its own primordial memory of floating in soft, warm dark. *Don't stop!* I would have given almost anything for her to continue, but of course she finished, bundled me in towels, and put away her pitcher and pan. The cold room assaulted me. When the two women left me alone I wept, long, shuddering sobs.

It's dusk now, and the room is no warmer. Anne's tender ministrations notwithstanding, I cannot think of a single reason to go on. I can't bear to look at the wound, can't believe I will ever learn to live with it, will ever walk again, make love again. I will not run down the beach, swim, climb mountains. I will always be helpless, dependent on the kindness of friends. I will never lift my leg around my lover's neck again; I will watch him avert his eyes when I undress. I will not push a supermarket cart, plant a garden, cut wood, walk a dog.

I am stained with my own blood. I cannot wash it out.

Tuesday

S NOW. I CAN just make it out through the filthy window screen. My visitors tell me I have a fine view of the Hudson, but I'm rarely erect enough in bed to see it. Am listening to old jazz: Red Norvo, Sidney Bechet, Slam Stewart. The flakes look like bits of window screen breaking loose and falling.

"I wonder if I'll ever build a snowman again," I muse aloud, morosely self-pitying, to Ellen and Lucy. Ellen has smuggled the child into my room in her cello case. Though this ward seems to have no particular age restrictions on visitors, Ellen and her niece both passionately love cloak-and-dagger.

It is a tone of voice Ellen hates. (So do I.) Quick to take her cue, she announces that she and Lucy have been building a snowman on Ellen's front lawn.

38

"It's not really a snow*man*," Lucy corrects. "It's too short for a snow*man*."

The snowman is Lucy's height, Ellen explains. Turning to the five-year-old: "So what is it, if it's not a man?"

"A girl. A snow*girl*."

"Then we'll have to take the Groucho mask off," Ellen says. "Girls don't have moustaches."

"*Snow*girls do," Lucy says.

Ellen—who likes to repeat to her friends her conversations with other friends, as if thereby to introduce them to one another—tells Lucy, by way of explaining my mood: "Kate feels sad sometimes, she feels like there's a big bloodstain where she had her operation and she can't wash it out."

More than once Ellen has been accused by Lucy's mother of forgetting the child's age.

Lucy ponders. She climbs up onto the bed to sit beside me, circles my neck with her arms, studies me. Her small face, dominated by her aunt's large brown eyes, is thoughtful. "You should tell the doctors," she says finally, "to clean it up. *They* made the mess. *They* should clean it up."

I've been telling Ellen about the perverse satisfaction I get from solving petty tactical problems of hospital life: how to water my plants, wash my nightgown, transfer my typewriter from dresser to wheeling tray table—how to do these things without, of course, any help. By now the nurses are so used to my self-sufficiency that they answer my occasional summons on

39

the buzzer with looks of mild surprise. Reminds me of my four years alone in the woods: the stubborn pleasure of needing no one. Silly business when you're paying two hundred a day for all those nurses. A point of honor? To whom am I proving that I can do without?

At least here the test is safe: if I fail, they're ready to step in, fuss over me, chide me for trying to do everything myself. In Maine I could have failed and no one would have found me until the spring thaw. Nor would anyone have looked.

Here is a brief instruction manual for typewriter transfer: (1) Crank tray table down to dresser level. (2) Clear it of assorted litter: toilet paper, breakfast thermos, paper cups, tissues, etc. (3) Position it next to dresser. (4) Unhook trapeze bar overhead and extend to full length. (Usually it's kept hooked high up on itself, well away from my head.) (5) Inch body down toward foot of bed. (6) Grip center of trapeze bar and lean out over floor as far as you can lean, across tray table. (7) Grasping typewriter by rim, drag toward you onto waiting tray table. (8) Crank tray table up to just the right height. You want it to graze your knees when placed in front of you. (9) Roll tray table into position.

I of course sabotage myself by doing everything alone; all that activity causes great pain in the wound. What's more, I am foreshortening my stay here: yesterday my surgeon, hearing of my hikes to the bathroom and examining the nicely healing hip, updated my projected discharge from the middle of next week to this weekend. In an environment that takes such excellent care of me, this is indeed self-sabotage. I am, after all, peaceful (when not in pain) and productive. For the first time in thirty years—no, the second time; I forgot last year's hospital stay—I feel safe. Like an orphan finally adopted, I am awestruck by such nurture, and terrified of being sent home.

They *touch* me, these women! How exotic, how utterly delicious! They wash my hair, they rub my back with lotions. They seem saintly to me in their swift, kindly attentions. Not a drop spills on the bedclothes.

A poignant comment on my childhood, I suppose, that I should be so dazzled by nurture. I have no memory of being touched, ever, by my parents. They were too preoccupied with hating each other to remember that their only daughter should sometimes be touched. Lost in the momentum of that hatred, they settled into the comfortable, deadly familiar nest of connubial routine. Like Cocteau's enfants terribles, they let no light into their world. She sniped, with excellent precision; he muttered, sulked, drank, went out at night. Each morning she counted the empties from the evening before. She was too well-bred to spit.

Here is what puzzles me: I know that other children-turned-adults have known similar hunger, growing up. We may in fact be a majority. Why, then, are most hospital patients so eager for discharge? Is it a reflection of the general standard of hospital care that *anything* else appears better? Is the quality of their out-of-hospital lives actually better than mine? Not likely.

Is it that they associate hospitals with pain? On the contrary, I associate my life outside with pain. Not that I am comfortable here but rather that here I am prepared for pain, expect it, prefer it (almost) to the more diffuse, pervasive, debilitating hurt of daily living in the Real World. The sharpness of physical pain here is bracing, a cold gust of wind in a closet, a held breath finally let out.

Are they frightened by the specter of death all around them? What about the human malaise in New York City faces? That angry, jaw-set hopelessness. At least here there is a name for it; here something is done about it.

Are they simply bored? I am spoiled rotten, yes. My friends, my books, tapes, radio, plants, my writing—an embarrassment of riches.

Could they be lying? Mouthing the appropriate convention, privately yearning to go on being cared for in their clean (or not-so-clean) white rooms forever? Too proud to risk public humiliation by admitting their need?

Is my need grotesque?

Are they enraged by the powerlessness of The Patient? Yes, oh yes! And certainly most are treated less kindly than I by hospital staff. Old women seem especially to elicit hostility; they are rebuked most readily, kept waiting the longest, patronized most cloyingly. They seem the ideal target for overworked staff: old men are less pliant, younger people less resigned. They comprise the "untouchable" caste among patients, and their manner often seems both to reflect and to anticipate the treatment they receive: the querulous voices and petty complaints, pointedly ignored by staff along with more substantive grievances, defeat emanating from them like a slow pulse.

What bourgeois naivete, to wonder why people want to go home! I am, after all, white, middle class, attractive, educated— a Brahman. I'm a private patient in one of the finest hospitals in the country, thanks to the generosity of my friends.

And yet the question lingers. I remember my first hip operation, three years ago, performed in a city hospital where standards were different: six beds to a room, sadistic nurses, patients howling with pain all night long. The Snake Pit, they called it. Even so, I wore my ID bracelet for two months after being sent home.

Wednesday

I TAKE A SECONAL every night. This means that every morning I spend my first few hours in the throes of a sleeping pill hangover that lasts until about eleven. The taste of the pill, naturally varying from pill to pill, is always in my mouth when I wake. Seconal is not as lingeringly bitter as Dalmane.

But then I have a right not to like Dalmane, having swallowed a bottleful five months ago, followed ten hours later by the unforgettable charms of a stomach pump. I sometimes think the flavor of those capsules is permanently grafted to my taste buds. Behind each exquisite spoonful of strawberry ice cream will always be that acrid ghost.

Of course, they don't know about that incident here. They would be aghast. I'm obviously regarded as the Best-Adjusted

43

Patient On The Block. How easy it would be to save up a stash! I've already unintentionally accumulated four, set aside on nights when painkiller seemed to be enough. The nurses never stay to watch me take their offerings.

How pretty all the pills are, grandly presented in their little white fluted paper cups. The shiny green ones especially—vitamins, I think, or are they iron?

Where were we? Sleeping pill hangovers, like this one yes, webby sleepiness in the morning that can't be shaken off until it's run its course. Like a tick that won't let go until it's gorged. Robbing my beloved mornings of their clarity.

I remember a sleeping pill hangover of six years ago, in a cabin in Maine. I'd been taking pills nightly for several weeks. My solitude was stunning, frightening; too many years alone in the woods had begun to unhinge me. I woke that morning to a blizzard, spectacular even to my sleep-clotted eyes. By this stage of winter I was no longer sleeping in the big bedroom; I'd felt small and lost in that bed, and no light got through the single northerly window. I'd moved instead to a little cot on the windowed porch overlooking Bear Pond, where the sun woke me every morning, and after that I never set foot in the bedroom except to collect each day's clothes from my dresser. Woke to this blizzard, glanced at the clock: the mailman must already have made his rounds; it was very late. I rose, unsteadily dressed myself in warm snow gear, and started out toward my mailbox up on the hardtop, half a mile away at the other end of my dirt road. Snow assaulted, pounded me, buried me up to the middle of my thighs. Where was my road? It crossed a field of stubbly baby white pines that had all been swallowed up; nothing now intruded on that great level stretch of white. I tried to remember the road's configuration, but sleep and snow were filling up my brain, and the brilliant white hurt my eyes. With every step the urgency of reaching that mailbox became more pressing: I *must* get there, maybe someone had written to me, someone from Outside.

One foot in front of the other. Wobbled, fell into the soft white depths six times. Hard to get up; it pulled like mud. Suddenly there it was in front of me, the mailbox, and yes, here was a letter from Barbara, my poet friend in Wisconsin. With it was one of her bright little line drawings on matboard, done with felt pens of a thousand colors—reds, oranges, greens that all started running together when the snow touched them, a patch of color so magical in the midst of all that whirling white that my brain leapt, my heart leapt into livingness, my blood started up again. I turned to go back, splendidly alert, and looked at the trail I'd left coming up. It beetled to and fro across the snowfield, aimless, helpless, interrupted by little sprawled clearings where I'd fallen. I could not help laughing, until the tears came.

The Dalmane, five months ago, was not really so unpleasant; only the aftermath was dreadful. The event itself was clean, simple, near complete. I didn't hesitate for a moment; Mark's just-arrived letter went with me to the bathroom, where I fetched my pill bottle, to the kitchen for a paper cup, and on to the dining room to locate my purse. Gathering up the blue flannel blanket, my movements swift and efficient, off I drove to my favorite beach, where I knew no one would find me. The paper cup and pills and letter sang softly to one another inside my purse as I drove, song lyrics made of words spoken by the doctor whose office I'd just left, jumbled together with the words in Mark's letter. The two men seemed to have exchanged identities, each making the other's pronouncement: Mark was saying my leg pain is chronic and untreatable, resulting from massive muscle loss and consequent stress to the leg, and that I should consider having an electronic device implanted subcutaneously which would "interfere with the pain message" but would of course involve certain risks. And the doctor, a physiatrist— what on earth was a *physiatrist?*—was saying that he could not see me anymore, his wife and children came first. Polite crooning came from inside my purse, to the tune of "Happy Birthday." I had just turned thirty.

It was the fifth of September. People were scattered about the sand in little groups, sitting on their blankets. Mostly Greeks frequented this beach; I loved their language, loved that no one knew me and that I did not understand one word of the myriad conversations around me. Each time I went there I lay back, lost in the rhythms and inflections of their speech, in the dark-eyed kids playing at the water's edge, in how tenderly the men played with their children. Lost in the old women in their long black dresses, sitting on folding chairs or flat on their blankets, legs stuck out in front of them like sticks, watching the kids. Lost in the young women, who always sat together; lost watching the men fish with nets. Each family brought music to the beach, Greek radio or tapes. They'd back their cars up to the sand, park, open their trunks, set their radios or tape decks in the open trunks, and along the sand string great lean-tos made of sheets, I guess, attached to one another and to the car trunks with rope. Those lean-tos lined the beach from end to end like a gypsy camp, and always the smell of lamb cooking over charcoal, and the music, and the beautiful men.

Crossing the street to the souvlaki stand (I used a cane in those days), I locked myself in the ladies' room and emptied my bottle of Dalmane, twenty-five capsules in all, downing each with a little tap water from my paper cup. It took a while. About halfway through I paused, glancing in the mirror, a little shocked, I think, but momentum kept me going and I finished

46

them off. Crossing back to the beach, I spread my blue flannel blanket on the sand as near to a large and boisterous family of Greeks as discretion would allow and lay down in the sun.

Drifting. Sky too blue to contain itself, achingly blue, as if about to burst. Long Island Sound stretched at my feet, wrinkled, thick, blue-gray. Small pattering of water on stones, a sweet domestic sound, like Sam lapping milk from his bowl. Kids' laughter rising and falling against percussive radio bouzoukis. I watched two fishermen work their net down the beach. Closing my eyes, I took them with me, gathered them into the intimate arc of my eyelids, hugged myself against their muddy boots.

It was the fishermen who saved me, I'm told. They'd put away their nets and were leaving the dark beach, long after everyone else had gone home. I guess they saw me there, curled on flannel, dreaming of fishermen, of dancing with their children, their wives. One of them picked me up, I guess, carried me to his car and drove me to a hospital, where someone stuck a huge tube down my nose, even though I distinctly heard him tell someone else it was probably too late . . .

Sleeping pills. They dispense them like candy here, and no wonder: it's practically impossible to fall asleep without them. Not that noise prevents it; this private ward is respectfully quiet at night. But there's the room's strangeness, even after ten days; the chemical smell of my crisp sheets; the smell of my body. I wash daily and manage to keep reasonably clean, but my wound is never washed, all the ointments and solutions mingle their own peculiar odors with the smell of dried blood and wounded flesh. Sometimes the room itself smells like one great bleeding wound.

Last year I was awakened throughout the night, every night, by my roommate old Annie, who was a fitful sleeper and had to make frequent trips to the bathroom. A spry seventy-three year

47

old, Annie was nearly defeated by the cancer that had claimed both breasts, her lymph nodes, her adrenal glands. Throughout the first week she was in great pain; those middle-of-the-night journeys from bed to bathroom were terrible ordeals for her, but then so was the effort of lifting her body and maneuvering the bedpan. Early on she decided she'd had enough of bedpans. I'd wake to the soft scuffle of slippers crossing the room, punctuated by the walker's clank. Opening my eyes, I'd watch her slow progress across a pool of moonlight, hunched forward in her shabby housecoat, whimpering under her breath, "Oh dear, oh dear," her voice so pitiful that even in my drugged stupor I wanted to leap from bed and run to her, hold her, stroke the pain away, wanting this with a violence that was dizzying. In those days I could barely move my own body, even to use the bedpan. To me it seemed the ultimate horror, that helplessness in the face of Annie's suffering.

This year my nights are different. Without the diversions of a roommate I tune in to other sleep-intruders. The bed, for instance, which feels like granite. How difficult it is to sleep laid out flat on your back like a corpse. Alien footfalls in the hall, quiet voices down at the nurses' station. And of course the blood pressure and temperature routine in the middle of the night.

Not that I mind this last. The middle-of-the-night nurses are my favorites, those guardian angels of the dark . . .

BLOOD PRESSURE

Light-
footed she appears
at my bedside   in quiet silhouette
her hands are never cold
lifts my thin sleepy arm
wraps the heavy band
around it   pumps and
pumps until my body roars:
BOOM. BOOM.
my bloodbeat!
the beat of my
life!
how the room
echoes   how
the old building
stirs on its foundation
how every nurse and doctor bows
down at the chorus
of our thousand
separate
beats   BOOM, BOOM, the beat
that oils the wheel-
chair wheels that makes the IV fluids
flow the beat the
rhythm
and the blues

Thursday

[V] ISITORS. TO BE hospitalized is to sign away your claim to private life and become a public figure, on call twenty-four hours a day. Dropping in is the official modus operandi. Doctors, nurses, aides, housekeepers, dieticians, social workers, and technicians all breeze in and out freely, day or night; friends and relatives are granted license to walk into your "home" without knocking, any time from noon to eight. Feels like living on a cloverleaf of the Long Island Expressway.

Most visitors call before coming, as I've requested. I try to stagger them so as not to be bombarded by eight at once. But it happens anyway; friends who plan to get here at two arrive at three and stay till five, sharing the room with students who arrive at four and the occasional drop-in colleague. There are only two chairs, so some people stand or perch upon my dresser or bed. They all look at me expectantly, as if I am about to perform magic. As if, by getting better, I could make their own lives right. Newcomers always seem slightly awed by the paraphernalia of illness, crowding excitedly into the room and stealing furtive, discreet looks. Only their children stare, openmouthed, though the adults probably would like to.

They want answers. They—my students Martha and Ernie especially—cannot understand how such a one as I could be "struck down." They look so frightened, the word "cancer" a paralyzed two syllables on their tongues. I try to comfort them, set them at ease, pass their cookies, cakes, candies. And we talk. Some of it is book and movie talk, gossip—but there's a difference here, a nakedness. We seem stripped of our traditional roles with one another; old power struggles and grievances fall away, we find ourselves on new ground.

How else to account for my having called Mark a few days ago? His secretary took the message and he called me back that evening when he was alone in the lab. We talked quietly for half an hour maybe, and the next evening he came to see me. He was shocked, as I'd expected, at the news of this last operation; he had not heard. (Of course he hadn't heard. Our paths have no occasion to cross anymore, not since he drew himself back into his own world of wife, kids, and a few billion stars.) I likewise had not heard of his coveted promotion to head researcher at the lab; nor was I aware of his daughter's graduation from high school or of his wife's recent (minor) auto accident. So we caught up on each other's lives, our conversation subdued; he sat in a chair close by my left side, exactly where he used to sit last year.

(The room was different, though, a double. Old Annie would watch us eagerly, pretending to sleep. She liked Mark and greeted him enthusiastically each time he came to visit, always offered him a treat from her latest box of cookies, always asked him to adjust her pillows, bring her a glass of water, close her

51

window just a hair. Once she startled him by asking him to empty her bedpan, which he did, gallantly. He concluded to me in whispers that the crone had gone a little soft in the head. I defended her vigorously: "You don't know what it's like to have a full bedpan!"

He brought me a gift the other night, a jigsaw puzzle, small and round, just the size to fit nicely on my little bedside table. One side of the box showed a photo of a butterfly, its wings brilliant orange and black; Mark turned the box over and I found myself staring down at a photo of a fat greenish-gray cocoon dangling from a twig. Clumsy and helpless one moment, mysterious the next, it looked as if it were about to spring free of its cardboard prison and astonish the world with its grace.

I used to call Mark The Emperor Of Hospital Gifts. He never came empty-handed; I suspect he devoted extravagant hours to the selection of each item. Intuitively appropriate in his choices, he brought me, for instance (last year, during the Demerol days), a print to hang on the wall opposite my bed, where I would see its muted, rich colors daily, a portrait of a woman sitting by a window in quiet contemplation, smiling faintly to herself. Two days later he appeared with a seashell, the loveliest I'd ever seen, a Banded Tulip he called it, said he'd picked it up on a Florida beach. I held it in both hands and traced the shiny dark-brown spirals, turning it round and round, amazed by its smooth, cool skin. When no one was looking I slipped my tongue across it, hoping to taste salt.

Should I have felt anger, melancholy, a sense of loss, the other night when Mark came to visit? He sat hunched and forlorn at my bedside, his throat jammed with tenderness, watching me anxiously with his great brown eyes. Perhaps all my anger was gone, having found its own voice in that one sweet, brutal act of rage on the beach. He'd heard about it, of course, months later, from a mutual friend, as I must have intended.

52

Anyway, how could I be saddened at the loss of so pathetic, so hangdog a countenance, stricken as he was with guilt and remorse?

Yes, I'll admit it: there are still bittersweet moments, recalling those first five dreamlike days he spent with me after surgery last year. He'd fast-talked his way into the recovery room and stood at my side, waiting for me to wake. "When you first opened your eyes," he told me later—and told our friends, too; it became his favorite hospital story—"this beatific smile spread across your face. I couldn't believe it; you were obviously in so much pain. What a smile!"

I remember swimming up out of that core of pain, the room spectacularly cold, colder than any cold my body had known, colder than Lake Placid under the ice, teeth rattling together and death, the metal taste of it, still chewing my dreams, swimming up and up until my eyes rested on a vertical form at my side—a man . . . Mark, oh Mark! Here to greet me, bring me back from that place, yes, drawing me up and out with his hot brown eyes. Smile, yes!

He used to try to describe the hours of sitting quietly at my bedside, watching my eyes glaze with painkiller, clear, glaze, hearing my voice sink into sleep mid-sentence. He'd say he felt he was sharing with me some terribly intimate act, more intimate than lovemaking. "I just want to take care of you, protect you!" he burst out once, trying to gather me into his arms. I submitted, saying nothing, groggily resting my head on his chest. He used to say my hospital bed was like an island where I'd been marooned and where he was unable to land. I looked stranded, he said. He'd sit by my side and I would watch yet another crack lay open his heart, his hands lying wretched in his lap.

Mark belonged to that group of friends who steadfastly held to their faith that I'd regain my old agility, though at certain moments I could see flickering across his face the idea of Cripples, slipping into and out of a veiled realm of unimaginable fate. Wheelchairs would present themselves and then roll off into corners where he would not see them. Leg braces, scars. "Don't worry, you'll be running down the beach again before you know it," he'd say.

He stayed for an hour and a half the other night. When he left I was exhausted and fell asleep at once, before the night nurse arrived with my juice.

What is it about this environment that transforms us all, my visitors and me, makes us new to one another? Staring at me, their looks are the look that must have been on my face, holding Mark's puzzle. Thinking: *the winged creature becomes a cocoon.*

Inevitably, I suppose, all their empathy, their pity, wears me out. The combinations of people who end up sharing a visit are sometimes improbable and occasionally disastrous; I find myself attempting to orchestrate their visits as if I were conducting a symphony. Each of my guests is emotionally taxing in one way or another; their connectedness to me is so naked here, so bewildering. *Why do they love me?* And sometimes: *The fools! What do they think I am?*

Only on the rare day when no one comes at all do I realize how much I need their distractions, their gawky smoothing of my bedclothes and watering of my plants. My mother's brownies, apologetically proffered, as if *she* were to blame for my illness. When no one comes to visit and late afternoon stretches into dusk, my heart starts to thicken, desolate. Anxiety sets in: I should be spending the time wisely, I have papers to grade—why on earth did I bring them to the hospital with me!—but it's no use; despair paralyzes my brain.

There are of course a few friends who neither call, visit, nor write. It's been true of each successive hospital stay; by now I can mostly predict who they will be. They're the scared ones, stunned by Cancer, incapable of acting on the simplest supportive impulse in the face of huge fear. Their response is denial, an attempt to insulate themselves from whatever demons have been unleashed by my illness. I wish I could respond to them in kind by denying their neglect. I am as stung by it now as I was three years ago, though I pretend not to care.

Those who've lost husbands, sisters, lovers, to cancer are often the worst. Willa's father died when she was not yet four, of a cancer that started in his knee. He lost his leg to it, including the hip—he was hindquartered!—before it killed him. Willa remembers being in her father's room when he died. Now she cannot speak to me, not even to send messages through friends; those memories of thirty-two years ago are still treacherous waters. I have betrayed her by falling prey to her personal nemesis. And yet she is not only a close colleague at the university but an old friend as well; we've counted on each other for over a decade, through bad marriages and love affairs, breakdowns, suicide attempts. And I will, I know, forgive her silence. I already do.

"Maybe she's busy," Lucy suggests, when I complain to her and Ellen about Willa.

Ellen, often her niece's foil on such occasions, says, "Busy doing what?"

Thoughtful, Lucy changes her tack. "Maybe she doesn't like it here. Maybe she's waiting for *you* to visit *her*."

Quite likely, I think. I explain that it will be impossible for me to visit Willa for at least five days, though perhaps when I get out—

"Why?" Lucy demands. "Why can't we go visit her now? You could hide in Ellen's cello case. Nobody will know."

All three of us exchange giddy looks, and the escape plot is hatched. The remainder of this visit and all of the next one are spent fine-tuning our plan, in hoarse whispers. Will I fit into the cello case? (Of course not.) Will Ellen be able to carry it/me? Can Lucy create a convincing diversion by wandering down the hall and claiming to be lost? No, that's no good, most of the staff already know her, they'd simply lead her back to my room and discover the empty bed all the sooner. A different ploy, then: Lucy will pretend to fall and start crying, while Ellen breezes out of my room and down the hall to the elevator, cello case in tow. Lucy, who will carry a little bag containing my street clothes, will meet Ellen and the cello case in the first floor ladies' room, where I will emerge and change clothes. Both Ellen and Lucy will wear their Groucho masks, just in case. This last prop is Ellen's idea. "You can't be too careful," she says, and Lucy echoes, "Yeah, you can't be too careful!"

(It does not occur to any of us to address how I'll get from the first floor ladies' room out to Ellen's car in the parking lot, or from Ellen's car into Willa's house. It is as if the change into street clothes will change the body inside the clothes.)

The people who know of my years in Maine seem to enjoy painting a dramatic contrast: total self-reliance then—chopping wood, hauling water, and so forth—total helplessness now. Whatever the threads that weave these two epochs together, they form a pattern no one (including me) sees very clearly. Why, people wondered, would anyone cloister herself in log cabins and farmhouses in Maine for four years, under conditions harsh enough to crack the strongest constitution? (Paradoxically, my friends tended to romanticize the harshness. Thoreau, etc.) And how is it possible that that same determined (naive, self-punishing) idealist now lies immobilized in a hospital bed?

Have they anything in common, those bitter years of snow

and this narrow bed? Certainly they're both tests of mettle. Peter would call them adventures. In sour Calvinist moods I sometimes see this powerlessness as a kind of Dantesque atonement for that former, sinfully arrogant presumption that I needed no one, neither family nor friends. That I could do without "God."

The self-pityer says, Why me? Didn't I pay my dues already, up there on the frontier?

The fatalist sees those years in Maine as a kind of preparation for, and prefiguring of, this crisis. Mark told me that one Demerol-clouded evening last year I said to him quite clearly, my voice flat, uninflected, drifting into and out of sleep: "I drank from this cup once before, in Maine. Just a sip. I memorized the taste."

K ATE IS REMEMBERING old Annie. They celebrated her birthday in the hospital last year. Kate's mother was there, and her cousin Maggie, and Annie's son and daughter-in-law and their three kids. Someone sneaked in champagne and gooey cake, and they sang "Happy Birthday" in two-part harmony, and Annie murmured, misty-eyed: "I love music."

Whereupon Kate turned to her mother and said, "She loves music," and her mother beamed. They decided on a few old English rounds, an impromptu birthday gift for Annie.

It was nice, having a roommate. I wonder what happened to old Annie?

After the birthday party Kate's mother began to bring sheet music, enclosed with her customary envelope of clippings. Singer in local choirs and an eager pianist, she always looked happiest, Kate thought, when she was making music. And prettiest, too: her face softened, its perpetual look of betrayal re-

58

placed by something sweet, almost childlike, the brow easing, the lips becoming fuller. Occasionally she would fret that perhaps they were disturbing other patients, but then she'd look relieved when Kate would start up a song. Annie's lusty snoring in the middle of a concert was generally enough to set her fears to rest.

Kate toys with the plastic flexi-straw in her juice glass, coasting back through seven years to the day her father slumped suddenly over his desk at the local newspaper office where he'd worked for a quarter of a century. Dead of his first heart attack. Kate had driven down from her cabin in Maine to the shabby old house in New Jersey to be with her mother. Lip-chewing, restless, she'd washed the ivories on the old upright piano. *Warm, soapy water*, one of her mother's carefully hoarded newspaper clippings had enjoined her. She'd closed the wooden keyboard cover then, but her mother had opened it again. "The keys yellow faster if you cover them," she'd said.

That evening after supper, Kate had stuck a little candle in a cupcake and carried it to the dining room table. "We never celebrated your last birthday," she'd stammered sheepishly, seeing her mother's look. It had been a spontaneous act; she'd wondered at the impulse all evening, surprised and vaguely embarrassed.

There had been flowers everywhere, sent by neighbors and friends. (*Is that what prompted this reverie?*) "Why do people send cut flowers," her mother had said, bitter. "They just die. Why don't people send potted plants."

The straw's accordionlike ribs make a pleasant series of pops when she stretches them out. Kate glances around at her roomful of greenery and flowers. *She's right: the potted plants are best.* It occurs to her that half the plants in her apartment were acquired during her first two operations. Hospital plants, she calls them fondly.

59

There are other mementos, too: the slender ceramic coffee mug with rust-colored curlicues, smuggled out of last year's room. And these gaily pin-striped flexi-straws, which she started buying by the box in 1975, after the first operation. Odd that such an innocuous act as sipping juice through a straw is now indelibly charged with memories of nurture.

Friday

ORNINGS ARE THE best, I guess, sleeping pill hang-over notwithstanding. In the afternoon a kind of ennui sets in, relieved (usually) by visitors. By evening the ennui gives way to anything from plodding anxiety to acute terror.

Not that mornings are pleasant. Nightmares, sleeping pills, stiffness from lying in one position all night, and leg pain all conspire to sabotage my mornings. Often I can barely move when I wake, and sometimes the combination of pills and night-mares gives me terrible headaches.

This morning I woke feeling as if I'd been beaten with a sledgehammer all night long. The hammer was still hard at work pounding a spike into my brain. I dreamed I was driving a huge tractor trailer, one I'd never driven before, didn't know where the brakes were, or headlights, or windshield wipers, couldn't steer it, didn't know where I was. A recurrent hospital theme, with variations. Once I was driving up a nearly vertical hill behind a flatbed truck that carried a load of giant logs, and the logs started sliding off the truck toward my car.

And another: I'm wandering alone through the woods, it's getting dark and I am lost.

I wake from these nighttime plagues and the room settles itself into an almost-welcome sight. Perhaps it's the function of nightmares in a hospital room: they sweeten the awakening, they make one—if not glad for Real Life, at least readier to face it. And why not? This room is so pleasant, filled with plants, books, prints, music, a large window. Gripping the overhead trapeze, I haul myself upright, inch my legs painfully over the edge, and crutch my way to the bathroom, very slowly. Two aspirins and a thorough washing-up later, feeling only marginally better, I make my way back to bed as if returning to the rack, perch on the edge, brush my hair, pin it back out of my eyes, dab a little color on my translucent cheeks, and settle back on the bed which has by now been cranked upright by the morning nurse, at my request.

In walks Melba, the aide, with my breakfast tray. Smiling irresistibly, she sets it on my bedside table and greets me with such animation that in spite of myself I feel my soul rising up out of its morning mire. Drawing the tray over my lap I inspect today's breakfast, ordered two days ago. My yellow menu order card is now tucked beneath the plate, presumably to prove the kitchen staff's efficiency and to head off complaints. Or maybe to identify that which might otherwise be unrecognizable?

"Poached eggs! I never ordered *poached eggs!"* Old Annie crowed one morning last year. The aide calmly pointed to the circled items on her menu order card, which bore her signature. Annie's petulance subsided, but when the aide left I heard her mutter grimly, "That's not *my* circle—I guess I know my own circles! I *hate* poached eggs!"

62

Coffee. Presented in a cheery red plaid thermos that holds two cups, the coffee here is improbably good: strong, hot, flavorful. It works; I start to revive.

On the worst of days, I've found only one relief for these morning blues: music. This morning, listening to a tape of two Irish fiddlers playing jigs, reels, hornpipes, I laughed and laughed, nearly lifted off the bed. All my life I've turned to music to haul me up from the bottom—or, in fits of self-indulgence, to keep me there. There's one Handel oratorio, for instance, that used to be a foolproof miasma-chaser, though I never called on its powers until late afternoon or early evening; it seemed too rich a pastry for mornings.

These days it's lust music rather than Handel: gospel, rhythm and blues, Motown, fifties rock and roll. There's a gospel recording from the thirties that can be counted on to whip me into ecstasy: I weep, I clap my hands and shout and grind my hips. I always dance alone, and my dancing is spectacularly lewd.

Dancing. Will I ever dance again, listening to Dorothy Love Coates?

Lucy, who loves music, is learning to play the piano. Ellen says that one day when Lucy was four she tried to crawl inside her aunt's baby grand while Ellen was playing. (A cellist by profession, Ellen plays the piano mostly for her own pleasure, occasionally accompanying friends in recital.)

"*Get down!*" Ellen roared, lunging, fearful for the instrument. And then more calmly, her intercept having succeeded: "Your body will damp all the strings and then I won't be able to get any music out of them. The strings have to have lots of air around them to *vibrate*, see."

"But—" Lucy protested, her face dark. She'd placed a stool beside the piano as if mounting a horse; now she slumped, cheek against its flank, stroking the sleek curved wood and glaring at Ellen. "Why can't I catch it? I won't hurt anything. I want to make it keep going. It always *stops*," she complained, her voice rising, almost in tears.

"What always stops, honey?"

Lucy climbed down off the stool, tossed her head, stamped her foot. *"Music!"* she shouted.

Ellen, telling the story, bites her lip. "I didn't handle it well," she says slowly, remembering. Suddenly her huge eyes fill with tears and she looks away. "I used to feel like that, when I was her age," she says, talking to herself.

I still do, I'm thinking. I tell her how, when I was eight or nine, I'd stay up late at night, after my parents were both gone—my mother to bed, my father "out"—put Poulenc's "Gloria" on the hi-fi, turn out the lights, and curl up in a battered armchair in the living room. The music created me, I became what I knew it required of me: a sea creature in an underwater world, green and weedy, diaphanous. My people eddied and swelled about me, all of us naked and serene.

Music and black coffee having finally salvaged my soul, and breakfast behind me, I settle in for a solid stretch of work on this journal, or letter writing. (Right now I'm in the middle of a letter to my old friends and political comrades Cora and Ed, who've moved to England.) Shortly before ten I'm interrupted by Mamie, the housekeeper. I crutch out of her way, sitting in the little stuffed chair to watch her leisurely ritual of bed making, floor mopping, tidying. Mamie's Panamanian speech is so like music that whenever she's around I turn off the tape deck and try to engage her in conversation. (Not hard; she loves to talk.) Our casual chat helps soften a situation that fills me with anxious distaste: *I am lounging in an armchair while black folks clean my home.*

By noon both the room and its occupant are clean, doctors' visits are done, and my customary sleeping pill hangover has worn off.

Then my visitors start to arrive.

Ellen comes daily, except when snow prevents, sometimes with Lucy but more often alone. She brings me little offerings: yogurt, an apple, old issues of *Sing Out!* If her visit coincides with lunch, she settles cozily into the stuffed chair with her brown paper bag, and the smell of peanut-butter-and-banana sandwiches fills the room. On days when she's had no time to pack a lunch she picks morsels from my tray. I always order twice as much as I can eat, to provide for Ellen's sturdy appetite.

Each day she reports the latest hospital gossip: what she overheard the nurses saying about all the music that issues from my room (Henrietta loves the fifties rock and roll tape), and how the old man down the hall fell out of bed today just as Ellen was passing his room. He didn't utter a sound, his bones landing so quietly that Ellen had to summon the nurses, who came running and lifted him back into bed, chiding him gently for his silence: "That's what we're here for!"

Ellen likes the nursing staff on this floor almost as much as I do. What started out as a daily, brief exchange of greetings has by now become five minutes of jokes and lively talk. Whenever I hear her coming I turn off the tape deck and listen. "What news from the front!" she hails them, or "How's your cold today?" Or sometimes, "How's Kate?"

To which someone replies, "She's healthier than *I* am!"

For their part, the nurses seem equally taken with her. Make no mistake, Ellen is most impressive. Probably the tallest woman any of them has ever seen, she carries herself with such queenly erectness as to suggest an additional ten inches. Her mobile lips and wide-set, puckish eyes give her a look of irrepressible mirth. A mime as well as a cellist, she supplements her income by teaching classes in theatrical movement.

Last year Ellen kept threatening to sneak her cello into my room for a little concert. She never actually got around to it, my stay having been relatively short; hence her determination to play for me this time around. Two days ago she walked in, armed with cello case (containing not Lucy but the cello), music, and stand, sat down in the corner, and started tuning. I asked if any staff, seeing the bulging case, had ever tried to stop her, and she said no. She said all you have to do is stride in with great authority, as if you were delivering a package. Soon I was listening to a Bach cello suite and praying that no one would drop in, so that I wouldn't have to share her with anyone. Inevitably, greedy prayers notwithstanding, my doorway soon filled with an assortment of awed nurses and aides.

Ellen, thank you for that moment, the women all staring as if at an apparition, you with your long, full skirt and high boots, your bushy, nappy hair wet with snow . . .

In the middle of Ellen's visit today a new doctor stopped by and introduced himself as Doctor Ching, head of radiology. The name was familiar; Doctor Dickson had told me to expect him. He talked to me about cobalt treatments, his accent so thick I could only catch a word or phrase here and there. He seemed to be telling me when the treatments should commence and at what dosage, etc. Apologetically I kept asking him to repeat himself, and he kept politely obliging, to little avail. I tried to ask specific questions about side effects, genetic impact on offspring, and so forth, but he didn't seem to understand me any better than I did him. Finally he left, instructing me pleasantly to "think it over."

How remarkable that a man with such severe limitations in English should be sent to talk to an English-speaking patient about so complicated and serious a matter as cobalt therapy. He seemed kind enough, not the sort of person to inspire verbal abuse, so I saved my invective for Dickson, to whom I planned to readdress my questions. But Dickson has already deferred, on the grounds that radiology is not his field! Ellen, who sat quietly in her corner throughout this bizarre exchange, was both amused and appalled; she says I should insist that someone else be sent from radiology, an English-speaking doctor.

Ching's departure was followed by the arrival of Peter and, close on his heels, Steve Pulaski, who's taken over my Creative Writing and American Novel classes at school. Five minutes later my neighbors Beth and Jeremy stopped by to report that yesterday Sam had to be taken to the vet (constipation: he ate a mouse), but that he's fine now.

Dusk was falling. We sat quietly in the half-light, talking about radiation. All of us being over thirty, we recalled the bomb shelters and air raid drills of the fifties. The theme had variations, based on year and geographical locale: Beth, who grew up in Brooklyn, remembered all the schoolchildren being made to crawl under their desks during drills; Jeremy said his teachers made the kids file into the corridors and sit along the walls with their heads between their knees. Steve, who's forty and grew up in northern New Jersey, recalled that he and his schoolmates had to wear dog tags. It was years before he understood that the purpose of dog tags was to aid in identification of bodies that were mangled beyond recognition. He thought they were shiny and fun, like his monogrammed pencil box.

Radiation makes your hair fall out. Radiation eats up your body. Touch a frog and you get warts. We believed these truths with equally passionate innocence; they were part of our collective generational subconscious. Radiation was linked with the apocalypse; we understood in the marrow of our little bones, though we never said so, that the world had gone mad. I remember ducking my head and freezing, eyes squeezed shut, every time I heard a plane fly low overhead.

And I remember Tommy Corcoran, second-grade class clown who, during one air raid drill, was found on a closet floor curled in fetal position. The teachers could not persuade him to get up, and nothing they did or said could stop his crying. Finally they called his mother; we all sat gaping as she gathered him up in her arms and took him home. She didn't seem to mind that he'd wet his pants and that the pee was getting all over her clothes.

Tommy didn't come back to school for several days. When he did, a man started coming to take him out of class for a while. We all agreed that he was the crazy people's doctor and that Tommy Corcoran had "had a fit." But, though wetting your pants was The Unpardonable Sin, none of us felt much like teasing him.

Cobalt. Another new chapter. An Adventure, Peter would say. A Learning Experience.

Speaking of new chapters, I'm told I may be sent home on Monday. Ellen has offered to put me up in her home until I can graduate from crutches to cane and can manage my apartment stairs again. Beth and Jeremy will keep on feeding Sam and watering my plants, and the university will continue covering my classes until I return.

Feb. 25

20 St. Julian's Court
London SW 27 ORS
England

Dearest Cora and Ed,

Thank you for your good, kind letters. I cherish and draw strength from them, as I know you intended.

I too want to make some sort of statement, as much for my own sake as for yours. Somehow our correspondence has become the vessel for weighty self-revelation on both sides, eh?

I'm in the hospital still, quietly spending my thirteenth day. Today for the first time I made my way outside these four walls and down the hall, one foot in front of the other on my wooden crutches, to the lounge at the end. Stood propped against a Coke machine, pressed my nose on blessedly cold window glass, and looked down at New York City, five stories down. Business as usual: nurse crossing the street, punks on the corner, garbage in the wind. I watched the jivey way the punks moved, laughing, slapping their thighs. Watched a woman and child hurry hand in hand past the punks toward the hospital entrance.

After my hot, deodorized bedsheets, cold glass felt like *life*. Like ice cream in July and then a romp under the garden hose. Like running in and out of the fountains in the park. Like swimming my five-year-old heart out in Barclay Pond, tearing out of the water and across blazing sand to the blanket where my cousin and I were building forts and looking at the lifeguards. Already I could swim out past the ropes, dive down, touch bottom, and come up grinning, clutching handfuls of mud.

I must have stood for fifteen minutes, dangling like a scarecrow on my crutches. Someone's private nurse came into the room behind me; I turned and she looked at me curiously. I asked her to pull a chair over near the window and she nodded and did so, politely, and left without a word. I sat and looked down at the punks. I couldn't take my eyes off them.

Finally the pain in my hip sent me back to my room, even more slowly than before. Collapsing on my bed, drawing the covers over my head, I lay without moving. I'd done too much, I knew. How terribly frightening, to venture out of this room alone. A kind of agoraphobia sets in after so many days of confinement. Of course I'm not supposed to walk unaccompanied till I'm stronger, but I push myself. I must, else this immobility and weakness and pain could go on forever.

But let me give you a medical report. The operation

seems to have gone well, despite some folks' dire fears. The tumor appeared to be still well contained; my surgeon removed what he regards as a minimum of muscle tissue and a piece of my pelvic bone. He's generally optimistic, though as for me I've heard surgeons before him twice make the same claim—that they thought they'd "got it all"—and so have arrived at a healthy, if faithless, wait-and-see attitude. By way of ensuring an end to all these cuttings he recommends cobalt, five weeks of treatments, five days a week, "just to be sure." Treatments are to start some two weeks after discharge from the hospital, which looks like this Monday, if all goes well. I plan to spend the first few weeks at the home of a friend who'll care for me till I can manage the two flights of stairs into my own apartment and can get back to work.

Prognosis, after all that, is said to be very good; obviously, cobalt is supposed to improve my odds. The dosage is what they call "mid-range": 5,000 rads, in case you know anything about radiation. I wish I did; wish I were a little less susceptible to my cold-war-baby mystique surrounding radiation. Having grown up with fallout shelters, air raid drills, the works, I find the idea of a force capable of destroying tissue without being seen or felt an unimaginable horror, in the way that anything of mythic dimension is unimaginable. They assure me that the only likely side effect will be a mild burning, similar to sunburn: peeling skin, etc. They concede that one ovary might get irradiated, but they say I only need one anyway, and if mutations were to occur they wouldn't appear in my children but in my children's children. I didn't ask why. Since I have no immediate prospect of childbearing (who the hell with?), this question concerns me less than many others. (I know that sounds glib, but children seem more and more remote in my life. That could of course change . . .)

The incision is impressive, over a foot long this time (last year it was six inches), rampaging up and down my side. After I developed a pretty savage allergic skin reaction to the tape used in the dressing, they removed all my bandages and swabbed me down, and now I'm periodically doused with cortisone cream. My caretakers want the air to get at it, so whenever I'm alone I draw back the bed-clothes and hospital gown. This has its advantage, I suppose; being forced to look at it in all its naked hideousness, I've grown used to it, almost fond of it. It serves as a kind of badge, a measure of the epic interior voyage I've traveled in the last two months.

Cancer.

That's part of the statement I wanted to make. The word: *cancer*. It's at the center of this little navigation into the heart of darkness. I say it often, *cancer*, though my friends tiptoe around the word. Perhaps if I understood its meaning I'd tiptoe around it, too. In fact, I say it in order to understand it, I say it and listen to its reverberations. I roll it around my mouth like a grape, to taste it, let it burst upon my senses. *Cancer*.

My friends were amazed at how I "took it" that last week before hospitalization. There was nothing to be amazed by, really, I simply didn't comprehend the fact—I mean its full proportions only came to me in flashes, little deadly epiphanies in the middle of the night, when no one was near. Now I can gaze at this messy serpent on my side and understand what has happened, and my understanding is calm, even—is this arrogant?—serene.

And yet I'm terrified. Not of cancer but of leaving this safe, sheltering prison-womb, going out into the world I looked at a while ago from the lounge window. How will I live? What will I say, coming home from The Front, about what I saw and felt here. What I learned.

The rest of the statement is this: I died, Cora, Ed. It was too much, that whole last year. When I finally confirmed, at Christmas, that the tumor was once again spreading through my hip, that this time I might lose my leg to it—I let go. *Okay, you win,* I said, and I died. And now I find myself here, in a peaceful little tomb full of promise, and at last I have faith that out of the pieces will emerge something new. It hasn't happened yet, but I lie here waiting, profoundly calm and patient. At least it wasn't boring, my life; I look forward to the new one with fascination. It will be different. I think it will be good.

My keepers here don't know of my death. With them I maintain the appearance of cheery recovery—as indeed I *am* recovering, in their terms, grandly. We keep up an exchange of festive good humor. Even my daily journal believes me to be a deeply healthy, if temporarily incapacitated, individual of great strength who is fighting the good fight, with periodic interludes of panic, grief, despair. My journal records a good-hearted, "courageous" (ugh) effort at daily functioning, an effort of the will that is, by and large, successful.

Indeed, my very dreams seem uncertain whether I am alive or dead. They're filled with scenes of imminent destruction from which I only sometimes emerge. Nor am I convinced of the possibility of life each time I look at my body, despite its clear evidence of mending. The only persuasive sign of life in me these days is my lust, which sometimes runs away with me. I don't recall being plagued with such devouring sexual appetite in hospitals before. And even this feels more like hopelessness than vitality: *Feel! Take!* my body seems to be saying. *There's nothing left. Take what you can now.* Like looters after a war.

Well. I guess all this doesn't sound much like calm serenity, does it. Believe whichever version you choose, dear friends. I don't quite know which *I* believe; at any given

73

moment, some arbitrary state of mind prevails: faith, faithlessness, grief, serenity, fear, despair. Perhaps the language—what to say to "the folks back home"—will find itself as these things sort themselves out.

Meanwhile, I am miraculously able to talk to you. (I've become a private bird; I unplug my phone for longer and longer stretches each day. My friends must think me a bit dotty by now. Why pay for a phone, etc.) For that I thank you.

Much love,
Kate

Monday night, Feb. 27

L EAVING IS NEVER right, never gives us what we need. No matter how we handle it, we wish we'd done otherwise.

I yearned, this morning, to slip quietly out a back door. But of course there were forms to be signed; the departure must be made official.

Not that I wished to bypass good-byes. On the contrary, I *wanted* them, the closure: Mamie, Henrietta, Eleanor, Melba, Anne the German. Rabinowitz, Barnwell.

But hospital departures aren't like that. Nothing quite *ends* (so how can anything begin?), except that at some point one looks up and finds oneself *outside* the building, not inside. Shouldn't there be a brass band? Or keening, or a procession? A solemn liturgy, attended by every single member of the staff? A party: music, booze. Something, *anything*, to mark the passage.

None of my favorite staff was on shift when I left, and those who were there took it all in stride with the brisk, preoccupied air of professionals who'd seen a thousand others come and go before me, for whom this event had no more significance than the opening of one particular maple bud in spring. (They *all* open, and sooner or later they all drop.)

Dickson did look in on me before my discharge, admonishing Peter—who'd come to drive me to Ellen's place, Ellen being at work—to "take good care of" me. (He seems to think Peter is my lover.) It was the one real leave-taking, and I valued it. Ironically, of them all, Dickson is the only person I'll see again: there'll be about a year of follow-up appointments.

Even the notorious hospital convention of escorting patients out in wheelchairs—a rule having to do with liability insurance, I imagine—seems designed to rob this event of closure: the institution relinquishes its claim only grudgingly, disgorging its charge from the jaws of its equipment into the world at the last possible moment.

I suppose this kind of exit does have one subtle payoff for those of us not consigned to permanence on wheels: any brief sojourn in the chair makes us fervently grateful for its brevity.

Still, one longs to stand up and stride grandly out the door, hugging the women—those beloved handmaidens of healing— one last time: *Good-bye, good-bye . . . Yes, I'll come back and visit, yes, I'll write, we'll be Best Friends, good-bye . . . Remember me.*

Wednesday

*E*LLEN CARES FOR me tirelessly. She seems to anticipate every need and deftly intercepts the asking, minimizing my sense of helpless obligation. Her movements have a graceful, unthinking economy; watching her fly from one activity to another—settling pillows on her couch for my comfort, chopping vegetables at her kitchen counter, stirring soup—I marvel: nothing is wasted, the segues are all so seamless, effortless.

Not that she never makes mistakes. Last night while whipping up a creamy mushroom soup she became engrossed in telling the story of her mother, who died of respiratory failure resulting from multiple sclerosis when Ellen was twelve. She got to the part about her mother's first use of a wheelchair when abruptly she stopped and, wooden spoon in hand, peered into her cast-iron pot.

"What's the matter?" I said.

She'd forgotten to buy mushrooms. By the time we finished eating (she threw in carrots instead), the soup had dried in her hair where she'd clunked herself with the wooden spoon, as punishment. She spent the next half hour in the shower.

No wonder she bears the yoke of nurturer with such clarity about the role: she was born to it. When her mother's illness was diagnosed, Ellen was six. Another six years were taken up with doctors, tests, physiotherapy, wheelchairs, and bogus "cures," while her mother's body slowly wasted away. Her father, alternately a child-batterer and molester, finally left home the year before his wife died, though not before he'd managed to break his eleven-year-old daughter's nose one night when he came into her room and woke her; when she tried to resist, he threw her against the bedpost. Ellen showed me the funny bump on the bridge of her nose. "It gives my face character," she said.

The eldest of three children, she'd learned all the household chores by the time she was ten: she cooked, cleaned, changed her baby sister's diapers, shopped for groceries. She turned the pages of her mother's books and finally, during the last year, read to her mother—Verga, Colette, *Alice in Wonderland*. "Half the time I had no idea what I was reading. . . . But I was a good reader; I read with feeling even when I stumbled over words. My mother would sit there with her eyes closed and her head thrown back—she was a grand woman, an indomitable spirit, my mother—and she'd listen attentively and nod sometimes. . . ." And Ellen the mime rumpled her hair to show her mother's disheveled appearance, lifting her chin proudly, closing her great dark eyes.

She says she used to sleep with her mother, nights when she was afraid to go to her own room. She knew she'd never tell what scared her, and the woman never pressed, welcoming the child into her lonely bed.

For four years after her mother's death, Ellen's father periodically showed up on the doorstep, saying he missed his daughters. Finally an elderly aunt succeeded in having him put away, and a year later word got back that he'd mercifully strung his leather belt over some institutional ceiling water pipe and hanged himself. "I used to wonder if it was one of the belts he used on me," Ellen mused (he sometimes tied her up in bed). At that point the aunt, who had moved into the household to help out as her sister's health worsened, became the official guardian of the children. Together she and Ellen raised the two younger girls.

When Ellen speaks of these things, my hands curl into dizzying fists. A skinny black twelve-year-old tomboy sits before me, hunched in a chair at her mother's side, stumbling through the sensuous prose of Colette, lamplight honing her cheeks, her long, bony fingers turning pages. I want to seize that child, pluck her back from her mother's illness—how selfish is disease!—pluck her from her father's vile hands, pluck his eyes out, bludgeon him with my crutches.

How did she endure? Burnished (when one expects her to be burnt to a cinder) by years of pain, she glints like old gold. She is impossibly, fiercely whole. And it is fatuous and self-indulgent of me to speak of having died and not yet come to life again. Ellen's mother is dead; her father is dead. I am alive.

ELLEN REMEMBERS BEING TWELVE

Ellen remembers being twelve
her father's tongue waggling
between her legs
she remembers her fifteenth year
the bribes and   when all else failed
the chloroform
she remembers being seven
his lap   his huge
hands
Ellen who has cured me of
self-pity   remembers
being twelve

Thursday

*E*VERY MORNING AND night I do my leg exercises. The nighttime round is done in Ellen's company; the morning round is done shortly after my babysitter arrives. (Yes, babysitter: my friends are taking turns while Ellen's at work, until I'm more mobile. They cook my meals and keep my spirits up.)

Not only do the exercises hurt more than anything should be legally permitted to hurt, they're also profoundly distressing. They're my private, twice-daily Armageddon: Good (my "will to survive," I suppose, though at the moment this seems like the tedious invention of a soap opera writer) in mortal combat with Evil. (Ah yes, the Big C.)

Last year a physiotherapist came twice a week to Peter's apartment, where I convalesced until I was strong enough to move back home. His name was Arthur. He sat by the sofa-bed in Peter's living room, and each time I tried to raise my leg he pressed my ankle down—simulating leg weights, he said—all the while rattling on about his wife's 1968 Dodge Coronet and how many junkyards he'd visited to find a new cross member when the old one gave out. Throughout this loopy chatter he never seemed to notice that tears kept springing to my eyes.

This year Doctor Dickson's response to my question about seeing a physiotherapist was, "You already know it all. Now do it!" It's true, I do remember all the exercises. How could I forget such nastily predictable celebrations of pain? I start on my back with straight leg raises, both legs, followed by front knee bends and then by a dreadful little number, each leg tracing a circle in the air. Then onto my belly for more straight leg raises. Last year Mark, watching this particular ordeal, beside himself at the anguish in my face, lay down on Peter's living room rug and tried to do what I was doing. His leg barely moved. Male ego bruised, shocked at the extremity of pain, he railed: "They have you doing exercises even *healthy* people can't do! What do they think you are, an *Amazon?*"

After that I avoided doing exercises in Mark's presence.

The rear leg raises are followed by the cruelest ones of all: side raises. My first attempt, a year ago, was at the request of a hospital physiotherapist who appeared at my bedside and said, blandly conversational: "I want you to lie on your side and raise your right leg in the air." Innocently I obeyed and, turning, raised my leg—that is, my brain executed the split-second, instinctive process of raising a leg. The leg didn't budge. Aghast, I stared at it and tried again, teeth clenched, imagining it gathering itself like a heron for flight. It lay benignly on the bedclothes. Sweating, limp, stunned by the betrayal, I looked at the doctor. I was beaten.

"The muscle that governs that activity was removed," he was

saying helpfully. "Don't worry, we're going to try to get the muscles that are left to compensate."

It was, as they say, a moment of truth, my body's first resounding defeat. It marked the start of a slow process of coming to terms with new limitations, a process that even now seems barely under way. I think I expected sheer will to lift that leg. I had, after all, spent twenty-nine predisability years convinced that my body could do practically anything it wanted. Even the first operation in 1975 didn't slow me down much; in terms of physical well-being I was like a spoiled upper-class kid: *of course I could still raise my leg, because I wanted to.* My old friends Cora and Ed, with whom I did union organizing in Maine, call it "the aristocracy of the fit": that solipsistic, arrogant assumption that nothing could possibly impede my body's perfect sovereignty.

During the year that passed between my second and third operations—a year of steadily diminished mobility and often dazzling pain—I still (and even now) sometimes stumbled on traces of that attitude in myself, dressed up in other clothes. *This is my doing,* I'd mutter darkly. *I've sabotaged my own creative energies, stifled my soul.* (How? By doing what? It was never clear to me, but the guilt was resounding.) *The blockage has taken on physical dimensions; it's concentrating in my hip. If I change my life, get my soul in order, the tumor will disappear and the blockage will be freed.*

What dreck! Intoned by people who sit in pious self-appointed judgment on those of us with cancer. Cancer, it seems, is self-inflicted, a just punishment for the moral crime of "unfulfilled energy" that turns against the body, laying one open to various "poisons." Where is the documentation? And who among us is so purely "fulfilled" as to have the right to cast such a stone?

It's almost parodically bourgeois, isn't it, this looking inside oneself for the source of all ills. One remains the *actor* at all times; the concept of being wrongfully acted upon by a social or political order becomes—what? A smokescreen? An easy excuse for "not taking personal responsibility for one's life"? What about the epidemiological studies that show 70 to 90 percent of all cancers to be environmentally caused? What about nuclear waste? What about the air we breathe, the food we eat, the water we drink, and what about my childhood in one of the most heavily industrialized (per capita) states in the union?

Unfulfilled energy, shit.

Sunday morning

S NOWING OUT, AS hard as in last night's dream, in which I trudged across my snowy field in Maine, head bent, surrounded by white. Today is my sixth full day out of hospital, my twenty-first day in captivity.

Captive. Sabotaged by my own body. I sit here seething, glaring at this pillowy snowfall, caught in the web of my dream, the taste of powerlessness it leaves behind. In Maine I was fighting forces much too great for me: wind, snow, stunning cold, and of course loneliness. It was hopeless and I knew it, but I persisted, doomed and so absorbed in the minutiae of the struggle that I forgot its hopelessness. (Self-reliance, ha.) This time the enemy is me, the crumbling temple of my cancerous body, stitched together like a Raggedy Ann doll.

Today the last bit of scab came off in my soapy washcloth.

The scar is clean now, its lower five inches a fine, straight red line diagonally crossing the top of my thigh and meeting, at its upper end, last year's roiling serpentine scar lined on either side with shiny white stitch knobs. These two paths converge for the next six inches and then the knobs stop, the messiness stops and the fine red line continues for another inch or so to my waist. Its overall shape is a crescent, encompassing a wasteland of sunken buttock, bruised yellowy-brown, the skin appearing stretched and glassy. All the way around the periphery is a wide band of flaked, raw-looking red skin, the remains of my allergic reaction. The wound area itself has begun to swell; today it's a puffy, spongy brown. A hematoma, Dickson calls it. He says he may have to drain it if it doesn't go down.

My sleeping is still difficult, at best. No matter how I sort out my limbs among the bedclothes, nothing feels good for very long, and every time I shift positions I moan softly, and each moan wakes me. Ellen says it's a problem of strategy, a matter of outwitting myself. "We're all babies in our sleep anyhow," she says. "Shouldn't be too hard to outwit a baby."

Sunday night

Speaking of babies, the babysitters come daily. They seem to take pleasure in their role; they want to do *everything* for me. They hustle about Ellen's kitchen like adolescent sweethearts playing house. The ignominy of being babysat does not occur to them. Only Ellen understands that if cancer doesn't get me, cabin fever—this helpless sense of imprisonment—will.

Today my cranky brooding peaked—or bottomed out. "You remind me," Ellen remarked, "of a caged tiger."

"At least a caged tiger can pace," I snarled.

86

"You want to pace?" Exasperated at last, she faced me, hands on hips. "So pace! Here, *I'll* pace for you!" And she stalked to one end of the kitchen and back, forth and back, her expression now poignant—the trapped, innocent beast—now noble, now dark with animal rage, her movements so springy, so tense and muscular and catlike that my initial laughter died on my lips.

She stopped abruptly, sat down on the kitchen stool, selected an apple from the fruit bowl, and bit in, calmly surveying her chastened charge. (Actually I was awed, not chastened.)

"C'mon," she said after a silence, "we're getting out of here before you drive us both to drink."

"But it's blizzarding outside," I protested feebly.

She was already pulling on her boots. "Where's your snowsuit?"

"It's not a *snowsuit*, it's a *coat!*"

"*Coat, shmote.*" She stuck a woolen stocking cap on my head and wrapped a long scarf round my neck. At the same moment we both caught my reflection in the hall mirror, a swaying figure on crutches in a red nightgown, blue muffler, and orange stocking cap with green tassel.

I should have known better than to think she was kidding. Twenty minutes later she had somehow managed to bundle me onto an old-fashioned sled she'd saved from her childhood, the kind with a little wooden back. Down the street she towed me and around the corner to the deli, where she parked me by the door like a baby carriage, with instructions to "wait here." She reappeared toting a brown paper bag, which she handed to me, twinkling. Inspecting its contents, I found two hot bagels dripping with butter and cream cheese.

"Since when do delis serve *hot* bagels? With butter *and* cream cheese? What a goy," I muttered, watching butter ooze out onto my snowsuit.

Ellen giggled, hauling the sled back around the corner and parking it by a fire hydrant. "I told the guy they're for a helpless invalid, and he heated them," she said. Hitching my legs down off the sled, she swung me crosswise, pulled off my mittens and her own, and plopped down beside me. For the next twenty minutes we sat together by the fire hydrant, gobbling bagels and cream cheese, licking our fingers, and cackling over bad jokes, the blizzard swirling around us.

March 9, 1978

20 St. Julian's Court
London SW 27 ORS
England

Dear Cora and Ed,

This letter is intended as a hurried update of last week's progress report on Kate. You must have spent a small fortune on that call! Though I only spoke to you briefly while Kate was getting to the phone, I feel as if I've known you for years. She's very fond of you and mentions you often.

She had a major setback two days ago, about which I'm sure you'll be hearing directly, when she gets over the initial blow. Right now she's in her room; she said she wanted to sleep so I left her alone, but I know she's not sleeping.

I took her to the surgeon for her first follow-up since her discharge from the hospital a week before. Being nosy and a worrier (and pushy, too; my friends call me "Commissar"), I asked if she'd mind my presence during the examination. She of course is too polite to say no, so I was there when the twerp casually informed her that she'd better "get used to the idea of using forearm crutches." Kate looked blank and asked him what he meant, and he described those aluminum crutches with cuffs that encircle the arms. Still she looked blank. She said, "You mean, until I get back the strength in my leg," and he said no, he meant indefinitely.

It was terrible, she looked as if she'd just been thrown off a cliff. He acted as if this news should come as no surprise to her. Since she was too stunned to say much, I butted in, pointing out that we had all heard him tell her, the day after surgery, that the operation had gone well and he didn't think there would be "any interference" with her "motor ability," whatever the hell that meant. He replied that the hip had suffered too much trauma to a relatively small area over the course of three surgeries in as many years, that she'd lost too much muscle to support her body, and that the stress that was bound to result if she attempted to walk without adequate support could cause much more serious problems later on. He didn't try to justify his earlier statement; he seemed to be pretending not to have said it.

I don't frankly know what to make of it. Had he been lying to her in the first place, to keep her spirits up until he felt she was strong enough to take the real news? Kate says he's not the type, and I think I agree. The alternative is that her prognosis has changed in some way. He assures

90

her that she's healing beautifully, although today he had to drain what seemed like quarts of fluid from the wound, which had puffed up like a cantaloupe.

That in itself was ordeal enough, without the news of the crutches. He used one large syringe, and each time he filled a tube he'd detach it and hand it to his nurse, who'd pour the disgusting-looking stuff into a little pan and hand him a clean one, which he'd immediately fill. After a while all four of us lost count, and in the end the nurse had to add up the dirty tubes to figure out how much fluid had been drained off. He'd been kind enough to warn Kate beforehand that "this is not going to feel very good," and sure enough, she lay there on his examining table with tears streaming down her cheeks.

She never just plain *cries*. These huge drops roll out of her eyes and wander down her face. But of course you must already know that. I tell her she should learn to bawl; I even gave her a little demonstration to show how it's done. I'm sure I'd find a good bawl a lot easier to witness.

When most of the fluid was gone he placed his palm in the hollow where the tumor had been and pressed, and there was a squishy, bubbly sound. It was nauseating. Then he trussed her up in an ace bandage so tight she can barely move; he says he wants to prevent the wound from filling up again.

The tight bandage makes it hard for her to get into and out of bed without help, nor can she really sit up. This new limitation, piled on top of her already-minimal mobility, would be enough to do anyone in. Not to mention the pressure on the wound, which is very painful. Dickson says he wants her to get a tight elasticized girdle and wear it for a week, until the danger of another hematoma is past. He says the bandage isn't good enough, soon it's going to start slipping.

All in all it's been pretty awful for her, and I'm afraid she isn't doing very well. Up until Tuesday she seemed terrific, as I told you on the phone. Of course, she's a stubbornly private person, and I'm never quite sure what happens in her head when she's alone in her room. Maybe someday I'll meet you, and we'll talk. I do ask questions, but the picture that emerges is far from complete. Lately she's been crying a lot when I play my cello. (I'm not *that* good. Then again, maybe that's why she cries.) And sometimes I wake to the sounds of nightmares coming from her room, and I go in to her and wake her.

Does it seem strange that *you* might be able to answer *my* questions about Kate, when I'm her oldest friend? The fact is, though we've known each other since college, the relationship didn't actually take flight (second flight, I mean, the first having been our undergraduate time together) until five years ago, preceded by a long stretch of separate lives. The odd truth of it is, though I know a good deal *about* Kate, and though I know the present-day Kate (probably about as well as I know myself, which may not be saying much), I can't really say I know where she comes from.

I'll give you an example. I know that during the four years alone in Maine she was making a living at various odd jobs (waitress, construction worker, etc.), doing a little journalism, and organizing a union. (Isn't that how you-all met, as organizing comrades?) It seems that when the union folded she found herself severely isolated; she went through a gradual decline that eventually culminated in a kind of emotional collapse. I guess she had a couple of good years before the bad ones, but in the end what she mostly seems to identify with Maine are the emotional scars.

When I say I don't know where she comes from, I mean

I don't know *why*: why Maine, why union work, why the depression, etc. Recently I asked her, and she responded, "Why not?" I asked what made her leave Maine, and she said it had become "too dark a place" for her, that she had no longer been "effective." I gather that toward the end she was abusing pills pretty heavily (sleeping pills and Valium); I think she felt that a complete change of scenery might help her get out of that hole. She wanted to start over, just as she'd wanted to start over when she went to Maine in the first place. She's a great believer in new beginnings, our Kate.

I'm sure I'm not telling you anything you don't already know. As for me, I've had to piece it together; some of this is speculation and secondhand information. It was her old pal Peter, for instance, who filled me in on the drug dependency part; I guess he thought I ought to know, since the doctor now has her on a strong pain med and a sleeping pill.

The trouble is (and the reason for all this snooping into Kate's life): she won't say what she needs, partly because she insists on that rather self-righteous lots-of-other-people-have-much-harder-lives routine and partly because she learned early on in life that her needs would not be met, so why risk rejection by expressing them? Which sometimes makes it tough to know how best to be supportive.

In my heart of hearts I think silent sufferers are selfish. It is, after all, a privilege to share in someone else's experience. Be that as it may; we who are Kate's friends take turns guessing what our next move should be. Of our hardy little band, I'd say Peter, who's disabled himself, has proven to be the best guesser. He comes twice a week to help out while I'm at work. Not only is he great fun to have around, but he's super-responsible and he knows Kate better than almost anyone. I've come to lean on him pretty heavily for help in dealing with her; in fact I wish he could move in here for a while, to take some of the load off me, but he has too many commitments in the city. Sometimes it's a scramble for us all, finding aides for the other days.

Or rather, finding the *right* aides. Mark—who's still married and about whom you already know, so I'm not betraying confidences—phones her regularly, but I haven't encouraged him to visit. (Apparently neither has Kate.) Gorgeous he may be, but he's also so morose about her illness, so guilt-ridden, and so confused about what he wants that he doesn't exactly liven up the place when he's around her. In all fairness I should add that he doesn't push himself on her, and anyway she seems as confused as he is. There's no question that he's still absolutely nuts about her and that he's on his very best behavior when he's with her.

If it weren't quite so risky I'd call him and ask for his support right now. Frankly, I think the news of the forearm crutches was devastating—the idea of being a permanent "cripple." That's the word she uses.

I've begun to consider inviting her to stay on here as a member of the family, so to speak, since I can't quite imagine how she'll manage alone anymore. But we'll see. Certainly I'll encourage her to stay until the next ordeals—the cobalt therapy, which is scheduled to start on Monday, and the transition to forearm crutches, which Dickson says could be purchased "any time she's ready"—are out of the way.

Time to start supper. Before I go, let me try to talk about something you mentioned on the phone. If Kate has spoken highly to you of my caretaking abilities, it's only because of the years I spent caring for my mother, who died before I was in my teens of what used to be called a "wasting disease." That was (gag) thirty years ago, and perhaps memory has softened the edges of those years.

Nevertheless, this nursing stint seems infinitely harder, even though Kate's condition, unlike my mother's, is not degenerative.

Maybe it has to do with the difference between children and adults. I don't think I ever really *empathized* with my mother; there were too many years between us, and anyway she was *my mother*. Nor did it ever occur to me in those tender years to question the *justice* of my mother's illness. It seemed a matter of fate, I suppose, and no more arbitrary than any other part of this ill-arranged world.

I guess justice is an archaic notion these days. But I'm an old-fashioned girl.

Hope I meet you the next time you come to the States. We have much to talk about, eh? Thank you for your support, not only of Kate but of me.

Warm good wishes,
Ellen DelGiorno

Bodies.

Endlessly particular. Long, knotted, brittle to the touch. Glossy, seal-brown, draped on the sand like elegant shawls. Oceans of flesh hugely pillowing the bones, pale as white slugs.

Bodies that move through the world on straight, strong stalks of legs. Bodies militarily erect between wheelchair wheels. Bodies that end at the tops of thighs. Bodies in braces, that jerk like rabbits just hit by cars. Bodies that swing across the street on crutches, jaunty as monkeys in trees. Atrophied bodies hung between crutches like laundry on a line.

Blue-veined folds of bodies, calloused feet with corners on the toes. Broad freckled backs, freckled faces, freckled white hands. Long splintery hands. Scabby suppurating sores, snotty noses, oily hair. Bodies crisscrossed with veins, like crazed glass. Crazed bodies that clump their hands in fists and cleave the air, knuckles meeting glass, meeting cheekbones, knuckles smearing tears out of eyes.

Muscles. The muscles in the hands that grip the cliff edge, the toothbrush, the lover's cock. Muscles of one body brushing against the muscles of another body, muscles that cause the body to dance, disco, the twist, muscles twisting, leaping like fish, muscles pressing up beneath their envelopes of skin.

Skin lumpy with pimples, corn-fritter brown, hardening in death. Skin soggy with sweat, slippery with come, skin beneath the eyes limp with tears. Puckered skin around the lips, lips that open, laugh, sing "Cry me a river," sing "There's not a sweet man that's worth the salt of my tears," lips meeting other lips, lips chewed by nervous teeth, teeth biting fingernails, fingernails picking scabs, picking noses, plucking eyebrow hairs.

Embrace the body, vulnerable, motley, run over by that tractor-trailer, age. Stretch marks, shiny tire tracks of years, reliable as tree rings. Tender second chin, amiable companion to the first. Soft wobbly pouch of belly, pouched eyes, forearms, thighs. Feathery hair sliding back across the scalp. Scars: glassy trickles or vast mirrored lakes.

Sweet body, sweetly soiled, imperfectly perfect.

And the heart. That secret, wet, pulpy thing, steadfast or stumbling. Embrace the heart that nearly beat itself to death, waiting for cobalt.

*T*HE FIVE WEEKS of cobalt treatments settle into a fixed
routine: her neighbors Beth and Jeremy pick Kate up
each morning and drive her to the hospital, accompany her to
radiology, wait, drive her home.

Despite her agility on wooden crutches, Kate hates the long
walk to the radiation therapy room, down a corridor lined
with wheelchairs containing propped-up, cobweb-colored little
bodies in hospital gowns. She sees her friends recoil from the
bony gray figures that already stare in an attitude of death.
Chattering, solicitous, she hopes to distract them lest they link
her—as she sometimes links herself, with dreadful resignation—to these spectral comrades. They are conflicted, Beth
and Jeremy, being goodhearted souls; they want to feel compassion, but fear prevents it. Their eyes cloud, revulsion wag-
ing war with its more socially acceptable cousin, pity. The

Art + Environment

If I Die Before I Wake
Being Human

1. What stages does Charlie go through as he stru

2. Why does Jackie want Charlie to stop thinking a

3. How does Jackie change? Why?

4. Why has Charlie's mother avoided talking to hin

5. How has Charlie changed at the end of the vide

latter, it seems to Kate, is fast losing ground. In fact, the farther they progress down the cancer ward, the more her friends' faces seem to harden.

Yes, turn from them! she exults, *embrace the living!* Nastily she averts her face and then, catching herself, smiles guiltily at this one slumped between his wheels like a marionette laid to rest, at that one with the barium-lined white lips. She remembers a magazine story told by an elderly man whose illness had gradually limited his vision and finally blinded him. He described the behavior of his fellow senior citizens who, seeing his dark glasses and red-and-white cane, would brazenly step in front of him at the supermarket checkout line. The old man, whose sight had not yet left him completely, was bewildered and stung; his daughter tried to console him: "Your peers abuse you most because they have the most to fear."

I am one of them, Kate tells herself, knowing her attempts at solidarity to be spurious at best, refusing to succumb to the hateful cruelty of the healthy. Nevertheless she is disturbed: might it not be a necessary form of self-preservation to turn from the sick? Might not alliance signal defeat?

She enters the radiation therapy room with relief. Beth and Jeremy take her coat and seat themselves in the waiting area. They are about to say good-bye but she is already gone, unceremoniously departing into an open room, her crutches soundless on the red carpet. A short woman in a white coat follows her. Clanking machinery, the two women's voices chatting quietly. Then the white-coated woman emerges, alone, calling over her shoulder: "Okay, don't move now, and we're off!" She pulls the door shut, steps into a little control room, and presses a switch. Kate's neighbors stare dumbly as a red light flares above the heavy door bearing the sign: CAUTION HIGH RADIATION AREA.

The woman in the control room is sitting at her switches, watching a small television screen; all patients, Kate has re-

99

ported, are observed during treatment on closed-circuit TV, in case they move. Beth and Jeremy shift their weight uneasily. The woman pours herself a cup of coffee and watches the screen, vastly bored. What if she forgets to turn the machine off! Magazines in their laps, the two stare at the ugly yellow-and-purple sign, conversation stilled, stomachs lurching.

The light goes out. (Ah, timer controlled, Jeremy concludes.) Vanishing into the red-carpeted room, the radiotherapist can be heard greeting Kate as if they have been parted by a very long journey. More clanking sounds, and suddenly Kate appears, moving rather stiffly on her crutches. For a moment she is framed in the lead-lined doorway, smiling at her friends under the now-extinguished red light. Beth registers a flicker of déjà vu, recalling—or does she?—an airport somewhere, meeting Kate as she got off her plane. That remote, private look, abstracted. Beth thought then that in Kate's face she saw, or imagined she saw, a ghost of resistance. As if the pilot had landed the plane against Kate's wishes, as if she would have preferred, if anyone had asked, to stay in flight forever.

The two embrace her. Jeremy sees her search their faces and knows she is observing how drawn they look, how full of doubt.

Each time Kate steps into the treatment room and approaches the enormous gray machine, she sorts through her various cobalt fantasies for the one that will divert her this time. Settling herself on the hard, narrow pallet, watching Kelly lower the plate over her hip, she tries to reconstruct her first cobalt experience. "I must have been waiting for the sound of a motor," she'd written to Cora and Ed. "I heard a click followed by silence and assumed they'd turned the machine on and then, for some reason, turned it off. It was not until a second click followed the long silence, and suddenly the terribly empty room filled with doctors and technicians, that I understood. The radiologist explained: 'When we turn on the machine, a glass vial of cobalt particles clicks into place and immediately starts bombarding you with gamma rays.'"

The second day she was ready for it. She noticed that the sound started as an odd clatter, followed by the click. Then silence, the empty room. She stared into space. *Gamma rays are penetrating my body, destroying my tissues.* The doctors had said that gamma rays are not selective, that the goal of radiation research is to perfect the depth and directional specificity of radioactive isotopes so that a minimum of healthy cells are eliminated in the process of wiping out cancer cells.

Kate saw the gamma rays as hard pellets stabbing her cells, saw the tiny helpless cells recoil, cytoplasm heaving like storm tides. On subsequent days she developed variations: sometimes the gamma rays were invisible spears that impaled her on the pallet; sometimes they burnt her cells to cinders, she watched them curl and hiss and blacken.

The cells of my body are tiny bottles filled with life elixir. Gamma rays are gouging holes in these fragile containers, my fluid is oozing out. Soon the surface of my hip will dampen, then my whole body will be wet and I will wrinkle and shrink like an empty balloon, I will dissolve like a salted slug.

I will not lie still while my life fluid pours out of me.

Resolute, she contrives a scheme: mid-treatment, she will sit bolt upright and peer into the glass vial. This would, she reasons, achieve four ends. (1) She would glimpse, once and for all, what (surely) no human eye has seen: her nemesis, the Dread Cobalt Particles. *Are they blue? Greeny-blue, aquamarine? The color of the Dead Sea, of blue-green dead eyes glinting up from the sea floor.* (2) She would effectively halt treatment, for how could they continue to irradiate a blind madwoman? (3) She would avenge

101

her torturers, who'd lie awake nights, horrified at what they'd done. (4) She would no longer be forced to witness her body's slow death.

The plot elaborates during subsequent treatments. She'll have to move quickly, before Kelly can turn off the machine. Perhaps while she's pouring her coffee . . .

Monday

PETER 'S IN THE kitchen cooking up a storm; Ellen is at night school, teaching people to talk with their bodies and hands. Have I mentioned Ellen's magnificent long-fingered hands? Dark-skinned, more the product of her father's African blood than of her Sicilian mother's, their gestures have a grand, tempestuous sweep. They're never still, leaping into motion as soon as she opens her mouth to speak. Yesterday she was sitting beside me at the kitchen table reciting a recipe when I surprised her by seizing her hands and pinning them in her lap. "Now repeat what you just said." She of course didn't miss a beat: "Mmnff, hnnff," she sputtered, her lips flattened by the invisible gag.

Peter's storm is Japanese tonight. He brought his own wok. Usually I try to help out with supper, cutting vegetables, grat-

103

ing cheese, whatever. Perched atop my cushions in Ellen's kitchen, I answer my babysitters' questions about where the cooking oil is kept and how to turn on the oven, thanking them every few minutes for troubling themselves until, in a fit of impatience, they exile me to my bedroom. Peter banished me tonight before I had a chance to annoy him with my gratitude; he says he'd rather do it himself.

He brought his salsa albums. He says he likes to boogie when he cooks. The sight of Peter boogying to salsa on his wooden legs always thickens my throat with something like joy. What he lacks in grace he makes up for in exuberance. And certainly his hips are not wooden.

Peter's enthusiasm for this babysitting stuff knows no bounds. My disability seems to have unleashed in him a veritable frenzy of caretaking. He's like a ten year old on Mother's Day, desperately trying to do the right thing. Is this the first time he's found himself in the relative position of being the able-bodied member of the party? In the hospital he took great delight in pushing me up and down the halls in a wheelchair, singing "Pardon me boy, is that the Chattanooga choo-choo . . ." When a nurse reprimanded him for all his noise he sulked: "Jeez, you'd think we were in a *library*. . . ."

Ah, here he is making his entrance, bearing his Japanese storm on a tray. He's wearing a bright red handwoven Guatemalan shirt, which looks just fine with his ponytail. Two pairs of chopsticks protrude from the hip pocket of his jeans.

I think he'll play for me later; I requested "There Stands the Glass," and he promised. And I'll try like hell to keep my composure, afraid he'll stop playing for me if all I ever do is cry.

I know better, of course. Peter and his guitar are here to stay.

Saturday, March 25, 1978

[L] IKE AN EARTHQUAKE. Like shock waves rising up out of the center of the earth. Betrayal: nothing known anymore, nothing certain, the earth itself—beloved, trustworthy—rising up beneath the feet, roiling, shattered. One shock after another, the little calm space preceding each almost more deadly than the violent tremors themselves.

I bought my forearm crutches today.

It's now three A.M. I've just finished a letter to Cora and Ed in London. I told them of the crutches, that I may be using them forever, unless medical technology invents a way to give me new muscle. Doctor D. says the day will come. Many years off, of course, but he's confident.

I told Ed and Cora that the crutches are horrible, they drag and clank against me like chains. They fall down every time I try to lean them against a wall. The cuffs hurt me, already one of the hinges has caught the soft flesh of my inner arm and pinched it black and blue.

They are hideous: shiny anodized—what on earth is *anodized*?—aluminum with steel-gray plastic hand grips and cuffs. Plastic and metal. My old crutches were rubber and wood. They looked like young, growing trees, their wood curved like dulcimers. They told me and the world that soon I would be All Better. *Don't worry*, they said, *she's in good hands. We're taking care of her. We're on the side of the living*.

I told Cora and Ed that these new ones smell of death, of permanence. They are like coldly expeditious public institutions—there's no caress in their touch, they set themselves against me from the start. I cannot bear them, can't maneuver with them. They seal my fate.

They taunt me. They're cruel.

The honeymoon is over, I said in my letter. No more pretense of "getting better." I am *not* getting better. My leg exercises hurt terribly, still, they're no easier now than they were when I started. I lie on my back and lift my knee toward my chest; the leg sways drunkenly to and fro.

I did *not* mention in my letter the funny scream I heard coming from my throat, a high-pitched Hollywood scream, how I threw the crutches across the room and started jumping up and down on one leg as hard as I could, my right leg, screaming, *"I'll kill it, I'll finish it off!"* until I gagged and could no longer climb to the top of one breath to launch the next breath, and Ellen and Peter and Beth and Jeremy—for wise Ellen had invited them all to dinner—seized me and held me still, and hauled me over to the couch and circled me and said, "Take a breath," and, "Okay, now take another breath," until my breathing came back, and I slumped against them and looked around me and discovered that Ellen, indefatigable Ellen, had sunk down on the floor, weeping, covering her ears. It was Peter who had taken charge, who made me breathe again.

They called Doctor Dickson and made an appointment, to see if I really did kill the leg.

And now they've hidden my pills. Peter says that for the time being, if I want a painkiller or a sleeping pill I need only ask. He decided to stay the night; he's on the living room couch, fast asleep. I can hear him snoring.

The pain in my right leg is a spectacular bonfire. Peter offered me a Demerol. I said no. I want the pain to burn me alive.

Tomorrow I will find those pills. All of them.

DREAM

Dappled woodlot golden with fall leaves.
The cripples are being punished.
The cripples are being made
to walk on their hands each cripplebody
stretched on an aluminum
frame like a long snowshoe. They hold
themselves horizontal   about two
feet above the ground.
This is very hard They keep stopping
to rest. They're used to it
by now but I'm not I keep
stopping to cry.
The cripples don't notice. They wander
to the end of the dirt road
and back   quietly
musing. A few upright people
among them my two friends
police the cripples.
My friends stand silently
beside me.
When I cry my elbows buckle,
my forehead touches earth.

*K*ATE, WHAT ON EARTH are you doing?"

Kate looks up. Seated on an overturned milk crate in Ellen's suburban garage, she is surrounded by a sea of newspapers. Her expression changes from what looks like guilty, caught-in-the-act embarrassment to confusion.

"Mark!" She winces. "I suppose Ellen told you about my jumping up and down."

Mark doesn't bother to deny it. He stands, hands in jeans pockets, unlit pipe in his mouth, right smack in the late afternoon sun so that Kate has to squint and shade her eyes to see him. She wears baggy overalls and a sweatshirt; a thicket of yellow frizz untidily frames her face. She's lost weight; the bones of her face stand out. Though they've spoken frequently on the phone, Mark has not seen her in two weeks.

"You're in my light."

As he moves around to the other side of the pool of newspapers, she sees that he is wearing the heavy brown handknitted sweater from Norway, her favorite (he knows). She notices how it wraps itself around his dense shoulders and how his jeans hold his long legs. Flustered, she bends over her work.

"What *are* you doing?"

"What does it look like I'm doing?"

"Sanding your crutches."

Kate doesn't look up.

"Were you getting splinters?"

"Very funny. I'm going to paint them," she snaps.

"*Paint* them?" Mark echoes stupidly. He stares, unbelieving. One crutch lies on the newspapers, thoroughly scratched; beside it is an aerosol paint can.

Kate shifts the bad leg. Her composure regained, she ignores him.

He stands watching for a moment, fascinated, then squats in front of her, hoping she'll look up. "I haven't said hello yet," he says, and he leans across the newspapers and kisses her, his usual quick hello kiss, too tender and, as usual, a fraction of a second too long.

She smiles at him in spite of herself.

"So these are the famous forearm crutches." Mark picks up the unscratched one and examines it. His fingers ride over the smooth, shiny aluminum, stop at the little height-adjustment buttons, push one in experimentally, tug at the molded plastic hand grip, play with the cuff hinge. "Ugly buggers, aren't they," he murmurs finally, looking pained.

Kate has been staring at his fingers moving hypnotically over the metal. She shrugs and looks up at him; their eyes lock awkwardly. *She's so strong*, he thinks, looking back at the crutches. *I'm so weak*, she thinks, glancing again at his jeans.

Abruptly he stands and, taking the crutches from her, asks, "Do you mind if I try them?" Without waiting for her reply he

110

starts out across Ellen's driveway, jerkily trying to synchronize
arms and legs.

"You look like a drunken centipede," Kate observes.

Ever since she came home with the crutches, everyone has
wanted to try them, like kids with a new toy. Their lack of
coordination never fails to amaze her. It occurs to her now,
watching Mark, that over the past few years she's become an
expert in the use of crutches, and that her friends' spastic lurching to and fro is nothing more than the healthy body's rejection
of a foreign object. She envies Mark his clumsiness, remembering sourly the colleague at school—he taught Victorian Lit—
who remarked to her last fall, "There's nothing quite so elegant
as a beautiful woman who walks with a cane."

"Yes, it makes a charming adornment." Kate smiled sweetly.

Some nights ago Ellen took her to a party at the home of
friends. Kate curled up in an armchair by the fireplace, watching
the flames, listening to her friends' quiet talk punctuated by
laughter, stroking the black cat that slept on her lap. His glossy
fur pleased her, shining against the red of her long skirt. Someone was always getting up for more wine or coffee. No sooner
would one person return from changing the record on the turn-
table, then someone else would get up to stoke the fire or head
for the bathroom. Watching the choreography of their bodies as
they moved in and out, crossing and recrossing the room, standing and sitting, turning, stooping, straightening, she dropped
her head back on the cushion and caught the thought before it
fled: *At last I act the part of a Cripple. Three years, three operations it took
to tame me.*

It was at that same party that Kate first detected in herself a
new quirk of mind that she regarded as conclusive evidence of
finally having crossed over into the no-man's-land of Cripples.
Once or twice during the evening, looking on as a Healthy
Person got up from a chair to move about the room, she almost
blurted: *Look out! You'll hurt yourself, you forgot your crutches!* The

111

next evening it happened once as she watched someone in a TV drama get out of a car. Later that night when a character in the novel she was reading jumped to answer a knock at his door, Kate actually winced!, oh, the pain of forgetting crutches, as she herself still occasionally forgets, climbing out of bed in the dark room to fetch a glass of water, the stubborn leg reminding her as soon as she takes her first step.

What does it all mean? "A refusal to acknowledge," she writes in her journal, "my differentness? If I am helpless, then everyone else must be, too?" She is aware that she's become profoundly sensitized to other people's bodies. Sometimes she imagines herself inside them, hunkered down, hidden, hoping not to be noticed, contracting their muscles, pumping their blood, obligingly helping their organs and tissues to function . . .

"Are you really going to paint them?" Mark is calling from the driveway.

"Yes." Kate is determined not to explain, to anyone. Useless even to try.

"What color?" He hefts himself into the air as if mounting stilts.

"Green. Give them back!" she shrills, suddenly annoyed.

He stops instantly and returns to her side, his brown hair catching the sun. It's been the first warm, springy day of the year; pale fronds of forsythia lining Ellen's driveway are about to explode in that lemony brilliance that always brings a lump to Kate's throat. One rapturous cardinal split open the morning at six and then kept her company all day long, and now two woodpeckers can be heard drumming on opposite sides of the house, like ritual celebrants.

Spring with Mark two years ago was like no other spring in Kate's memory. Endless walks through the woods, admiring skunk cabbage, skipping stones at the beach—a corny spring. Their first lovemaking happened then, in a dazzling green meadow, sun pouring down on their two bodies that met each

112

other perfectly, perfectly except, Kate recalls, that she had not thought to bring her diaphragm, so he had to restrain himself with her, which probably made it all the more glorious. She remembers with what authority he touched her and how she blazed, burying her face in his chest.

"Why?" Mark is inquiring.

She thinks hard. "I like green," she says vaguely, staring at his chest.

"I mean, why paint the crutches?" he persists.

Kate sneers. "You're afraid I might violate their natural beauty?"

Conceding the point, Mark shrugs and hands her the crutches, deciding not to ask why she thinks it necessary to sand them first.

Contrite, she says, "Do you think the paint will stick?"

He knows her too well to try to stop her. "I don't know, you might try a coat of primer first. . . ." He stands in the sun, just outside the garage, reading the label on the aerosol can.

Something in his stance catches Kate off guard and she blurts, "You're looking more and more like those gangling daughters of yours every day."

He laughs and then, suddenly ardent, squats on the newspapers beside her. "Did I ever tell you," he says, "how much I wanted to have a child with you?"

"Yes." Kate inspects the crutch in her hands, aware that the next-door neighbor's Lhasa apsos have been yapping for several minutes. "Lapsang soochongs," she calls them. She hates dogs that yap. "Damn fool monsters," she mutters, glowering at Mark, who looks startled. "Those dogs," she adds. "Well, kids, too. I hate kids. Good thing we never had any."

Mark perches on the hood of Kate's car and stares at her, perplexed. "What's wrong with kids? I thought you liked—"

"They're crude! They point at me and poke each other and shout at ear-splitting volume, 'Mommy, what's wrong with *her!*'

113

They back off when they see me coming, as if I were some kind of giant insect. Their eyes devour me . . ." She sands her crutch fiercely. "They're uncivilized beasts. I hate them."

Actually, it's not so much that they stare, for adults do that too, though more guiltily. It's their cold, flat, animal curiosity that always brings to her mind Lawrence's description of a bobcat's stare: "conscienceless," he called it.

"That's how they learn," Mark protests. "They learn by doing what's wrong and having patient grown-ups explain the difference . . ."

He speaks with such tenderness that Kate suddenly wants to cry. Mark often makes her feel that way, for some reason. She believes him to be the best of fathers; it's easy to imagine him spending time with his daughters. Sometimes the mere vision of the three of them together is enough to make her throat jam. *Used to be enough*, she corrects herself.

"Kids *are* cruel," he agrees. "But they can't be any worse than those heal-thyself adults who keep telling you to cure your illness. They're the ones who drive me crazy. At least kids have the excuse of being kids."

Kate pulls a letter from her overalls pocket and hands it to him. "Look what came in today's mail. It's from someone I haven't seen in ten years, a guy I hardly knew in college. I have no idea how he heard about me."

A clipping flutters out of the letter. Mark picks it up and reads aloud, "EST CURES CANCER."

Kate started a file of clippings sent by her friends (*"Friends!"* Mark snorted when she told him about it. "With friends like that. . ."), which she satirically labeled "CANCER CURES." (Mark was not amused.) By now it contains sworn testimony to the efficacy of everything from six almonds a day to mudpacks, enemas, psychic healing, and "visualizing." This last method, vaunted in a clipping that arrived during her first week of cobalt treatments, exhorted her to adopt a "positive attitude" while undergoing treatments, on the theory that her own negative atti-tude had brought on the illness. "Dramatic remissions" had been experienced "even by terminally ill patients" who had so done, the author claimed. The article continued: "There are five psy-chological steps that precede the onset of cancer: (1) a child-hood decision to repress negative emotions, e.g., hostility, anger, and resentment; (2) the experience of highly stressful life events, often involving some form of loss; (3) the emergence of a problem that seems insoluble. . . ," and so forth.

Each time a new clipping arrives Kate registers several min-utes of anxious, bleak self-doubt: *What have I done wrong?* The thought is paralyzing. Usually she manages to clear her head by talking with Mark, whose contemptuous dismissal of such "pseudoscientific claptrap" stems, she knows, as much from his pragmatic socialism as from his careful, classical scientific train-ing.

"Why do you even bother with these creeps!" he stormed once last year, having stopped by her apartment on his way to work intending to surprise her with a toasted corn muffin and a kiss, only to find her in tears over a particularly condemnatory clipping that had arrived moments earlier. "They're arrogant, self-righteous sadists! They want to think *you* caused your cancer because they can't stand the thought that *they* could get it too! Here, eat this!" And he slapped the muffin on a plate and thrust it, glaring, in her face.

Kate's tears dried halfway down her cheeks as she nestled gratefully in his arms, at once amused and admiring. "I value your anger," she told him on his way out the door. "It's instruc-tive."

He grinned at her over his shoulder, boyishly modest.

But Mark saved his best analytical invective for "the media blitz on cancer." Shortly after the corn muffin incident, inspired by a recently published collective review of several new books by social psychologists on cancer, he wrote a letter to *The Times*

115

book review editor. The letter appeared in print just as Kate entered the hospital for her second operation. Ellen spotted it and brought her the clipping, and Kate taped it to the wall beside her bed. "It's the essence of bourgeois thinking," it argued, "to ignore the material and social causes of things. It's more than that, it's part of a general offensive that you find everywhere these days—particularly in pop psychology—the main thrust of which is an attempt to convince people that if they're not getting what they want, the problem is their *attitude*. Cf. 'prosperity consciousness training.' It all amounts to blaming the victim, which is of course very convenient in these straitened times. But what it attests to more than anything is the inability of our present system to provide people with what they need. . . ."

Mark glances through the EST clipping and hands it disdainfully back to Kate. "Where's Ellen?"

"She had to leave for work a little early." Kate pauses, wondering. An incredulous frown creases her face. "Are *you* my babysitter this evening? I told her I'd be fine by myself . . . She must be mighty nervous about leaving me alone," she drawls, looking at him.

He stands, half in the garage and half out, hands in pockets, unsure what to do next. A pool of dusky sun lights part of his face, glinting in his brown hair like shiny chestnuts, the silver streaks now gold. "She said she wanted to see me before she left for work," he explains, ignoring her tone.

"To show you where the pills are hidden, in case I ask for one?"

He tries to change the subject. "Does Ellen ever *not* work? Every time I turn around she's off to work."

Kate lays down the crutch she's been sanding and studies him. "She works two evenings a week," she says finally, "on top of her day job. She's trying to save up lots of money. She wants to start her own business, she says."

116

Mark brightens. "What business?"

She pauses. "Aluminum siding." They roar, vastly relieved that the moment has passed. It is, in fact, one of Ellen's favorite pronouncements, uttered with just the right blend of wry self-deprecation and working-class pride.

There is a silence as each contemplates the other, Kate dusting her hands on her overalls, Mark lighting his pipe. The evening air is getting cold. Kate's hungry and tired, her hip aches from sitting too long, and Mark's company is making her cranky. She wants a drink and yearns to say so, but undoubtedly he'd interpret it as an invitation to stay. She decides to get rid of him first and then mix herself a drink. *Look, Mark,* she'll say, *do you really think it's such a good idea—*

But Mark is already getting up and moving off toward his car, saying, "I brought you something." Closing her mouth, hugging herself to keep warm, she sits down again on the milk crate and watches him open the door of his grubby sports car. His long legs in worn jeans are most excellent, she thinks as he stoops to lift a box from the back seat. He has a way of carrying himself that gives her an oddly persistent sense of déjà vu. Nervously, she tells herself it's inevitable, given the amount of time they spent together, all memory of which she's attempted to bury for the last seven months. Something stirs her now in the set of his dense shoulders inside the dark wool, and how he walks very straight, without tension. He returns to her with the box in his arms, jerking his head toward the warmth of Ellen's kitchen; Kate follows him meekly indoors.

"You go lie down," he orders as soon as they're inside, but she lingers to watch him set one after another cardboard carry-out container on the kitchen table. "Chinese Cuban," he explains as she pokes her nose into each little box, adding sheepishly, "I was in the city on business—"

Kate bends confusedly over the containers, averting her face. She knows he bought the meal at their old favorite restaurant,

117

and she suspects from his hasty explanation that he made a special trip. His gallant bustling about the kitchen both annoys and moves her; as she eyes him setting the table, pouring wine, warming food in Ellen's copper pots, it comes to her: *He's afraid! The hidden pills—*

Before she can carry this thought any further, Mark has lit candles and, turning out the overhead light, lifted his wine glass to propose a toast. But Kate is already halfway through hers, chewing the glass thoughtfully. At length he inquires, trying not to sound plaintive, "How are the cobalt treatments?"

Absent, Kate shrugs. *What did he tell Pat this time, when she asked where he was going?*

Say it now. Open up your mouth and say it: Look, Mark, do you really think it's such a good idea . . . Unaccountably, her last swallow of wine lifts her and drops her squarely on the beach, where she lies among the Greeks, drifting sweetly. The sense of déjà vu has returned and is now flooding her. Something to do with Mark's arms? He used to carry her off to bed sometimes in those splendid arms, she'd put her head against his chest, and he'd place her on the bed and proceed to undress her with his slow, sure hands . . . *It was like an ineluctable force, those rides in his arms to bed, his arms were like—his arms—* The image stops dead, resistant. She burrows deeper in the arms.

The fishermen! Who carried me in their arms . . . *I tried to hold my head up and rest it against that chest but it kept falling back, it weighed too much, but then some hands picked it up and put it against the chest and held it there where I wanted it* . . . *The fishermen carried me back to life* . . .

It is her very first recollection of having been rescued by the fishermen in the nearly seven months since they found her on that beach. There's been one persistent memory, a doctor's voice in a hospital and then something huge being jammed up her nose, but nothing in between the sweet drifting on the beach and that doctor's voice saying it was probably too late. She clings to the image now, amazed. *Did the fishermen undress me?*

118

No, of course the fishermen did not undress you.

Did my father ever carry me to bed?

No, your father never carried you, or touched you, or remembered your name.

Mark carried me to life! Our bed was our life, our bed was Life—

But it was Mark whose actions sent you to the beach!

"Kate!" Mark has crossed over to where she sits slumped in her chair, her head fallen back against the kitchen wall. She feels elated, and very weak. "Kate, what's the matter!" He squats before her, hands on her shoulders.

With difficulty she rests her eyes on his, which are clouded with fear. *What did the fishermen look like? Brown eyes. Greek eyes. What were their names?* It is unspeakably exciting to Kate that at last she remembers the fishermen. She thinks she is in love with them.

"I think I'm in love with—" she croaks, stopping at the look on Mark's face. *What on earth* . . . He's picking her up in his arms, saying something about not letting her pass out on the kitchen floor, saying he shouldn't have brought wine, he'd forgotten she was on pain medication. Unable to think of anything to say, she says, "I'm sorry," and rests her head on his shoulder. "Just like in the movies," she giggles, "the memory-movies," and quietly lets him deposit her on her bed and stroke the hair from her eyes.

The room is warm and dark, curtains drawn. When he asks her, "Kate, are you all right?" he sounds as if he's about to cry. She begins to sob uncontrollably.

"You shouldn't have done that, you shouldn't have carried me in here, the fishermen, the fishermen—" Frightened, Mark crushes her to him as if he could squeeze the delirium out, until she gasps for him to loosen his hold. "They carried me back to life," she's saying. "They undressed me."

Lying very still then in his arms, her trembling subsided, after a silence she beseeches, "Undress me."

He thinks she means, Put me to bed, tuck me in, take care of

119

me, but she lies back, pulls his head down to her, and kisses him. Slowly his long-fingered hands begin to regain their authority, finding the buttons of her overalls, pulling off her baggy sweatshirt and the sweater underneath, finding her hard nipples. "I don't want to hurt you," he murmurs, trying in vain to pull down the overalls without moving her hip, so that she's obliged to roll first to one side and then to the other to help him.

It's not until she lies naked beneath him, and he sits up in bed and draws the curtain aside to see her lit by the high, brilliant moon . . . Not until he looks down and sees the conflict in her face as she looks back at him, does his mind crowd with doubt. "Kate, are you sure—" Her hands fly up and cover his mouth but he takes them in his own and continues, holding them against his chest. "You're distraught. You don't know what you want. I don't want to take advantage of you."

Does this sentiment sound quaint to her ears? Kate often gently mocked him with that word, in the old days. Thinking he's never seen her so beautiful, staring at the sharp protrusion on her right side, where they cut away part of her pelvic bone, he adds irrelevantly, "I shouldn't have brought wine, it was thoughtless—"

Kate's hands free themselves without much effort and guide his own to her breasts. Finding his shoulders, she again pulls him, unresisting, down to her. "Don't talk."

How shall I open my legs? "The muscle that governs that activity was removed . . ." Who was that doctor? Suddenly she recalls one of Dickson's rare attempts at humor. "What you need," he said with something approaching a leer, "is a very fat man." They'd been discussing physiotherapy. Too astonished to think of the perfect, swiftly cutting rejoinder, she said nothing; even now, remembering, she winces at his bad taste. *I guess*, hands admiring Mark's narrow hips, *you're not what the doctor ordered.*

"Do *you?*"

120

Mark considers the question. "Do I what?"

"Do you know what *you* want?"

Bare skin prickling against his rough, nubby sweater wool, she waits.

"I want you," he says at last, quietly.

The room seems to darken and brighten all at once. Kate feels herself sinking into the center of the bed, as if the weight of his body—oh his sweet, lean body—is pressing her down through the bed, through the floorboards, down to the center of the earth. They look at one another. She cannot make out his eyes very well but she's long ago memorized their look when they study her, as now, from above. Is there any reason to think that this time their expression might be different? Is there any reason to think that *anything* might be different?

Resentful of the intrusion, she nonetheless observes her mind scouting cruelly ahead. Where will she be after he spends himself in her? And where will she live after Ellen's—for she's decided to move, having grown entirely too dependent on Ellen, and her own apartment occupies the top two floors of an old frame house. For that matter, how will she manage at work, with office and classrooms on the second floor of an elevatorless building? How will she do her laundry, clean, shop for groceries? And who will bustle about her kitchen preparing supper after she leaves Ellen's, while Mark is sitting down to a cozy meal with Pat and the kids—. The thought of him with his family hits like a fist. "*Mark!*" she cries out, convulsing.

Mark shifts his weight. "Am I hurting you?"

The familiar smell of him fills the room, pulling her back. She shakes her head. Blend of sweat, his musky beard, his sweet, clean hair. And wool, heavy raw wool, damp and steamy now from her tears and so heavy she can taste it, the taste joining with the ghost of red wine still on her tongue.

My scar! He'll rip open my scar . . .

How will I spread my legs?

121

He left me!
He'll leave me again.

She takes his hand and places it in the hollow left by absent bone and muscle, challenging him to flinch, but nothing happens, his fingers merely trace and retrace the scar's full length, innocent and curious and light, as if reconnoitering terrain. Gradually her fear falls away, and the grief, and anger, chipping off like moulted skins . . .

Sweet dark room. Flawed man, sweet tender weight, caress this shiny rivulet of flesh, anoint it with your tongue. Let the body forget, let the heart loose its worried bands of muscle. Let the heart start to remember. Remember what? Mark? The skunk cabbage, the toasted corn muffin and the kiss? No, not Mark, not the fishermen, not my father. Let the heart remember how to beat: slow and easy, voluptuous. Let it love that beat. Let it dance.

August 10, 1978

I'VE JUST SHOWN Peter this journal. His idea, not mine; he says that as the journal's Official Muse, he has the right to see it.

An acidulous muse, to be sure. "So why did you stop? It's been over four months! Quit fuckin' around and finish it!"

(He's flattered, he says, by the depiction of himself. Especially "that stuff about the broad back.")

"How will I know when it's 'finished'?"

"Well," he amends, "it may never be *finished*. But at least you could set the record straight about your pills. We did give them back to you, you know." Turning toward me to bat a mosquito, his sunglasses reflecting two tiny images of me beside him, he adds, "Write about your move. Write about living alone."

He stretches his legs. We're sitting in two identical folding

123

canvas chairs in my postage-stamp suburban back yard which, like Ellen's, manages to be both poignant and banal. A splendid old willow squats beside us, its fronds drooping in our laps, covered with cottony wads of seeds that drift in the air like lazy snow. Off in one corner of the yard is a lilac; at our backs is my little vegetable garden, which Ellen planted and which she tends weekly in her rolled-up jeans and straw hat with limp, frayed edges that remind me of my willow fronds.

Why *did* I stop? After moving out of Ellen's (and out of my old apartment) in May, I think I lost the sense of urgency that originally impelled me to write things down. At Ellen's, and surely before that in the hospital, I felt so demeaningly helpless and was so constantly surrounded by people that journal keeping—and certain other acts of defiance, like unplugging my phone—afforded me my only shreds of privacy and self-assertion. Privacy in my new life is a more thunderous presence than the most obstreperous roommates or visitors. And the demands of living alone so preoccupy me that journal keeping seems a luxury.

I got off to a rather bumpy start, occasioned by Mark's departure with his family for Utah; he'd been transferred to another lab. His moving day and mine coincided, which was just as well; I was too busy supervising my sweaty, patient little band of movers—Ellen, Peter, my students Ernie and Martha—to think about anything but paint and scrubbing windows and where to hook up the telephone. Like a bustling funeral full of relatives and detailed arrangements, Moving Day and its aftermath made so many demands on my attention that by the time I was alone with the fact of loss, Mark had been gone almost a week. Ellen later told me he'd planned it that way. I was almost as grateful to him for this kindness as I'd hated him for leaving me the first time around.

In paranoid moments I suspected him of having requested the transfer—even of having orchestrated our dramatic rapproche-

124

ment that night at Ellen's, by scheming to play babysitter. He'd said again and again that he could not reconcile the pieces of his life, felt torn in two; what better deus ex machina than a "forced" permanent relocation, sans guilt, thousands of miles away? During those first few weeks I grudgingly admitted that it had ended rather comfortably, even affectionately. And now as I write, three months later (poor Mark! He deserved speedier recognition), it occurs to me that what he gave me that night at Ellen's—the meal, the tender lovemaking—was rare indeed, the kind of opportunity that offers itself once or twice in our lifetimes: the gift of closure. Unfinished, painful business finally finished, the loose end tied not by my customary bold leaps and forcings but of its own accord and through the grace of Mark's gentle soul.

He did not write. Neither did I. At last we'd both moved on.

I rest in my yard often, sometimes facing in toward the house so that I can look through the windows—the back wall is made entirely of glass—to the quiet, sleepy living room within. Seen from outside it has a dreamlike quality: so bright and calm a space after such dark chaos. Often I'm unsure which is the dream, this well-ordered little patch of light or the darkness that preceded it.

Nighttime is particularly confusing. When sunlight scatters from the rooms, and my leg is dizzy with pain from trying to pretend it can do anything, and I crawl between the sheets and the vastly empty bed unfurls around me, I feel that other darkness encroaching on the sturdy, safe daytime world. It's hard not to panic, then.

I do seem to be proving what I set out to prove: that I can live alone. The question begins to reshape itself: *At what price?*

My doubters were legion, chief among them being Ellen, whose kitchen wall sports a blown-up photo of her favorite (Parisian) graffiti, "SOYEZ REALISTES: EXIGEZ L'IMPOSSIBLE!" (Be Realistic: Demand the Impossible!). When I finally tracked

125

down a suitable accessible house rental and moving day was imminent, she sat me down in my new, bare kitchen and said, "Kate, let's talk cooking."

She wanted, she said, to put me through my paces.

"How will you chop vegetables?"

"I'll sit at the counter on a stool."

"Show me."

"How can I? There's no stool."

Swatting aside my objection with an elaborate *Why me, Lord?* look, she started to clamber onto an imaginary stool, whacking her knees ostentatiously against the lower cupboards.

"Hmmm. Okay, so the kitchen needs a few adaptations. Maybe the landlord—"

"How will you set the table?"

"I'll put everything on a little cart with wheels, like those dessert carts in fancy restaurants."

"How will you move the cart into the dining room?"

Silence. "Push it with my feet?"

"On *these* broken tiles? Better eat at the kitchen table and forget about the dining room."

"But how will I set the *kitchen* table?"

And so on.

During those first few weeks I did in fact confine my meals to the kitchen table, which I managed to set by passing dishes from cupboard to counter to table while sitting on my stool. I also improvised a technique that has since become my basic, if graceless, mode of locomotion in the kitchen: abandoning crutches, I grab the sink or counter and drag myself like a twenty-five-pound sack of cat kibble.

Then I discovered, to my amazement, that with some lurching and teeth-gritting I can walk with *one* crutch for a few feet, freeing my right hand to carry things. Triumph! I began to eat my solitary suppers at the dining table, complete with placemat and stemmed wineglass. In the end, this one-crutch routine may create more problems than it solves, but I persist out of sheer stubborn "pride"—that is what our culture likes to call it—or, as Ellen would have it, masochism. In fact, it causes spectacular pain, the remaining muscles in my leg (calf, thigh, groin) being apparently ill-equipped to do what I'm demanding of them. (Perhaps they'll toughen up if I tough it out?)

"Why?" Ellen railed that day, confounded. "Why put yourself through this crap? Find a roommate! Get yourself a sugar daddy to—"

"Sugar *parent.*"

"—a sugar parent to help you with the daily stuff."

"In exchange for services rendered?" I hissed.

"Kate, why are you always setting up tests, always proving something to yourself? Life doesn't *have* to be so hard—"

"Whose life?" A cheap shot, I knew. She'd paid her dues many times over.

Tactfully she held her tongue; eventually she dropped the roommate question. After all, she understood perfectly—as everyone who knew Ellen knew—The Test, the need to be alone.

Anyway, coping mechanisms are boring, I tell Peter. Everyone copes, on one level or another. What interests me are people's responses to disability, which Peter and I have been jovially analyzing and grouping according to type, over Bloody Marys in my yard.

"There's the One-Foot-In-The-Grave mentality, first of all." He settles comfortably back, poking at a scrap of lemon floating among his ice cubes. I'd given him one of my carnival-striped flexi-straws hoarded from hospital days, which he'd promptly removed with a disdainful curl of the lip.

"'Now that your wings are clipped . . .'" I intone, mimicking the doleful sentimentality that is the hallmark of this group. We've found by comparing notes that the One-Foot-In-The-Gravers are more vocal around me; Peter expresses amazement

127

at the numerous strangers who comment or commiserate, on first sight of my disability.

He's almost never similarly addressed. Apparently, there is a newly disabled "look." Do people take his limp for granted because they cannot imagine him without it? I am invariably taken for a sports accident "victim" (what a dreadful word)—skiing, usually. Peter, on the other hand, evidently is assumed to have been born "crippled." ("How gauche," he smiles.)

Those who've known me over the years, who recall my former strength and agility, tend to be the most cloyingly morose; clearly they believe they're witnessing the beginning of the end. Whereas strangers can usually be persuaded that my condition is stable, my "old friends" grimly cling to their certainty that Death has me by the hand.

The ones who haven't seen me since the advent of my tumor can be downright bizarre. Peter has reported sitting in on conversations that opened with something like: "I knew her when she used to chop firewood in Maine!" As if documenting a Hollywood matinee idol's career before her alcoholic decline. This would be followed by a curious kind of one-upmanship in which memories of Kate were traded for their athleticism!

"Tacky!" Ellen once crowed, recounting a similar scene in the hospital waiting room. She'd sat quietly listening for some minutes before bringing the exchange to a hasty close by jumping from her seat and cheerily exhorting the group: "Say, there's a sale on coffins this week, shall we all show our support by chipping in?"

The Healers—Mark's specialty—are equally maddening. "Faith," my young fruit and vegetable man earnestly entreats. Dominic's large brown eyes meet mine for a moment before he resumes sweeping sawdust. He wears a tiny, pretty gold cross on a chain, nestled among his chest hairs, and an open-necked plaid shirt. "You'd be surprised . . ." he adds, and then lets it drop. "Here," rummaging through his fruit, "if you won't take my faith, at least take a bite of my banana."

There's something accusatory underlying even Dominic's disarming admonitions. "All you gotta do is believe, and live your life right" is not very far from Mark's pop psychologists who say that attitude is all. And it's *everywhere*, this view; scratch an apparently rational, well-informed citizen and lo, a Faith Healer is revealed. Even my goodhearted neighbor Beth once said to me: "If you convince yourself you can do it, you'll be off those crutches in six months."

Ignorance? But Beth knew that I had very little hip muscle left, that muscle tissue does not regenerate, that the remaining muscles in my leg were already compensating as much as they were able, and that my one-crutch walking brought on murderous pain.

Did she regard my pain threshold as that of a self-indulgent infant? Did she believe I'd sold myself a defeatist bill of goods? What about all my efforts to live independently, in defiance of "sensible" advice?

There seems to be something inherently immoral, according to her view, in a principled acceptance of the fact of disability. Does Beth's God love disabled people only when they hate themselves, striving to be something they're not, disguising what they cannot change? I think of "reconstructive" breast surgery, even (in some cases) of prosthetic limbs, which Peter considers an uncomfortable nuisance, worse than no limbs at all. (But he's habituated to them, he says; he thinks he couldn't adapt, at his age, to life in a wheelchair. Neither could I.)

Some months ago I embarrassed a concert hall full of people when a school colleague with the best of intentions and the sensitivity of a slab of suet approached me during intermission and eagerly urged me to pay a visit to a spiritualist healing spa in New Mexico. I looked her in the eye and said, "What is it about me you would like to change?"

She drew back, offended. "Well, wouldn't you like to walk without crutches?"

A paragon of self-control, I contemplated a dozen or so bilious comebacks and said instead, quietly, "I'm a little busy for health spas." I was settling smugly back in my seat when a voice issued from somewhere near my bowels, "And besides," building with every syllable until it might have shattered glass, *"what the hell's wrong with crutches!"*

"What the hell's wrong with compassion?" Peter's voice is sharp. "You're the one who called yourself 'helpless, dependent on the kindness of friends.'" He seizes the journal and, riffling through it, locates the offending passage.

I expected him fairly to hiccup with glee at my story. Irritably I play with my drink, holding up the glass so that the ice cubes glint in the sun. "I wrote that in the hospital. I *was* helpless at the time, dammit!"

"When you wrote that, you thought you'd always be helpless. You thought all disabled people were helpless."

"So big deal. I've changed. I'm smarter now."

"Not so smart. You still think people in wheelchairs are helpless . . . But the point is, look at what you had to go through to get smarter. Why can't you allow your friend to be a little dumber than you? She's where you were a year or so ago. She hasn't had the same golden opportunities for growth," he adds dryly.

"Look, when perfect strangers walk up to you on the street and say 'May I pray for you?', are you hearing an honest expression of compassion or are you being patronized?"

"Your friend's not a perfect stranger. Her motives were sincere," he lectures. "She saw you struggling with the crutches . . . Naturally she wanted to help. You can't fault her for that."

130

"I didn't *struggle*, I *walked*. Anyway, crocodile tears," I glower, "are not my idea of compassion."

This is not what I mean to say. I don't want to argue; I want to tell Peter that disability was still relatively new to me then, that all the way home from that concert I cried, raging, my grief a brand-new wound. Instead I say, sulking, "People in wheelchairs *are* helpless. They can't go up stairs, they're stuck at the bottom. Of *everything*. Anyway, look who's talking. *You're* the one who's refused to use a wheelchair for the past thirty years."

Peter's dignity prevails over this tasteless bit. "Not because I think they make people helpless," he says quietly, and lets it go.

We sit together in silence. Sam, curled on Peter's lap, crosses to mine and starts kneading my cut-off jeans. He was prematurely weaned, I tell myself, though in fact I have no evidence to support this fiction, the cat having been a foundling. At any rate he seems transported, suckling on blankets, sweaters, whatever's on hand. Which shamelessly melts my heart.

Quietly Peter and I watch him now, like indulgent parents. Next to his little patch of wet denim is the bottom of my scar, a two-inch stretch peeking out from under my shorts. It's changed color by now; the raw-meat look is gone, softened and faded by sun to a dusky purple-gray, the color of heather, of distant rolling Shenandoah mountains. I've come to like it, I think of it as the color of history.

"It's hard," I blurt, interrupting my own reverie. "My disability is history now, I mean, I'm pretty well reconciled to it, until some asshole comes along and says, 'I have a cure.' I do a double take: *A cure for what?* Not that I forget that I'm disabled, but I forget that people think it's so bad. It always brings me up short. It's like they're trying to rip the scar open again."

Peter reaches over to pet Sam. His broad, hard-bit hands are battered for those of a guitarist. I love him for that. He's always complaining halfheartedly of broken nails. He has a way of sitting, slump-shouldered, neck thrust forward, that seems to apologize for itself at the same time as it issues a challenge. His knee joints used to look monstrous to me, poking through his trousers; now I forget they're there.

"Most folks mean no harm," he repeats gently. "You'll get used to them. They need educating, is all." He glances up at me and back down at the cat. "That's *our* job," he adds, and he touches the stray tag end of my scar. A light, fleeting gesture. His fingers return to the cat.

"I do my teaching in the classroom!" I flare. "I'm busy, I have better things to do than—"

"Y'know, you're turning into a Bitter Nasty Ol' Crip!"

Bitter Nasty Ol' Crip is our code phrase, adapted from Ellen's proud, ironic mother, who coined it (Ellen says) in self-deprecation.

We smile. The air between us sighs. Sam stretches, yawns. Restless, I crutch toward my vegetable garden and study my crops while Peter studies me. One more month and we'll be sinking our teeth into warm, fat tomatoes. And Peter will watch the juice drip on my bare knees.

Peter likes me in shorts. His admiration notwithstanding, I refused to wear cutoffs throughout most of this summer. The scar seemed too ghoulish, snaking up over the waistband and down from the bottom of every pair of shorts I owned. By late July I broke down and even started wearing my bikini at the beach, eliciting curious glances and, occasionally, shock.

People apparently think they know what disabled folks should look like. I startle them; clearly I'm not helpless, not pathetic or sickly. A supermarket clerk who gave me a hand with my groceries last week confided that she'd gone against the advice of her boss, who had dramatically insisted that I'd be offended by an offer of help. "She's an independent woman!" he'd proclaimed, having for some time watched my weekly battle with shopping carts from his vantage point high up in the manager's booth.

Men seem particularly bemused by the sight of me, as if they expect disabled women to be asexual, as if they wish the scar were uglier, not so seamlessly a part of me. (Do most non-disabled women have the same view of disabled men?) I'm rarely harassed anymore—ah, the little fringe benefits—in bars or on the street. At times men's stares seem suspicious, as if the crutches might be nothing more than a sympathy ploy. One beefy, watery-eyed fellow actually accused me outright, hastily withdrawing his judgment when my friend the bartender suggested that an apology might be in order if he didn't "wanna get decked."

Other men—Mark was one, the supermarket manager was not—seem almost relieved, viewing my circumstance as license for unbridled chivalry. Tripping over themselves to open doors, clear paths, carry packages, they tend to set in motion a welter of contrary emotions. I object to this kind of male fussing as I have since the dawn of my understanding of feminism; the difference is, now I often need their help. And loneliness prickles through my body like heat through not-quite-frostbitten toes.

INCIDENTAL

He is new to her, he's seen her
        at concerts, he asks her out
for seafood, they end up at
        the beach where she stumbles
on her crutches over muddy
        stones, weeds, as he moves quietly
beside her, watching, making no attempt
        at talk
Back in his car she looks
        away at the dark sweet-smelling
water glistening on the stones
        while he plays a tape of
Bach transcribed for classical
        guitar, a slow sad prelude
She stretches
        the bad leg and lets her eyes
drop to his hand
        on the stick shift, lit
by the glow of Bach and dashboard,
        and to his thighs
in their tailored
        jeans and remembers
how he carried her up the restaurant
        stairs and set her down, casual,
as if she were a child

AKE A LIST, she thinks. Maybe if you see it all listed in front of you in black and white, things will be clearer. You'll see where you could cut back, what you could drop.

Kate's list starts with the luncheonette where she picks up *The Times* every day. Some three miles from home, it has a candy counter, cigars, a soda fountain, booths. Being near the train station, it draws commuters. She parks as near as possible to the door—sometimes right in front, sometimes farther down the lot—drags her crutches from the back seat, and steps inside. Short and sweet, this errand, most of the time, though occasionally there are commuters ahead of her, or the overworked Greek waitress is serving people at a booth, and Kate stands, swaying, and waits.

From there she drives a mile or so down the road to Spyro's, another Greek luncheonette in a small shopping center. No *Times* here (she brings the one she's just bought), but they do have the best corn muffins on Long Island's South Shore. Settling down at her favorite table in the front window she orders a corn muffin, grilled, easy on the butter, and a cup of black coffee. Customers seated at the counter, turning to glance at her solitary figure basking in October sun, are struck by how she dips into muffin and newspaper as if luxuriating in a bubble bath. Indeed, that first bite, first sip, first headline is a high point toward which everything else—the dailiness of her life—leans in anticipation. She stops here only twice a week; to come more often would be an undeserved self-indulgence.

Parking is harder at this luncheonette; she usually ends up some twenty yards from the entrance. Though Spyro's is only three doors down from the supermarket (her next stop), it's a long walk on crutches and an even longer walk from the supermarket exit door back to her car with a cart full of groceries. Leaving Spyro's, she scans the parking lot adjacent to the supermarket entrance, hoping the single handicapped space will be empty. Mostly it's not, and most of the people who park there are usurpers. She watches them trot out of various stores as if walking were like breathing—left, right, in, out. (*It used to be,* she thinks with a sudden intake of breath. *It used to be.*)

Perhaps once every two weeks or so she lucks out—the space is empty!—and lurches the twenty yards from Spyro's back to her car in hopes of reparking before another driver claims it. The usual clumsiness of disengaging arms from crutches, slinging them onto the back seat, settling behind the wheel and arranging her legs slows her down. Sometimes the crutch cuffs catch on her clothes, or one of the hinges nips her forearm. Sometimes her open car door starts to swing shut, knocking her off balance just as she's fooling with the crutches. The metal hinges have started to poke tiny holes through the car's vinyl back seat; in her zeal to reach the handicapped parking space before someone else gets there, she rips one upholstery hole wide open.

And hurrying hurts. The hastier her movements, the more her calf and thigh muscles seem to tighten and the more loudly they cry out later in the evening. She dreads this crying out. She dreads evenings altogether. But that is later; this is now; there are groceries to buy.

By the time she arrives at the handicapped space, it's taken. She didn't see the driver; she must have been maneuvering her car around the lot, or still fighting with her crutches. She peers at the driver's side of the windshield: no permit. Her eyes fill, a rising lump of rage mingled with panic turning the corn muffin to bile. (Panic? That the driver might stride out toward his car just as she's sitting there? Might look into her face? Might read what's written there? She avoids glancing in the mirror at such moments; too frightening. And what if not only her face but her actions suddenly spoke for themselves? What actions? What would she do?) Hesitating, casting about her, she sees that the closest empty space is the one she just left, and she heads back.

SUPERMARKET is the third item on Kate's list. She only shops twice a week, unless there's something she's forgotten, since the supermarket is immense. Thank god for Melissa, who defied her boss and started giving Kate a hand. Though she feels guilty and vaguely decadent accepting such handouts, she gives Melissa her shopping list and sits in the front window while her young friend goes up and down the aisles. Melissa helps her through checkout, sees to it that she doesn't have to wait long on line, pushes the cart out to her car, and places the bag of groceries beside Kate on the front seat.

The supermarket, then, is not so bad, as long as Melissa's there. Of course there are days when she's not, having called in sick or having switched shifts so she could spend the day with

137

her boyfriend, and Kate does for herself, turning chalky with pain in the checkout line.

Dominic's fruit and vegetable stand is all the way at the opposite end from the supermarket, next to a florist, so she must cross the lot, park the car again, get out the crutches, and so on. But Dominic's is easier: there's always a space right in front. Still, isn't this an errand she could drop? Couldn't she buy her produce at the supermarket, with Melissa's help? But Dominic has lustrous dark-leaved spinach in loose bunches, not like the limp cellophane-wrapped mass at the supermarket, and juicy (not mealy) nectarines and much better tomatoes. Almost everything at Dominic's is locally grown, or was, during the summer months. The aroma, when Kate first walks in, seems worth a high price, as does Dominic himself, greeting her as if he has done nothing all morning but wait for her entrance. (Might this be true?) She loves the sawdust-sprinkled floor, treacherous for crutches but evocatively fragrant. She loves the pungent heaps of fresh basil. Perched on Dominic's stool, she tells him what she wants and he selects the very best, carries her bag out to the car and flashes her that smile. As she slides behind the steering wheel she thinks suddenly that dark-eyed Dominic's smile is like that first bite of her biweekly corn muffin. She cannot give it up. Besides, she reasons, a vegetarian like me can't afford to cut corners when it comes to produce.

There's LAUNDROMAT and BANK, both once-a-week stops. Laundry is a nightmare; she yearns for someone else to do it but can't figure out who to ask and can't afford to pay for the service. There's never a parking space in front, so she ends up double-parking, hurrying inside on crutches to find someone willing to carry in her bag, and hurrying back out (for which haste she later pays, in spades) to find a parking space down the block. When she first moved into this neighborhood Kate tried to fold her clean clothes at the laundromat, alongside the harried housewives who helped lug her bag to and fro. But the folding tables were all chest-high, which meant she had to stand. Finally she gave up and started jamming the clean clothes back into her bag in a bunch. Of course, it makes for more work later, since crumpled clothes have to be ironed, another task for which she has not yet improvised a satisfactory technique. Measured one against the other, it's a trade-off, she concedes; in fact, folding clothes at the laundromat is probably easier than ironing, but at least when she stands at the ironing board in her bedroom no snot-nosed little kids stare openmouthed or bump into her and make her lose her balance.

Should she ask for Ellen's help with laundry? But Ellen is holding down two jobs, in addition to which she faithfully tended Kate's garden all summer. Kate has declared herself emancipated from Ellen's protective care. No no, it would be downright parasitic, asking Ellen to do the laundry.

As for BANK. Clearly something must be done about BANK. For a while Kate experiments, arriving at various times of day, to no avail: the long lines are always there, snaking back and forth along roped-off aisles. She wonders if the people are actually props, extras paid to form a line and stand there until she finally either makes her deposit or gives up, tears salting her eyes. Do they all disperse and go about their business as soon as she stumbles out the door? She studies them; they seem convincing enough. One observation above all impresses her: whatever bank her disabled neighbors use, this ain't it. She has never seen so much as a cane sully its wall-to-wall carpeting. Probably *sensible* disabled folks use drive-in banking; this bank has no such service. Should she switch banks? But she chose this one carefully for its free checking and high interest rates on savings. (Savings! Ha!) Should she ask the tellers to let her circumvent the lines? She did that once, but the looks she'd gotten, or imagined she'd gotten, from others waiting on line made her heart freeze. Could she do her banking by mail? Risky: she'd be adding two or three days to the time it takes for her deposits to

139

clear. Considering how many checks she's already bouncing, this seems unwise.

SHRINK. (Speaking of bouncing checks.) The thought of dropping this twice-weekly "errand" that eats up her salary at an alarming rate fills Kate with longing. Her psychotherapist appointment takes her on a forty-five-minute drive to a tree-lined street of Tudor houses on Long Island's monied North Shore. Parking the car beneath a huge silver maple, she crutches the slate front walk which spans an immense country-club green lawn, climbs the stairs, buzzes, steps into a carpeted waiting room.

Once inside the office she sits beside Doctor Weitz's desk and talks, and Doctor Weitz stares, her thick, stolid face inscrutable. As if I were an alien, Kate thinks. She talks about her dreams, her parents, her childhood. I'm depressed, she says, and Doctor Weitz responds that it's normal to be depressed at facing the transition from years of active life to being Handicapped.

Therapy was a Liberty Memorial social worker's idea. She looked in a spiral notebook and gave Kate Doctor Weitz's name and phone number. "Adjustment counseling," she called it. It seemed like sensible advice: of course she'd need help adjusting—who wouldn't? As months went by and her muscle pain seemed not better but worse, Kate noticed that the depression and sense of loss climbed correspondingly, so she increased her weekly visits from one to two. Doctor Weitz was glad to see Kate dealing so realistically with her situation. Eventually, if Kate "stays with it" and continues to talk about her dreams, parents, childhood, Doctor Weitz says the depression (oh the grief!, that clots her passage from one day to the next) will subside.

When fifty minutes are over, Doctor Weitz looks at the clock on her desk and says genially, "I'm afraid our time is up," and Kate reaches for her checkbook (fifty dollars) and then her crutches. Retracing her steps, she heads back down the long front walk to her car.

Drop therapy? But what will take its place? Kate recalls a brief, unprofitable exchange with Ellen on the subject. The two women were sprawled on sofa and rug in Ellen's cluttered living room. Nearby lay the companionable cello, on its side; her friend had been practicing when Kate arrived.

"Well," Ellen started, and stopped. "Well. We could build you a sixty-foot imitation slate path and some fake stone steps, and you could walk up and down them to a fake Tudor manor house. Better yet, we could hire a hotshot set designer—my sister knows one who does terrific work—and you could pay your hundred a week to *him* instead of Weitz." Getting into it now, leaning forward on the sofa, she paused, scooped a handful of peanuts from the bowl in front of her, and continued with her mouth full: "You could set your clock to drive around in your car for exactly three hours a week, and you could sit behind the manor house prop for another hour and forty minutes a week. I'd be your timekeeper. Hell, for a hundred bucks a week I'll bet the set designer would throw in a little role-play. *He could be Weitz!*"

Ellen's contempt for most practitioners of psychotherapy was not unlike Mark's. "Very funny," Kate said, not enjoying the joke. Too close to home; her own head spins with doubt.

So, what to drop? There are other irregular errands: the stationery store for typing paper, envelopes, and so on; the post office when she runs out of stamps or needs to have a package weighed. And sometimes the bagel store, where she treats herself to a twenty-five-cent sesame or poppy, still warm from the oven. But stationery supplies are among Kate's favorite forms of commerce. She loves the displays of appointment calendars, the neat stacks of manila envelopes of every size. She wanders happily from aisle to aisle, forgetting why she came, trying out pens, admiring desk blotters. And as for the bagel store—no, no. Dropping the bagel store would be like dropping Dominic's. That sour hot-dough rush, the moment she opens the door . . . *Drop that? Where are your priorities, Kate?*

As for the post office, it's a hard one: park in the rear of the building, crutch around to the front, climb stairs, stand on line. But who to ask, if she delegates? She's always in a hurry, where the post office is concerned; the package *must* go out in *today's* mail. Anyway, she visits the post office less than once a week.

There is, of course, one item missing from the list: school. But school doesn't really belong here, she reasons; this is a list of *optional* errands, any one of which could be eliminated to spare Kate physical stress. The purpose of the list, after all, is to identify activities that could withstand judicious pruning. One can't very well prune one's livelihood, so why bother to include it?

Impeccable logic, but still something rankles. Never mind. She skids away, grumblingly writes down: SCHOOL.

(Will school prune *itself* from the list? There've been rumors about the new department head, due to be installed next month. A by-the-book academic notorious for budget-slashing, his appointment is being viewed by many as signaling the end of what some in the administration have referred to as "sloppy liberal excess" on the part of the outgoing English Department head. One of which excesses has been the retention of the department's resident loudmouthed—now strangely silent—troublemaker, Kate Meredith, despite an embarrassingly sparse publishing track record. But her students adore her; only an outsider with no dues to pay would dare tamper with such fervent loyalty.)

SCHOOL. Kate stares at the word. Shrugs, finally conceding avoidance. She does not want to deal with SCHOOL. Doesn't want to think about the two flights of stairs she has to climb twice a week to get to her office, descend to get to her American Novel classroom, ascend again to get to her Creative Writing class.

Couldn't she let one of those strapping young students carry her up and down sometimes? No. Out of the question. It was one thing to be carried into restaurants by dates—that voluptuous sense of nurture, overlaid with a flippy sexual jolt. (Ah, Mark!) But transferring such pleasures to her job would be something else again. *That* was play; *this* is work. To mix the two seems perilous, especially where students are concerned. There are laws, written and unwritten, governing such power relationships. Things could get rather muddy.

Not that her students would object. Once, just once, she did consent to being carried when the pain was visibly bad, and they squabbled among themselves over who would "get her." She smiles at the vanity, granting it a minute and a half before hauling herself back, as if jerking a dog past an obscenely seductive tree.

In Creative Writing last week, Kate assigned her students an exercise: write a fairy tale. She gave them only one restriction: each student's tale should address a specific problem in his or her life, one that seemed to admit of no solution. "Identify the crisis, big or small," she told them, "and then translate its components—the everyday stuff of your lives—into fairy tale terms. Start with 'Once upon a time' and take it from there, all the way to the end.

"In other words, invent a solution. It doesn't have to be a happily-ever-after finale. It could be the opposite.

"Try," she added, "to think about how fairy tales differ from Life. And how they resemble it."

They looked hopelessly puzzled. She tried to explain: "Sometimes it's easy to get lost in detail, in the pileup of surface minutiae . . . To lose sight of that other dimension, *depth*, the Mythic . . . To lose our sense of the overall arc of meaning . . .

143

This is as true of the way we live our lives as of the way we write—"

She stopped herself, tremulous: *Come back, Kate.* Thirty seconds of disorientation later *(Who are these people? What was I just saying? Why was I saying that to them?)*, pawing through her brain's clutter, she recovered her anchor and went on to make a reading assignment: the Brothers Grimm and Oscar Wilde's *The Happy Prince.*

Kate sits, vaguely staring at her yellow kitchen table, the list in front of her forgotten. Sam rearranges himself on her lap.

For all their bemusement, the students gamely accommodated themselves to her fairy tale assignment. What a charitable bunch, what generous spirits! She intends to move them along from the personal to the political next week: identify a major social problem in your community (local or global), translate it into mythic terms, carry it to a conclusion. She drafts an example to read aloud:

Once upon a time there was a sleepy, happy village where all the people worked together and helped each other out. One day an evil giant happened by and decided he wanted to live there. This giant, in order to live in the manner to which he was accustomed, set up a huge estate and forced all the villagers to work for him. The villagers were too afraid of the giant to try to stop him even though, if all of them had banded together, they could have overpowered him. Eventually some of the villagers got sick and weak from breathing his breath, which was a poisonous gas. But the other villagers were too afraid of the giant to stop working and care for them. One by one the sick and weak ones died, leaving fewer and fewer villagers. After a while there weren't enough left to tend the giant's huge estate, and so the giant moved on in search of a new village.

The villagers who were left held a meeting to discuss whether or not they should send an emissary to the next village to warn its citizens what would happen if they didn't overpower the giant right away, while they were all still alive and strong. They agreed this was a good idea, but no one volunteered to be the

144

emissary, and it never occurred to them that they could go to-gether as a group.

By this time, since only a handful of villagers were left, they decided that in order to repopulate their village they'd better have lots of babies. And so they did. But all the new babies were born with three arms and three legs, owing to the giant's poisonous breath, which had gotten in their genes.

When the giant heard about this strange phenomenon, he decided to move back to that village, reasoning that villagers with three arms and three legs would be able to do even more work on his estate than regular villagers with only two arms and legs. What he didn't know was that, along with their third limbs, the new generation of villagers had inherited the giant's poisonous breath, which no longer affected anyone in the village. When the giant returned, they joined hands in a great circle around him and breathed on him all at once, as if blowing out candles on an enormous birthday cake and making a wish.

Three times they breathed, and on the third breath they got their wish, for the giant perished.

Skating back to last week's discussion Kate realizes, sinking, that she forgot to give her class an example of the personal-problem-become-myth. Somehow she'd gotten off track—or had she deftly avoided it? She remembers Ernie leaping in, as was his habit whenever Kate seemed about to drift out of reach or when he sensed a polite embarrassment on the part of his fellow students at one of their teacher's more bewildering unorthodoxies. Or when, as was the case last week, "some jerk" gave Kate a hard time.

She lingers fondly for a moment over Ernie's gallantry. Along with solemn Martha, who never says anything in class but opens like a flowerbud when the room empties, Ernie is her favorite student. Why he should so often feel it necessary to rescue her is unclear to Kate, since her students in both Creative Writing and The American Novel seem, for the most part, a receptive and nonjudgmental lot; then again, Ernie undoubtedly knows them a good deal better than Kate does. In addition to which his rescue missions are, of course, Ernie's way of scoring points.

Last year a handful of students came to the hospital to visit Kate. Of them all, Ernie and Martha—themselves newly, fiercely friends—showed the most steadfast devotion, returning several times, calling her at Ellen's to arrange a visit (which ended up getting snowed out), even helping lug boxes on Moving Day. They'd all just met one another, serendipitously, that semester, Martha and Ernie having enrolled in a course Kate was teaching, one she'd invented and persuaded the "sloppy liberal" department head to underwrite on a one-time trial basis: Working-Class Literature. She'd turned them on to Meridel LeSueur, and they in turn had told her their stories, Martha in her quiet, purposeful way, Ernie with that mix of flirtatious bravado and naked emotional need that was his hallmark.

Martha, a southerner with chocolatey, round, slow speech, is the daughter of miners; her mother made history as one of the first women to harvest West Virginia's coal. The mine collapse that killed Martha's dad was what galvanized her mom to organize, together with other women miners and miners' wives, a relief organization that, while feeding hungry families from its soup kitchen, doubled as an aggressive political force around black lung and mine safety issues. Martha's feelings about her mother's work were understandably ambivalent, since every hour the locally famous organizer spent at the union hall meant one more hour her eldest daughter had to spend at home, caring for three younger sisters and brothers.

Eventually the family moved north, Martha's mother having taken on the care of an ailing sister who'd followed her husband's job to Long Island. She also "had notions of bettering her daughter with a college education," Martha recalls. Eighteen years old when she landed in Levittown, Martha wasted no time in dropping the "hokey" Sue from Martha-Sue.

Last year an otherwise nondescript get-well card found its

146

way to Kate's hospital room; on it Martha had written, in careful curlicues: "I never thought of my mother's work as heroic until I took your class. And I never thought I'd want to follow in her footsteps. Now I'm not so sure." Kate showed the card to Mark—who'd followed with vicarious zeal the adventures of Working-Class Literature and its student stars—and a moment passed between them that came as close, Kate would later reflect, as she and Mark would likely ever come to parenting: eyes full, hearts stretched, and some imprecise sense of investment, of achievement, no less genuine in Mark for his never having met the young woman.

The next time Martha showed up for a visit, Kate waved the card and gently teased: "So you're thinking of becoming an organizer, huh? Honey, organizers *talk!*"

Martha, who not only never spoke in class but never smiled, in or out of class, ducked her head slightly. She had a habit of foraging around inside her mouth with her tongue, as if removing bits of just-eaten food from her teeth, a look of somber preoccupation on her face. It was Martha's infrequent substitute for a smile. Ernie, always at his friend's side on these visits, snickered kindly and poked her in the ribs.

Rib-poking Ernie, whose dad was doing time for larceny, whose mom cleaned other people's houses, made up for Martha's solemnity with his own inexhaustible good spirits. His self-assurance at first shocked Kate, as if he were not entitled, as if he'd brazenly leapfrogged over those tediously gawky teenage dues Kate thought she remembered paying throughout her own college years. Such comfort with oneself seemed, well, dangerous in one so young.

Nearly ten months have passed since their first meeting. Ernie now talks freely with Kate about his visits to the medium-security prison where his father expects to spend the next two years, and about the middle-aged, upper-class, Harvard-grad writer who seems to have adopted his dad as a cause, bombard-

147

ing him with letters, packages, visits, and promises to usher his prison diary into print. Ernie's take on all of this ricochets from one extreme to the other, alternately amused, proud, grateful, and caustic, his irritation directed not only at "guilty liberal bullshit" but at his shrewdly disingenuous old man, who seems to have hit upon a career for himself (as a Jailbird, capital *J*) more enterprising than any he'd ever juggled on the outside.

Fairy tales? What does a tough-as-nails, sexy street kid, whose father's doing time, whose mother cleans houses, think of fairy tales? Kate ponders, recalling resident smartass Leonard Mayhew ("Mayhem," Ernie calls him), who insolently drawled when she finished explaining the assignment ("pick a problem in your life that seems to have no solution"): "What if we have no problems?"

And Ernie, smarter-assed by far, not missing a beat: "Now *that's* a fairy tale!"

Kate wanted to cheer. Coasting along what followed, she remembers how discomfited the students seemed by that part of the assignment, the part about problems. And who wouldn't be? *Identify the crisis . . .*

She feels suddenly leaden, constricted. *They have you doing exercises even healthy people can't do! What do they think you are, an Amazon?*

The voice is Mark's. Kate lays her head on the table, grotesquely humbled by the realization that she cannot fulfill her own class assignment.

Sam, curled on her lap, suddenly wakes and jumps down, rousing Kate from this bleak reverie. The list seems by now to be written in Chinese, so far has she drifted from its original mandate. She hauls herself forcibly back, landing once again on SCHOOL, trying to retrieve what it was that launched her on this journey.

Stairs—ah yes, the two flights of stairs. Let herself be carried up and down?

By whom?

By Ernie, of course. No doubt about it: Ernie would win every time. It's Ernie whose arms she might not disentangle from her own, once the stairs were behind them.

Well, so much for being carried. Crutches will have to do.

And what if those rumors about the new department head are true? Are Martha and Ernie and the rest about to be pruned (pruned? *hacked*.) from the list?

Kate looks around at the kitchen, an energetic space, its walls covered with photos: Lange, Kertesz, Frank. She wanders into the sunny living room, the bedroom. There's no reason to call this house hermetic—no, it's riotously alive. Every single object thrums with livingness, the air itself chunky with life—Mexican rugs, South American bedspreads, early gospel (at this moment) on the stereo. Books, everywhere books. The cyclamen's in bloom.

To call such an environment hermetic would seem obscenely self-indulgent, until it comes to Kate that what Martha and Ernie and the others provide cannot be duplicated by Mexican rugs and that, over the past seven months since cancer picked her up and dropped her squarely on a set of aluminum crutches, the social walls of her world have narrowed, claustrophobically shrink-wrapping her with Ellen, Peter, and her students . . .

But Sam wants his supper. It's getting dark and cold. Switching on the kitchen light, Kate feels a rush of grateful solidarity: *We're in this together, little guy.* She rises, pushing back the list, barely restraining the impulse to crumple and flush it down the toilet.

How about a different tack? Instead of pruning items from the list (since it seems to defy pruning), could Kate expedite the awful arrivals home at the end of each day?

Theoretically no worse than any of the preceding ordeals, these homecomings are nonetheless dreaded more than any other moment of the day. Supermarket groceries, Dominic's spinach and tomatoes, *The Times*, bagels, envelopes, typing paper and, on teaching days, her books and papers—all must be schlepped from car seat to kitchen table or desk.

Improvising, Kate takes to sporting a giant canvas bag into which she stuffs everything, hooking the handles over one crutch grip. It *should* help, and does—if you call that help, the bag slipping around on the right crutch, banging against her leg, throwing her off balance.

Thus does problem solving become a way of life. And why not? Kate problem-solved her way through thirty-one years before a whole new and absorbing set of problems presented itself. By now she should be a pro.

But she doesn't *feel* like a pro. The canvas bag mitigates certain physical, logistical problems, but the dread of coming home lingers, illegitimately festering. Backed into a corner she at last frames the question: why dread? What is the difference between the day's litany of struggles and this final one? Isn't it merely a matter of timing, of culmination?

When at last it comes to her, she's embarrassed by the simplicity: *Coming home, I'm alone.* Alone with *It.* There's no place else to go and no one to distract her. Need yawns open, bottomless, and before she knows it, just when she feels least prepared, it's evening.

Evening. The pain in her leg in the evening crazes Kate,

makes her scream. Before she moved into this house, Ellen did it all: *The Times*, groceries, bank. No burst of bagel heat or corn muffin in a sunny window or Dominic's smile or Melissa's easy chatter. Kate stayed home, and much more than her leg atrophied. Ellen cooked, Ellen washed dishes. And Ellen fretted that Kate could not—should not—do these things on her own.

Skidding away from the possibility that Ellen may be right, Kate tries to learn to gauge herself, on the reasonable assumption that if only she can stop pushing her body past its limits, it in turn will stop striking back. But how to ascertain those limits? There's a time lag between action and reaction: a whole day might pass, even two. How to trace the pain to its source? How to anticipate? She learns, for instance, not to squat (wiping up a spill, petting Sam); this single lesson takes seven months. Does that suggest that she is "slow"? Unobservant? Resistant?

She becomes a student of pain, its courtesan, its temptress. "Pain," she scribbles to herself in a note she later loses (she no longer keeps a journal), "creates its own sealed-off world: shuttered windows, locked doors. Nothing is let in. The frame narrows until the lens sees only pain. All sense of possibility, of future, is gone, along with past. Color drains, the world is seen in grisaille. Motion slows, the body swimming, purposeless, through air."

It is evenings that push Kate over the brink of self-pity. And it is evenings, finally, that bring back Peter's words: "You think people in wheelchairs are helpless."

"Pain = powerlessness," she writes. "Powerlessness = horror."

The back trouble starts in late November, Kate's eighth month of forearm crutches. A chiropractor speculates that one-crutch walking might have damaged her spine. Triggered at first by long stints at her typewriter or by long drives, lately it seems to be brought on by almost anything: too much sitting, too much standing. Hurrying. Lack of sleep.

When Kate returns to school after Thanksgiving break, the new department head calls her into his office to inform her that she has another six months under the present arrangement before the position she occupies (Visiting Lecturer) is eliminated. Nothing personal, he assures her; part of overall belt tightening. If she wants to apply for an assistant professorship, she should feel free. At the end of six months she'll come up for review.

The price tag for the position? "Well, if you got a couple of papers accepted for publication, we'd have a little more to go on," he says, cheerfully conspiratorial, as if giving her an inside tip.

Kate nods and goes home to her typewriter. Six months later she has produced nothing. She tells herself that the demands of teaching combined with back trouble have hampered her, but in her heart she knows she's tired—of teaching, of everything. When her bid for an extension of her contract is predictably turned down, her colleagues and students implore her to fight for her job. Kate cannot muster the energy. Anyway, wouldn't life be infinitely easier if she didn't have to climb all those stairs, and lug all those books and papers around? Besides, if she really wanted to keep her job, wouldn't she have come up with at least one academic paper? As for Martha and Ernie and the rest, why should school be the only pretext for contact? A true friendship, she reasons, should be expandable beyond its original framework.

In May 1979 Kate packs up her desk and drives home.

For the first time in her life, she finds herself on unemployment lines. She asks the woman behind the desk if her checks could be mailed to her. No, she must come in and sign for them, like everyone else. If she's *that* disabled, she shouldn't be

152

on unemployment, the woman says curtly, she should be on disability benefits.

What disability benefits?

SSI or SSD, she's told. The woman hands her two flyers. She takes them home, glances at them to see what the initials stand for (Supplemental Security Income, Social Security Disability), and throws them in the trash. She's not *that* disabled, dammit.

And so the list is modified: UNEMPLOYMENT, which necessitates a long drive to Hempstead, is added, and SCHOOL is dropped. The twice-a-week corn muffin becomes once a week; absurdly, her government check, printed on cheap bluish paper, won't stretch to cover the extra buck seventy-five.

It's now a year since Kate moved into her own place, against Ellen's advice. Darkly despondent, self-conscious about her odd new posture—a wincing stoop—she gradually, over the next several months, drifts away from both Ellen and Peter, whose disapproval she conjures, imaginatively embroidering on the theme daily. (*Ellen thinks I should quit therapy and move back in with her; Peter thinks I should use a wheelchair. Both think I shouldn't have let myself get fired.*) They, in turn, exhausted finally by their guardianship and discouraged by her "self-destructive" intransigence, step back. "'You can lead a horse to water,'" Ellen quips, "'but you can't make it grateful.'" And they chuckle together, a collaborative, sad, anxious chuckle that each privately regards as treachery.

Kate sinks, and sinks lower. And wonders if there is anything, anything at all that can break this fall.

January 11, 1981

Dear Ellen,

Surprised, eh? A letter from ol' Mark. It's been more than two and a half years since I last saw you; I've thought about you a lot, and thought of course about our mutual buddy Kate, wondering how you-all are doing. How long did the paint last on those crutches? Did you miss her much when she moved out? How did you fill the gap she left? (Forgive the impertinence, this stuff is none of my business.) You seemed indispensable in terms of the role you played in her life. That sort of dynamic, as exhausting as it must have been for you, can be fairly addictive, for both parties. Isn't it, after all, mightily gratifying to be needed, especially by someone you love? I don't think I've

154

ever seen anyone so skilled at meeting needs, both physical and emotional, as they arise. I often wondered where
you turned to get your own batteries recharged. I'm afraid I
did very little to help either of you during those difficult
days; my own inner turmoil left me pretty useless, as I
recall.

I'm writing because of a recent chance conversation I
had with my best friend from college. We've stayed in
touch, off and on, over the years, though since I moved
out here to Utah it's been hard to keep up with my New
York friends. Anyway, he called the other day to shoot the
breeze, and during the course of our chat he mentioned
this new quartet he's formed. (He's an amateur cellist.) He
seems pretty serious about the group, judging from the
amount of time he spends in rehearsals. Well, one thing
led to another, and from talk about the quartet he went on
to talk about his teacher, whom he wished I could meet
one day. Before he could say the name I scooped him: *Ellen
DelGiorno*, I said.

Kevin (yeah, Kevin Morse) was a little surprised. I think
he thinks of me as a functional idiot in matters musical, for
good reason. How I guessed was, he happened to name
one of the pieces he's working on with the group, in preparation for a recital in April: the Schubert C Major
Quintet. He said his teacher's been sitting in as the second
cellist. Since it was at *your* place, during one of my visits
with Kate, that I first heard a recording of the Schubert
Quintet, I took a wild shot.

At any rate, Kevin and I took turns singing your praises
to each other. God it's strange; all these years I never
thought to ask him about his cello teacher. How is it possible that your name never came up?

You can probably guess the next part, right? He wanted
to know how I knew you, so I told him. Turns out (as

155

you're obviously aware) he knows Kate, too; I guess he met her while at your house for a lesson, back when she was living with you. He even went out with her a few times. (I refrained, with difficulty, from asking if he slept with her.) He said he saw her recently at your place, after she'd dropped out of sight for a year and a half. He said she looked tired and thin and upset, she told him she's living on welfare now. And he said she was in a wheelchair.

Ellen, I'd ask her this question directly, but I'm afraid of interfering, or seeming to, in her life. Guess I'm also afraid of my feelings, still. I assume she's moved on with her life and I don't want to hold her back, drag her down, lay claim where I have no claim. So I'll ask you: what happened to her teaching post, and *why the hell is she in a wheelchair?* Has she gotten worse? Is there something I don't know? She seemed to be getting around fine on crutches, i.e., she gave the impression of strength, confidence, great courage. I hope she's not giving up on herself, though I could certainly sympathize with the impulse to throw in the towel. Kevin said he saw her get up out of the wheelchair in your kitchen while fixing herself a cup of tea. He said it was the strangest thing—she stood there as if nothing was wrong with her, until she grabbed hold of the counter to drag herself sideways. He said it didn't make sense that someone with that much strength and balance would choose a wheelchair over crutches. "Doesn't she realize how it looks?" he said.

Hey, *he* said it, not me. (I just *think* it.) But setting aside how those hideous contraptions look, she must know that the more time she spends in a wheelchair, the more she'll atrophy. Hell, all the hours I spent at her bedside, seeing her through two operations, I kept assuring her she wouldn't end up in a wheelchair. Now she's making a liar

out of me. What's going on, Ellen? Is it medically indi-
cated, or is this another impetuous decision she's made on
her own?

Gotta run. One last thing: I never thanked you for introducing me to the Schubert. Kate gave me a wonderful
cassette, I play it here at the lab when I need a pick-me-
up. (Some pick-me-up—what heartbreaking music.)

Take care. If you're ever out in my neck of the woods,
give me a ring. It'd be great to see you again.

Love,
Mark

Jan. 18, 1981

Dear Mark,

Jeepers, Mark. Lucky for you I'm so fond of you, otherwise I'd tell you what an asshole you are.

If you want to know what Kate thinks and feels and why she's doing what she's doing, *ask her.* I refuse to speak for her. I *will* tell you what *I* think; perhaps you'll get a note from her telling you what *she* thinks. (You didn't ask me not to show her your letter. K. and I don't keep secrets—not deliberate ones, anyway.)

She's out of work because the university canned her; she wasn't publishing enough dessicated academic papers. She's not job hunting either—too low on energy and morale. For now she's supporting herself on welfare, and no, it's not enough, which is why, as Kevin told you, she looks thin.

She spends most of her time (I gather) brooding. I haven't seen much of her until quite recently. Kevin told you correctly: she withdrew for nearly a year and a half, not only from me but, to a lesser extent, from her old surrogate bro Peter, too. I worried about her, of course, and (in answer to your question) yes, it did hurt when she left. I couldn't help feeling (I know this is ridiculous) that it was ungrateful and callous of her to split after all I did. That was *my* problem, of course; she needed to separate from me. Maybe I mothered her too much, I dunno. In those days there was always a kind of push-pull in our relationship—I mean she wanted to be taken care of but hated feeling needy. When she left, the air was cloudy between us; we never did quite resolve it. As you know, she's extremely private, which makes it hard to talk to her on some matters.

I guess I didn't make it any easier, my own issues having been as tangled as hers. In retrospect, I think that for me it was a kind of second chance at caring for my mother—as if by pulling Kate through, I could bring my mother back. There were also some control issues at work, I'll bet. Think about it: is there anyone quite so powerless as a little kid whose parent is dying? I've probably been paying dues in one way or another ever since I was twelve. Anyway, that's my dime-store analysis. All you wanted to know was if I missed her; aren't you sorry you asked?

Yes, of course I missed her something fierce. Who wouldn't? I was also mighty pissed. (Who wouldn't be?) Fat lot of good it did me. (Like raging against my mother for having the nerve to die.) I didn't realize until after

Kate was gone how completely I'd "consecrated" my life—her word—to her well-being, to the point of sublimating my own. When I tried to discourage her from moving out and living by herself I got the feeling she thought I was being manipulative, trying to perpetuate her dependence on me. I guess that's what you mean by "addictive." Now I can't help wondering if all this handwriting was on the wall all along. Am I the only fool who didn't see it?

My niece Lucy, who hates vegetables, sees things in much clearer terms. She says Kate moved out because she couldn't stand my cooking. When I point out that Kate's a vegetarian too, she glares at me. Tofu's not a *vegetable*, she says.

As for the wheelchair, frankly I don't think it's any of your business (or mine) whether Kate chooses a wheelchair or crutches. But since you ask, and since I know your concern is genuine, I'll fill in what I can. But fergodssake, Mark, don't be so *shy*. (Not to mention patronizing.) Write to her and *ask!*

She's just started using the wheelchair. When Kevin and I saw her two weeks ago she'd had it for all of two days. She hasn't yet made the decision to buy; this one's a loan from the local ambulance corps. She says she wants to "get the hang of them" before deciding to invest in one. Certainly sounds like a wise approach to me, considering the price tag on one of those suckers. Let the buyer beware, etc.

My initial reaction, when she showed up unexpectedly on my doorstep an hour or so before Kevin's regular lesson time, was much like yours. But then, I'm bound to have negative associations with wheelchairs (what's *your* excuse?): my mother's chair coincided with the final stage of her illness. For me it signalled defeat and certain death. Kate's situation is hardly comparable; her condition, unlike my mother's, is stable. (No, she hasn't gotten worse. Other than depression and a touch of malnutrition, there's nothing wrong with her.)

By the way, Peter (who's been disabled since birth and who saw a little bit more of her over that year and a half than I did) had the opposite response. When I told him, I heard him let out a deep breath and smile over the phone. Well I'll be damned, he said, Mazel tov! I was in a crabby mood and didn't feel like asking what he meant, but it came out anyway in the course of our conversation. And I'll tell you a secret: after that I found myself questioning my own reaction to the wheelchair. You probably should too.

When I asked Peter why Mazel tov, he said, Maybe Kate's decided not to make a calvary out of physical suffering. He said Frida Kahlo already perfected that art (thank you), so Kate might as well try something different. Then he said he bets the real reason for the wheelchair is, she can't join picket lines on crutches.

As for Kate, I didn't have to ask how she likes the chair; she seemed absolutely miserable, which is why I couldn't help wondering if she hadn't gone from frying pan to fire. But Peter says she's looked miserable for three years. Pain's an unflattering cosmetic, he says. I'd be miserable too, sitting in that thing. I think the ambulance corps must lend it out to spare themselves a trip to the junkyard. I keep wishing that before buying, she could try out a *good* wheelchair. Though maybe that's a contradiction in terms.

At any rate, I'm trying to learn not to judge too quickly. She's been somewhere you and I have not. And maybe, just maybe, it was a bit hasty and ill-considered of you to assure her she "wouldn't end up in a wheelchair." Peter says that, contrary to popular opinion, it's not a fate worse than death.

Bear hugs,
Ellen

P.S.: Well well, you and Kevin, college buddies and best friends! Somehow I'm not surprised; you have many qualities in common. You're both sweet and kind and patient and hardworking—and much smarter than your dumb questions would lead one to believe. Don't tell anyone, but Kevin's my favorite pupil.

*E*LLEN IS MIDWAY through a warm-up etude when the doorbell rings. Too early for Kevin, who's not due for another hour. This is the second interruption since she started; the first was a pair of Jehovah's Witnesses whom she sent packing. ("Are you *crazy*? Couldn't you hear me *practicing?*") She pauses, pretending not to be home. Another ring. Rising, setting the cello on its side, nearly knocking over her music stand, she mutters, "It's early January, what kind of lunatic would be *outside* in early January!" and flings the door wide.

The airspace in front of her—that place normally reserved for an adult's head—is empty. In the split second it takes for the brain to form assumptions, her eyes drop down, expecting to find a child. Lucy?

"Hi." Kate's expression is anxious, a little sheepish. "I inter-

163

rupted your practicing, I'm sorry, I heard you through the door,
I could come back later—"

Ellen remembers to close her mouth and compose her face.
Too late, she observes, reproaching herself as she bends and
kisses her oldest friend on the lips, for the first time in nearly
eighteen months. Awkward, bending so low to kiss not a child
but a peer. It jars, in a way that kissing Lucy does not.

They hold each other long and hard. *"Where* have *you been!"*
An Ellen-locution, the last two words equally stressed, as if
scolding a late, intimate dinner companion. As if, just as Ellen
had checked the casserole to see if it was done, Kate had run
out to pick up a bottle of wine and hadn't come back for a year
and a half. And Ellen had sat there, foot-tapping, steaming.
"And since when are you so *short?* Don't you know short people
make me nervous?"

She stands back and inspects the other woman's face, which
looks strikingly older now, cheekbones more angular. And
there's something cross-looking about the fine crevices that web
her forehead.

"How do you lift that baby out of your car?" She eyes first the
wheelchair and then Kate's beat-up '65 Falcon doubtfully.

"I don't."

"So what did you do just now? Ask a neighbor?" Glancing up
and down the empty street.

"I lifted it." Kate pulls off one glove to reveal a long red mark
where the chair raked her wrist. "Really, I could come back—"
She seems embarrassed by the injury.

"Oh no you don't, now that you're here I'm hijacking this
thing." She circles behind the wheelchair, pushing and grunting
ineffectually until Kate releases the brakes. The chair bolts forward, its footrests slamming into Ellen's front door. Both women
reach for the doorknob at once, Ellen's hand retreating first so
that the task of opening the door falls to Kate, who promptly
pulls toward her. But the wheelchair's in the way, and Ellen,

164

preoccupied, nettled, still recovering from her initial shock, does not think to back up until Kate finally instructs her, the words sounding more like an apology than a command. At last, all obstacles behind them, relieved almost to tears, in the same breath the two women giggle, and in the next breath they say in unison, "We should take this show on the road!" Linking pinkies, they smile, and the terrible first moments are past.

Ellen steers a path into her living room and sprawls on the sofa; Kate remains in her wheelchair. For several beats they regard each other, but it is not the reciprocal exchange of two equals; unseeing, Kate submits to scrutiny like a child being punished. Ellen, who recalls being accused by her friend of "abusing the privilege of eye contact," at last looks away and breaks the silence. "Want a beer?"

It is of course too cold for beer, but the plaintive face before her brightens, so Ellen retrieves two beers, cheese and crackers from the kitchen. "Great," she grimaces. "Let's get soused for Kevin's lesson."

"Kevin!" Kate rolls her eyes. "What time is he showing up?"

"I thought you liked Kevin."

Kate clears her throat distractedly, glancing around her. Mid-afternoon, a cloudy, inhospitable day. Wishing it were dusk, her favorite hour, Ellen imagines them watching the room fill with that poignant half-light that seems to quicken chairs and tables until they fairly vibrate, animate, glowing like flesh. Kate used to say that when dusk crept into Ellen's cello as it lay on its side it looked companionable, a friendly figure at rest.

Kate reaches behind her without turning her head—nothing's been moved, the room is exactly the same—and switches on the floor lamp. A look crosses between them that sadly acknowledges the intimacy of her gesture.

As if we were lovers, Ellen thinks. *Or more.*

"I didn't come here to talk about Kevin. Or *to* him," Kate adds, faintly sullen. "I can leave if you've got a lesson—"

"If you think I'm drinking *two* beers, you're mistaken." Ellen thumbs Kate's beer imperiously and looks at the familiar figure in front of her, unfamiliarly bent into a mechanical device made principally, it seems, of dirty blue plastic and rust. Not that she minds rust; it's the *vinyl*, that faded metallic blue, like every late-model car on the road. *Whatever happened to primary colors?* Ellen thinks, hugely irritated.

Does anyone ever look at ease in one of those things? She tries to remember her mother, but of course that was different. True, her mother's body (not unlike Kate's) rigidly opposed the chair. But it was not an intentional rigidity; MS—the spasticity of MS—dictated her movements. Kate's frame, on the other hand, folded into a contraption against which it clenches itself even in repose, is *choosing* to resist. There's no *surrender*, thinks Ellen the mime, practiced at analyzing the language of bodies; surrender, hell, there's a fundamental antagonism between chair and rider.

What did you come here to talk about? she's about to ask, but what comes out is, "So why the wheelchair?"

Kate's eyes are lowered when the question comes at her. She looks up quickly, her face flickering, dark. "Whatsamatta, doncha like it?" The shrill voice—Patty Gumchew, one of their favorite parodic inventions from the old days—ricochets around the room, startling them both. It doesn't last, for by now Kate is softened by beer, by the heat of Ellen's brown eyes, by this endearingly tumbled, pell-mell living room, so unlike her own careful space. "Pain," she says, dropping the word like a stone. Her head is turned away; she seems to be looking out the window, studying the husks of last year's broccoli in Ellen's garden.

When she next opens her mouth it's to say, pointing toward the bathroom, that she'll be right back. Shaking her head at Ellen's offer to push her, she jerks the wheelchair rims and maneuvers herself out of the room.

Alone, Ellen cannot help summoning the memory of a long-

166

skirted figure on crutches. Curious, she watches its progress across her mind's eye, that buoyant, springy authority radiating from her like a force field, catching up strangers in its vortex so that wherever she went, people looked, and looked again, wanting to be near her, to meet her. As if she had some glamorous secret, something clearly having to do with her body. More than glamorous, a secret so alluring in its mystery, Ellen used to think, it was enough to make everyone who watched that swinging gait want to run out and buy a pair of crutches. As if composure and personal presence could be bought, a handy accessory. Well, let the fashion industry package *that*. Stampede the prosthesis stores! Crutches on the cover of *Vogue*!

Was it all an elaborate compensation for loss? Was it theater? A carefully staged diversion from the central fact of disability?

Is *this* the "real" Kate? A piercing thought; Ellen leaps back from it, frightened, when it occurs to her that Kate may be having trouble in her cramped inaccessible bathroom. Admonishing herself for not paying attention, she starts to get up—

But no, here comes Kate, the chair blocky as a panzer, bumping into doorjambs and walls. Ellen looks into the red-eyed, smudged face approaching her.

In a flash the wheelchair stands empty, for Kate has thrown herself onto the sofa, one of her feet as it leaves the footrest giving a kick that sends the chair careening backward, almost (but not quite) into Ellen's cello. Ellen tries to think what to say to the woman lying in her lap, her face turned toward the cushions, until the answer comes clear. She gathers Kate in her arms, noting sharp points of bone protruding through the shoulders of her sweater. There is nothing to say. "Oh Kate, oh, Kate . . ." she says. The sobs that come winding up out of her friend seem to have no bottom and neither beginning nor end.

*K*ATE OILS THE WHEELCHAIR.

It's after midnight; January has just ended. She listens as the furnace kicks on, timing it: exactly one minute. Then silence, filling the air of her bedroom, a thick clot of no-sound, thicker than before the furnace-roar. Sam has been flinging himself about the living room from the moment she turned out the lamp beside her bed, an hour ago. He's like a cockroach, her cat, his nocturnal life a mystery: whenever she switches on the light, curious about the hubbub, he freezes, slinks, skulks. He will not share his secret, and this makes her lonely.

She looks at the wheelchair's lumpy, fat presence by her bed. Ellen called it a German tank, not without reason. Still the words stung, not because she is invested in the chair but precisely because she is not. No one will ever wax rhapsodic about its *lines*, she observes grimly.

In the dark bedroom it looks like another piece of furniture: a dresser, an armchair, California Mission thrown into a roomful of Victorian, irredeemably homely. But she remembers growing comfortable with California Mission over the years she spent in a shabby cabin in Maine, learning finally to like it, even to prefer its spare honesty to the coy indirection of Victorian elegance.

No Victorian *here* (her eyes roam from shadowy shape to shape): mattress on the floor, Salvation Army dresser, orange crates for bookshelves.

Useless to lie rigid in the dark; sleep will come, or not come, when it's ready.

A little Three-In-One oil, then, judiciously applied—why not? Nothing to lose and plenty of time to kill, she knows. (And plenty last night, and the night before, and every night for how many months now?) She wheels into the bathroom, where spilled oil won't do any harm and, settling herself on the linoleum, pins back her hair out of her eyes.

First the wheel axles, front and back. The footrest hinges. The hinge at the center of the folding mechanism. Using the shiny new fire-engine-red bicycle pump that Peter gave her, she pumps up all four appallingly spongy tires. This takes practice; air keeps hissing out as she tries to separate pump hose from tire valve. Gotta be quick . . . That finally done, she removes the front casters (half-inch wrench and a half-inch socket on a ratchet wrench) and extracts thick gobbets of hair.

Hair? Human hair, wrapped around the axles! Intrigued, mystified, she teases it apart with filthy fingers, trying to imagine its original color, now blackened with grease. *Carl would never use his fingers for such an operation*, she thinks.

169

Kate's new friend Carl—an ornithologist, specializing in birds of prey—dissects hawk and owl pellets, using watchmaker's tools to prize apart the hard nuggets of indigestible fur, hair, bones, and claws in order to study the eating habits of raptors. The sight of his persistent, steady hands laying open owl secrets is mesmerizing; she shivers and looks away, her eyes returning when he tweezes out, exhaling deeply, an especially distinctive shard of bone: a mouse jaw, say, or mole femur.

Actually it thrills her, those grayish regurgitated pellets—so unpromising, so like turds—suddenly yielding fine mysteries, fragile as flowers. But she resents Carl, as if his relentless hands are opening *her*. Such small and private objects, those pellets; is nothing sacred?

(Long before the spring hawk migration is under way, Carl will be her lover. This she knows, watching his hands.)

A compulsive hobbyist as well as a scientist, Carl cleans the bone scraps with tiny brushes, soaks them in bleach, dries them out on paper towels. Sometimes he goes farther, assembling them into skeletons, as if thereby to glue them back to livingness, though often key bits of bones are missing. Once, having retrieved from a pellet every single bone of a vole, he mounted its tissue-paper-frail form on a little velvet platform and set it on a shelf in his study. Kate felt sorry for it, not because its life had stopped in the bloody talons of an owl; what she grieved was this second death (he called it resurrection), so much more crass and inexplicable than the first, the creature's nakedness lewdly displayed, forever denied the dark loamy crumble back to earth. He could at least have arranged the vole into some approximation of its gesture at the moment of death: a paroxysmal twitch of pain, limbs splayed. Instead he sculpted the bones into a bland, tidy pose that seemed equally remote from life and death.

Kate imagines herself slipping unobserved into Carl's study,

170

carefully ungluing and regluing vole bones, tibia-to-jaw, meta-tarsus-to-skull. A manifesto: *Chaos, chaos, life as chaotic as death.*

As if I knew from voles. Anyway Carl's study is on the second floor of his two-story frame house; he carries her up and down stairs when she visits. So much for guerrilla archaeological deconstruction. Still, she can't help wondering what he'd do.

Staring down at the clot of greasy hair removed from an axle, Kate thinks of the piles of fur Carl somehow extracts from one average-sized hawk pellet. Such bulk jammed into so unlikely a package! Like those magic discs you could buy at the five-and-dime when Kate was a kid: soak them in water for ten minutes and presto! they blossomed into little sponges—yellow ducks, pink dinosaurs, green turtles, mushrooming like genies out of their improbable lairs.

She returns to bed (two o'clock now) and ponders, staring at the chair's stolid outline in the dark, dimly lit by the moon. Hair? How did it get there? *Whose hair?*

In the morning she's astonished at how much more easily the chair rolls. Zipping into the kitchen to make a pot of coffee, Sam leading the way, gaily trotting an inch ahead of the footrests, Kate remembers the scabrous, urine-soaked, car-flattened creature who found his way to her doorstep to die, some years ago. She brought him to the vet, who treated his sores and gave her pills and salves and eye drops and ear drops for just about every cat ailment known to veterinary science, gently warning her as she left that he didn't think the cat would make it. For two weeks she doctored him every four hours, around the clock. She remembers his bleating, squirming gratitude when at last he began to eat. How unexpectedly glossy was his new black fur; how sweetly he hugged her lap. How winsomely he nuzzles her now, arching his back, waiting for breakfast.

A *true* resurrection, she thinks, smugly pouring kibble into a bowl, and she the miracle worker.

Emboldened by last night's success, she returns to the

171

bathroom and settles herself on the edge of the tub. Swabbing the ambulance-corps chair with Iron-Out, watching metal emerge from its crusty orange skin, she coasts along on a current of déjà vu. What, when? Maine . . . the boat . . . another resurrection.

It was a small, badly battered fiberglass rowboat, her landlord's property, along with the little white cabin she rented and the not-so-little lake on which the boat bobbed. Sharp rocks had "stove up" its bottom during one bad spring storm, due to Kate's negligence. She should have dragged the boat ashore when she saw the storm coming. No choice now but to patch the holes, quick, before the landlord found out.

For seven weeks Kate tried to summon whatever it was she lacked to tackle the job; meanwhile the boat sat, overturned on two wooden sawhorses in her kitchen. (It was the only space in that garageless cabin large enough to fit a boat.) Repair a boat *herself*? She was as likely to speak in tongues. For seven weeks she circled the boat, cooking beans, washing dishes, pretending it was not there (though she could barely squeeze around it) and that she was not terrified. She began to stalk the boat, imagining that if only she could catch it unawares, she'd find it in one piece.

But the holes remained. Her nemesis. She glared at them, malevolent.

The patching of the boat, when it finally happened, was a sudden unheralded flurry of activity. One afternoon, without fanfare, her gut abruptly emptied itself of resentment and dread and she found herself doing it. And when it was all done—the cutting of fiberglass squares, the mixing-together of resin and hardener to just the right consistency (quick, before it got too stiff), the brushing on, sanding, painting—when, astonished by her own temerity, she could look at the shiny boat bottom upended in her kitchen and almost not know where the holes had

172

been, the heady gust of self-satisfaction, of *self*, that filled her lungs was dizzying.

Earlier that day, she'd visited the local boatbuilder's shop. Arville Beal, famous for his craftsmanship all up and down the coast of Maine, had been sanding a hull when Kate walked in. The raw wood fragrance that hit her when she first stepped through the door was like that sour dough blast at the bagel bakery: it knocked you flat, piercing every sense at once so that you wondered how you'd ever turn and walk out when your business was done—how you'd go on with your life as if you'd never set foot in this place. As if it were only a smell. Like certain sharp-etched, wise dreams that you can't bear to leave when the time comes to slide back into Real Life. Raw wood: sawdust, stacks of lumber, yellowy-white-gold, pungent, resinous, reaching out to embrace you the instant you walk in. You've been let in on a secret so intoxicating that you can no longer remember why other people in the world do what they do, instead of building boats.

The high-ceilinged space, meant to accommodate tall masts, reminded Kate of a cathedral, sun slanting in through southern windows and glinting off a permanently hovering sawdust cloud, the air grainy as an old photograph. Arville Beal looked small in this place, humbled by his wood. Wood dust, congealed in the pores of his face, limned the horizontal lines of his forehead and the deep parentheses at the corners of his mouth.

Kate had heard that Arville had a couple of assistants. To her relief, they were nowhere in sight when she stepped into the shop; Arville was alone, bent over his work. (She'd feel outnumbered, she was sure, by three men, and the younger two would have gawked.) Suddenly shy, Kate introduced herself and explained her mission. She was about to repair a glass (you didn't say *fiber*glass, she'd learned) boat that didn't belong to her . . . She wanted to do a good job . . . Could he maybe give her a

173

few pointers, let her watch him work for a while? She wouldn't bother anyone, she'd just sit quietly out of the way . . .

Arville promptly disabused her: Well, 'course he didn't work on glass boats, only wood. He paused, then asked if she'd ever worked with fiberglass before.

Kate shook her head. He asked, Well now what did she say was wrong with the boat?

Kate explained that it got stove up real bad on some rocks in that wicked storm last month. It was her fault, see, she should have hauled 'er in before the storm, so she figured *she* should be the one to fix the boat. She didn't add that the boat belonged to her landlord, who would not hesitate to charge her a month's security if he found out.

She heard herself slipping into certain rhythms, inflections, and turns of phrase that rolled off her tongue whenever she spoke with Maine people. Her own ludicrous version was a poor cousin to the true grace of Maine speech. In fact, Kate didn't much like this unconscious, chameleonlike habit of mimicking the speech patterns of "the natives" wherever she went, noting its onset with helpless distaste every time. She felt particularly foolish doing it with such a man as Arville, but there it was: she seemed unable to stop herself, as if a foreign power suddenly commandeered her tongue. It struck her as cheap idolatry, a form of theft. *Ah well, let it go, Kate. Clearly this man will forgive you, if he even bothers to notice. He's got more important things to do than fret about the petty vanities of people from away.*

Arville, steady-eyed, fiftyish, not much hair on top, surveyed her throughout her little speech. "So she's got holes, then, has she? 'Course if they're too big, you can't just patch 'er, like that."

Gentle voice, steady as his eyes, like a lullaby.

Kate nodded, demonstrating the size of the largest hole.

"I believe that'll take a patch," he confirmed, dipping his head once. "It's nasty, though," he added.

She nodded again, unsure whether he meant the hole or fi-

174

berglass. It was one of her favorite locutions, spoken with just the right emphasis on the first syllable, the second half of the word thrown away like an intake of breath. You heard it all the time, spoken of weather, an ill-tempered dog, road conditions, onerous work.

"You want to work fast, before she hardens up. Otherwise you'll have an awful time! Once she dries she's just like a rock! Just as hard," he repeated enthusiastically.

He paused. Was there no one to help her, then—. A statement, his quizzical eyes settling on her.

She smiled, shaking her head, liking him, a swooping burst of like. God, how it bemused them, this unmarried young woman living alone. Fixing boats!, no less, alone. Reassuringly she added: "Oh I'll do fine! Once I know what I'm doing, I mean, I fix cars and all, so I figure I can fix a boat . . ."

Without a word Arville turned to his workbench, rummaged among some cubbyholes, and turned back to Kate. "Here," he said, handing her two small sheets of fiberglass, "I don't believe you'll need more than that." Again he turned, pawed around some more and produced two squat little cans, a brush, sandpaper. Kate tried to protest, but he waved her off: "They're just scraps, is all. And them cans are pretty much empty, not enough left there for anything, I'd probably end up throwin' 'em out." He couldn't use "that stuff," he added, for the first time letting his contempt for fiberglass leak into his inflections. "I just keep it around, just in case."

She should cut out squares of fiberglass with scissors, he said, showing her how large they should be, what should be the ratio of hardener to resin, how to apply it, how long to let it dry. He piled everything in her arms and then, when she started dropping things, retrieved a paper bag from the jumble on his workbench.

"This is just like Christmas," Kate giggled, secretly thrilled.

Arville smiled, mostly with his eyes, and Kate could see he

175

was about to turn back to his work. The thought of leaving seemed suddenly unbearable. Summoning her courage, feeling even shyer than when she'd first walked in, she ventured: Would he mind very much if she just sat and watched for a while? She'd heard so much about his work—

Now it was Arville's turn to be shy. He rubbed the back of his neck and looked at the floor. "Well, 'course I don't work with fiberglass," he repeated in a tone that said that was that.

I've overstepped my bounds, she thought, shamefaced. *Pushy broad.* Turning to go, thanking him profusely, Kate said, to break the ice: "I might just start right in, soon's I get home. I like working on a cool day like this."

Gratefully, as if the favor had been hers, he chimed: "So don't I!"

Iron-Out forgotten, Kate has long since transferred herself from tub edge to floor, where she now sits beside the wheelchair, legs outstretched in front of her, leaning back against the wall as she recalls her subsequent few visits to the shop. She went back to report on her success with the boat, triumphantly recounting her technique and thanking Arville again. This time his assistants were there, and he said he didn't see why not when she asked if she could watch. She went back several times, occasionally joining them for lunch, observing their work, listening to their talk with astonished, silent happiness.

(They spoke of ancestors: whose great-grandfather had farmed that parcel of land that's now a fancy camp for rich girls, owned by a fancy rich New Yorker. They spoke of which clam flats had been closed due to pollution, which clamdiggers were hurting, and who'd been caught poaching on closed flats. They talked about the good blueberry crop that year, which growers were bringing down migrants from Canada to do the raking, and which local families who'd raked every year were forced onto welfare because of it. They spoke of which down-and-out greaser got caught breaking into which summer folks'

176

estate, who'd been nailed for raiding whose lobster traps, and who'd shot whose dog because it was suspected of running deer.)

Kate wanted to learn the trade, she lied, and they accepted her presence. People from away were expected to be odd. Anyway Arville liked her, she knew, he admired her resourcefulness. And he admired *her*, Kate, a slender pale young woman whose curiosity, like her curls, seemed a living thing, who laughed, asked questions, listened. Half the time, though, he couldn't quite make out what she was listening to, only that it wasn't always him.

As for Kate, surrounded by raw blond wood, its perfume, its silkiness under her palm when Arville let her stroke a freshly sanded keel—*she* knew, of course. But how to explain that in truth she was listening not only to him but to his wood?

Standing up, looking into the mirror at the room around her, she sees it now as if it were someone else's bathroom, a stranger's, voyeuristically glimpsed through an open window. Her mind's eye scouts out the living room, kitchen, bedroom, peering into each as if from outside, as if for the first time. Irrelevantly she computes: *how many years ago was that, Arville, the boat?*

Twelve. Twelve years. She met Arville not six months after moving to Maine, a year before she moved down east to help organize a farmworkers' union with Cora and Ed. The union would collapse, a victim of shrewd growers' intimidation tactics, and later, solitary Kate would, too.

She stares into the mirror. The house feels static, cold. *How small my life is! How bare.* She shivers. As if her home had just been airlifted and dropped into the middle of Antarctica. All that richness: Arville, his eyes, his gentle hands working the wood, his graceful, quiet voice, the farmworkers down east, and Working-Class Literature, Martha, Ernie, and the rest—*how small, how claustrophobic. My life as a Cripple.*

177

Is this what it's to be, then?

Pulling herself violently back, Kate picks up the Iron-Out and rag. Spoke by spoke, the ambulance-corps Everest & Jennings— Ellen calls it a dinosaur: "The chair time left behind and evolution forgot," she likes to croon—starts to quicken with new, rustless life. By the time Kate is done, its movement is practically jaunty.

*J*AUNTY? LIKE A fossil. She imagines herself sauntering into a showroom, saying to the salesperson: *I'd like to
see something . . . jaunty, if you please.* (Are wheelchairs sold in
showrooms? *Sauntering?* Never mind. In fantasy, in dream, Kate
saunters. She sashays. She moseys.)

*Forget the showroom, Kate. If what you have in mind is a dinosaur
replacement*—for calls have started coming in from the ambulance
corps saying her month is up, the ungrateful swine—*it sure as hell
won't come from a showroom, since things displayed in showrooms generally
cost money.*

What to do, then? Back to crutches? A heart-stopping
thought. Whatever else one can say of life in a wheelchair, it's
been mostly pain-free. And since sprucing up the dinosaur, she's
made some discoveries. Book fairs, for instance: the gorgeous
leisure of sitting in front of a publisher's display, of savoring

179

book after book *at her own pace*, not tyrannized by aching legs. And libraries! Rambling through the stacks all by herself, stumbling on dusty, mildewed treasures she's never heard of and wasn't looking for. Before the wheelchair (B.W., as Kate and Peter now say) she used to crutch into libraries and sit by the reference desk while a librarian—patient and generous and only slightly, subtly patronizing—fetched the items on her list. No surprises. No dirty hands. No fun.

And shopping malls. Predisability Kate *hated* shopping malls. Crutch life had seemed at first a ready-made excuse never to set foot in a shopping mall again. It didn't last; now she can't wait for the crass hurly-burly of each (rare) mall spree, though secretly she admits that logistical problems are still far from solved: pushing the dinosaur along, her arms always give out— the chair is stunningly heavy—before she's gotten where she wants to go.

And, of course, music festivals. Her favorite is coming up in June; can she pull a new chair out of her hat in four and a half months? Something to shoot for, a deadline.

Might as well at least look into the price of a new chair; no harm in asking. Reynolds Medical/Surgical Supply, listed under "wheelchairs" in the yellow pages, seems to have a corner on Long Island's market. She jots down the number, temper flaring at the lack of options, galled that her simple, physical need should be described as "Medical/Surgical." As if she were still back in the goddamn hospital. As if she'll never get out, as if some huge, malevolent thumb has her pinioned there forever. Bile floods her: *Forget it, just forget it, they can keep their stupid panzers.*

When at last she dials the number and resentfully blurts out her question, a man's voice informs her that the salesman is out to lunch and he can't quote prices. "I just fix 'em," he explains. Forgetting her mission, awash with relief, Kate instantly bonds with him, as if they were both veterans of the same campaign in

180

the same unpopular war. He's not some slimy hustler pushing Medical/Surgical Supplies on perfectly innocent people. He's a worker. Maybe even a craftsman, like Arville. His hands get greasy, he probably extracts wads of filthy hair from front casters every day. She imagines huge mounds of it, saved over months, years, piled on his workbench.

What a perfect opportunity for someone with Carl's compulsions! Kate pictures him soaking hair-mountains in vats of kerosene, followed by hot soapy water. Then what? He'd probably bleach the clean hair. Kate wouldn't. She'd sit and stare: golden blond, pitch-black, chestnut, and white, lots of white and gray. She drifts, conjuring the heads that held and relinquished those hairs, heads cushioned by pillows, heads precariously resting on their stems, heads topped by hats, bare heads, heads kissed by hot showers, by husbands, lovers, wives.

What to do with all these radiant hairs? How to pay tribute to such a tender, sacred crop?

In Maine, Kate's closest neighbor, Bud—local barber who doubled as game warden—used to save his clippings for her, stuffing them away in a plastic garbage bag. Kate used the hair to fertilize her garden; Bud swore it was better than cow manure. She wondered why he didn't use it on his own garden, but he said he couldn't be bothered. Kate loved to sprinkle the clippings like decorative garnishes along her rows of radishes and carrots, watching each day as the little sprigs of hair gradually melded with soil.

What would Carl do with the hair, having bleached it a uniform, antiseptic white? Stuff a pillow? Not Carl, no. Nevertheless Kate lingers with the pillow. In Carl's hands . . . Carl in bed, thrusting it under her hips—

"I'll leave a message for the salesman to return your call, then. Wanna leave your number?"

Suddenly loquacious, comradely, imagining her own blackened, greasy hand clasping his, Kate chatters to the wheelchair mechanic, enumerating her improvised repairs, boasting about the Iron-Out, the Three-In-One Oil. To her surprise, he chides her: No, she shouldn't have done that, oil breaks down grease. . . . See, grease lubricates the bearings and keeps out dirt, so if she broke that down, dirt'll start to get in. . . . And as for the Iron-Out, she should have used Brillo. She probably damaged the chrome.

"Ah." Briefly offended, Kate recovers her spirits by cheerily recalling that the wheelchair is not, after all, *hers*. Serves the goddamn ambulance corps right for lending out such a piece of shit.

Nonplussed, the mechanic pauses. Yeah, well. He's gotta get back to work . . .

It's Peter who suggests the local vocational rehabilitation agency: "Put your tax dollars to work! *You* pay their salaries, give those petty bureaucrats something *useful* to do for a change. Let *them* buy your wheelchair."

Peter, alone among Kate's friends, enthusiastically endorses her pursuit of a new chair. She loves him for this. Loves him for his conspicuous absence of smugness, his gracious willingness to forget whose idea it was in the first place, and how long the seed lay dormant before Kate finally allowed it to sprout.

They strategize, sitting opposite each other at a Greek restaurant near Peter's apartment in New York. Peter spears a stuffed grape leaf and holds it in front of Kate's mouth. "These are great," he coaxes.

It is one of his trademark eccentricities: he feeds his friends, no matter how full they are or how much they're enjoying what's on their own plates. His fork remains, midair, until the target either reluctantly opens wide or, as is Kate's wont, takes

Peter's hand and steers it toward his own mouth. Some people are annoyed with what seems to them an inappropriate intimacy; some are irritated by the interruption in their eating rhythms. Some feel infantilized, degraded; still others are disgusted by his unsanitary ways. Occasionally someone lashes out at him, invoking comparisons with a mother who force-fed her children or a manipulative sibling or spouse who feigns generosity in order to get bites of other people's food.

But subterfuge, Kate knows, is alien to Peter. In fact, he never accepts others' offers of food; he just wants to share his own, no matter how antagonized his dining partners. He holds out forkfuls of food to anyone and everyone at his table, regardless of the occasion. The most genteel, three-piece-suited, brand-new acquaintance gets a taste of Peter's falafel. *Lucky thing he's a musician,* Kate reflects. *He doesn't have to make the business lunch scene. He'd never cut it.*

To certain of his friends it is one of Peter's most maddening habits. Kate knows he can't help himself; she's seen him try to stop his fork, like a child's thumb headed toward the mouth. She's seen people snap, "Put it down!", seen him sheepishly comply, apologizing for offering a bite of Szechuan eggplant, contritely lowering his chopsticks—only to raise them five minutes later (snow peas).

"You'll probably have to prove you can't reenter the work force without a wheelchair," Peter says, brandishing the stuffed grape leaf. A veteran of this same agency, he tried several years ago to get funding for new legs, when his old ones wore out. "They wouldn't foot, so to speak, the bill. They said legs are an 'ongoing medical maintenance expense.'"

"As opposed to—"

"As opposed to a 'one-time capital rehab expense.' Like a wheelchair."

He plucks a cat hair from his sweater. Though Peter has no cats, he is forever plucking their hair from his clothes. Kate

183

wonders if they're *her* cat's or someone else's. More likely Peter's clothing spontaneously generates hair, lint, and bits of thread, so that even the nattiest of woolen jackets looks vaguely rumpled and untidy within an hour of his putting it on.

"But don't wheelchairs wear out too?" Kate is not thinking about wheelchairs. She's imagining Peter being turned down by this agency for a pair of legs. As if he'd asked for something extravagant. Peter The Tough, Peter The Resilient. The image of Peter as supplicant, begging for legs—for *legs!*—makes her acutely uncomfortable. How did he handle it? Indestructible Peter!

"Sure." He blinks, waving a hand in dismissal. "*You* figure it out. I've given up trying. Anyway, by the time your wheelchair wears out, they've long since closed your case. They probably bank on your not wanting to go through all the hassle of starting over as a new client. Or maybe they have some rule against recidivists."

Kate's not listening. Did he fight their decision? Was he depressed, did he take it as a personal rejection? How did he end up paying for new legs? Why did he never tell her what was going on? She remembers offhand references to the old legs— that they no longer fit, that they chafed.

And how was he expected to pay for his "ongoing medical maintenance expenses"? *Let him eat cake?*

Peter shrugs at her questions, runs his fingers through his thinning hair. Setting down his fork, he looks first at his plate and finally up at Kate, who has been staring at his hands. They seem to her at this moment a microcosm of Peter: intelligent, inelegant, made for work. Strong, stubborn hands, like her own, thorny with veins, resistant, indefatigable. So very unlike—Kate catches her breath at the blasphemy—the face that now returns her stare.

A candle burns on their table. *His face should soften in this light, should look young and sweetly eager, as it always does by candlelight.* She

184

wants to turn away, realizing that what has abruptly walked across his features is the look he must have worn when he sat across from some case worker's desk and received the news: *Sorry, but we can't pay for your legs.*

Kate toys with her food. She hates this agency she's never met. And she hates the man who sits before her, the tight help-less set of his lips. That he was defeated, that he allowed defeat. That he needed the Agency in the first place. Hates him, hates his wooden legs, his bitter voice saying to her now, "I *didn't* pay for new legs. I went around on the old ones till my stump sores got infected. Then I didn't go anywhere." He pauses, his voice stretched thin. "Lucky for me it was summer, my slow season, I didn't have to cancel any gigs. By the time they healed enough for me to walk, I'd gotten my income tax refund. I took my check down to the prosthetist and turned it into a down pay-ment on a pair of legs."

Stump sores float in front of Kate and disappear. The Slow Season: Peter bandaged, lying in bed, June, July, August in his airless New York apartment. What does not disappear is the image of his face, *this* face—same pale-boned jaw, same taut gray eyes—receiving the blow: *Sorry, but we can't—*

Peter continues (she wishes he'd stop): No, he didn't fight the decision. He couldn't deal with those goddamn bureaucrats any-more, he just wanted to get out of there and never go back. All their stupid forms, all their questions . . .

"*Could* you have appealed it if you'd wanted to? Was there a grievance procedure? Weren't you mad?" Kate's voice remains even. She imagines her hand slamming down, just hard enough to make the ice in her water glass jump.

"I guess I could have fought it. But I didn't. Maybe they beat me, huh?" Peter is hoarse, his eyes shining. "I was younger. I was alone—"

"You never mentioned one word of this to me when it was happening," she murmurs, imagining the water glass breaking.

185

"You were different then, Kate . . ." His voice trails off. He looks down at his right thumbnail. Broken, as usual. Kate's never seen a concert guitarist with so little respect for his nails.

"You mean I wasn't disabled."

Peter silently regards her.

"So you shut me out," Kate hears herself sulk.

"I didn't tell *anyone*," Peter snaps. "And anyway, just what do you think *you* did for a year and a half?"

"But why did you let me?" She's trying not to make a scene, sick of scenes, her words a hushed accusatory wail, barely audible. *So that's it,* she thinks as the question lobs its full weight back at her. *So that's it,* pretending to cough, damply unsure what "it" is.

Later, curled under blankets on Peter's sofa, listening to his sleep-thickened breath in the next room, she'll think about this agency, and a nameless dread will follow her to sleep. For now she submits to Peter's restored composure, grudgingly returning his gaze.

"I guess we both did what we had to do," he says.

"I'm sorry," says Kate.

She calls the Agency and requests application forms. A voice bombards her with questions: "Have you ever received vocational rehabilitation services before? What is your disability? When did you become disabled?

"Are you Certified Disabled?

"Are you presently working? Are you employable?" (Just as her dentist last week declared a broken tooth "not salvageable.")

"I just want a few forms," Kate says again, feebly.

"We don't *send* 'forms.'"

A pamphlet arrives in the mail, outlining the Agency's services, explaining the important terms ("Disabled," "Vocational

Goals," and so on), and detailing the steps she must take to become a client, the documents she must produce as proof of eligibility for services. There are answers to Frequently-Asked Questions, and a list of the various categories of people who do not qualify for services.

Kate studies it, coffee cup in hand, sitting in the dinosaur at her kitchen table. The little space heater she uses to take the chill out of her toes clicks faintly, signaling its intention to send a gust of heat onto her legs. Kate registers the sound fondly, its timid announcement seeming less a warning than an asking for permission. Her alarm clock has the same habit, its tiny premonitory click prefacing a five-second interval before the bell goes off. Kate appreciates both machines for their considerateness. Knowing she hates noise, they ask if she's ready.

A pool of February morning sunlight splashes on the yellow-painted table. Heat drenches her calves. Ah, black coffee, a lightning bolt of happiness that leaves her idiotically beaming at the pepper mill in front of her. To sit here at her yellow wooden table in the sun, drinking strong, just-brewed coffee from her blue-trimmed earthenware Italian mug . . . She glances back at the pamphlet and chucks it in the trash—who needs it—and decides to drive to the beach.

Two days later she retrieves the pamphlet, sodden with coffee grounds. (The ambulance corps has called again.) This time she notices little cartoons that accompany the text: a smiling, sexless man in a wheelchair sits opposite a smiling man behind a desk; a perky woman, also in a wheelchair, also sexless, smiles at a typewriter; a smiling man with hearing aids confidently strides toward a door marked "Executive Offices."

What would happen if for every "the client" she substituted "Jane," and for every "the Agency" she substituted "Dick?" (For every "disability," read "Spot.") She tries out a paragraph, then two.

Then she tries it out on Peter, who snorts appreciatively.

187

"Tell them you need voc rehab in order to fulfill your lifelong dream of becoming a satirist. If they ask for work samples, you're all set."

"More likely they'll ask for a dictionary . . . 'Uh, gee, *sadderest*? That's not one of our listed Vocational Goals.'"

Though she feels a little foolish, the Bullwinkle Moose voice seems a necessary foil to contain and deflect her anger, which otherwise threatens to swallow her and anyway is pointless, isn't it, might as well laugh. Are other client-applicants similarly offended by such baby talk? She feels a sudden tide of yearning: *Where are all the others, those happy cartoon crips? What would they say about their lives, if she could talk to them now? Peter, is all of this really worth it, just to get a new wheelchair?*

"I'm suffocating," she blurts aloud to the bathroom mirror, in the middle of brushing her teeth. A habit she's drifted into, over years of living alone: talking to herself or Sam, short phrases mostly, fragments snipped from the middle of thoughts. "Where *are* they?"

"It's a kind of claustrophobia," she tries to explain to Peter. "Here I am in my closet, dealing with all this stuff as if I were the only crip on earth. It's a stupid waste of other people's wisdom. I could be benefiting from what *they've* learned."

Pause. "Instead," Peter says, "you're reinventing the wheel."

"Peter gets off a good one." She raps the wooden knee beside her. Peter smirks.

After the fourth ambulance corps call she dials the Agency to arrange for an appointment, "to sit down and talk with someone."

A voice politely corrects her: "An *Intake Interview*, you mean."

188

The Intake Interview: February 17, 1981

THEY REMIND ME of IRS auditors, "implementing pol-
icy," "expediting paperwork" with an earnest, block-
headed zeal that confounds me, makes me want to laugh, cry,
scream.

I don't buy their occasional self-deprecating apologies for "all
the red tape," no, not for one minute. They believe in it. It is
this belief that gives rise to their placid sadism, that fundamen-
tally divides me from them, a division as deep, it seems to me
now, as that between poor and rich. They believe in the inev-
itability (and therefore the necessity) of their piles of forms full
of prying, suspicious questions.

The questions are endless. The ones they already asked over
the phone they ask again, along with an infinity of others.
There's a numbing list of documents to be compiled and fur-

nished to my "counselor" (*she's* going to counsel *me?*), demonstrating that I am who I say I am (social security card), was born when I say I was born (birth certificate), reside where I claim to reside (driver's license, car registration, utility bills), and am in fact truly disabled (complete medical records, including surgical reports, names and addresses of all doctors who ever treated me for my Disabling Condition, a recent letter from my current doctor affirming that I am indeed still disabled). I must furnish proof that I am Employable and that I have not set my Vocational Goals too high (full job history, including the exact nature of my assignment at each job, how long I held the post, what I earned, why I left).

Have I ever been diagnosed as having a mental or emotional disorder? Any history of substance abuse?

Have I been hospitalized for mental or emotional disorders or substance abuse?

In treatment now? For what? Take any meds?

Ever been arrested? Convicted? Of what?

What are my personal-care needs? Have I ever required any "special accommodations" on the job? What were they?

Am I Certified Disabled?

I ponder the source from which these questions spring. Prizing open the skull of this genial, neatly groomed woman who faces me—her desk a sort of shield to keep me from advancing too close—I find a cluster of assumptions: (1) The client-applicant is ineligible for services until proven eligible. (2) The client-applicant's Vocational Goals are outlandish, greedy, arrogant, must be trimmed down to appropriately humble scale. (3) The client-applicant's motive in seeking services is, until proven otherwise, to rip off the system. (4) The function of the Agency is to facilitate (favorite word) adaptation (second favorite) of client to job (client to world), not the reverse. (5) The client is a fraud. (6) The client is helpless.

Most pervasive of all, this last; its condescending flicker turns

190

up everywhere. Peel back the protestations of the most dedicated, selfless, even noble social worker, and there it is: the client is helpless. *Help the client.* (See Spot run.)

I sit, politely answering my counselor's questions. Somewhere in the large, low-ceilinged, factorylike space, subdivided by cheap modular partitions into dozens of small work areas, a copy machine hums, a typewriter clatters. Low murmur of indistinguishable voices from adjacent stalls. Smells of copy machine fluid and Mrs. Lowery-the-Counselor's hair spray.

I try to focus, but my mind strays to the others, glimpsed in passing (I asked directions to the bathroom in order to see what I could along the way), sitting opposite their own counselors in their own separate cubicles. (Undergoing their own Intake Interviews?) Patient bewilderment sags their shoulders. I search their expressions and what I see is offense, as if someone has just deliberately burped in their faces and they, embarrassed, taken aback, too dignified or fearful to return the insult, carefully pretend it was a sneeze: *God bless you,* they say.

So much hanging in the balance: a piece of equipment, a training program, something so costly one could save for years and never afford it. The distribution of power so terribly skewed, and so consistent in its terribleness: people in wheelchairs beseeching people who walk; people who can't hear beseeching people who can. Entreating not for a place in the sun but for crumbs, crumbs left on someone else's plate: *If there's enough money in the budget after we buy our new computer, we'll see about your college education.*

And how many will be persistent and resourceful enough to survive this paralyzing gauntlet? (If they weren't Certified Disabled when they came in, they will be when they leave.) How many will stay with it and assemble all the necessary documents, believing in their hearts that they're *deserving,* cleaving to this faith, undaunted even by the Agency's most degrading questions? The coveted equipment, the training program transmuted

191

into handouts, not entitlements. And who would quarrel with that most fundamental code of justice: *For handouts, you gotta scrape.*

Wheeling past them on my way to the bathroom, craning to look into their faces, I stop dead for a moment, caught by something I've seen. A frisson of recognition, as if I've spotted someone I know. And I have, for in face after face I glimpse Peter (that *other* Peter): *Sorry but we can't pay for your legs.* Defeat already consummated, rising from them like steam, defeat become a way of life, though in fact they may not (yet) have been turned down.

Small wonder, then, that the carrot dangles on its stick, and that the little dog dances. What dance, to what tune? Shall I look my own reprehensible dance in the eye?

A matter of liabilities. It is, for instance, a liability to maneuver the dinosaur too swiftly. *(Why should we spend money on a new lightweight chair for her when she does so well with bottom-line equipment?)* It is a liability to smile too readily *(Does she know something we don't?)*, to laugh *(She's laughing at us)*, to have an against-the-grain political perspective *(This one's trouble)*. To offer insights. *(She thinks she knows our job better than we do.)* Above all, it is a liability to seem self-sufficient. *(She doesn't need us.)*

At last the Intake Interview is over. I wheel outdoors, gulping air the way I imagine a fish, thrown back, gulps water. A racketing headache in my temples, I lift my face as if to the sun, though the day has been damp and cheerless as a cave, and bitter cold. Just behind me another client wheels out, one I encountered an hour or so ago in the bathroom. Middle-aged, with mole-colored hair, thin lips, small eyes in back of thick lenses, she emerged from her stall and advanced toward the sink where I was washing my hands. Settling herself to one side, she waited her turn, not meeting my eyes, her movements small, apologetic. Her nails were bitten to the quick. "Hello," I smiled hopefully, persuasively, but she would have none of it, her sullen demeanor defeating, finally, even me. Bad day, I told my-self, excusing her, but what lingered was the unsettling and thoroughly unreasonable impression of what Peter once dubbed "a crip who hates crips."

Now, seeing her approach a parked car, I try again. Maybe she'd just been turned down for a new wheelchair. Maybe she'd gone into the bathroom to cry. Benefits of doubts seem to be my stock in trade these days. "Some weather, huh?" Studying her face for a flicker of response, I continue doggedly, "Sooner or later this cold spell's gotta break."

Unlocking her car door on the driver's side, she glances up at my inanity with that same slightly furtive, rodentlike movement I noticed in the bathroom. "Winter is supposed to be cold," she rasps. Something in her expression directs my eyes to the sign above her car: RESERVED FOR STAFF.

"Ah. So you work here." I cannot resist, for by now her dis-comfort has begun to give me a sly pleasure. She's hefting her wheelchair—a dinosaur, like mine—into her back seat. Rudely I sit and watch her, forgetting to load my own, half expecting her to climb into her car and drive off without another word. What is it about the apologetic set of her shoulders, the angle of her head on its thick stem of neck? As if I've caught her at some-thing. And for whom is the apology intended? Not me, I think. *Au contraire.*

She nods, seating herself behind the wheel. Two small eyes glare at me out of a soft, unfinished face.

Carelessly I press on. "Are you a counselor?"

By now she has caught on to me and will no longer give me satisfaction. "A counselor. Yes." Her flat eyes, which are the same color as her hair, return my stare. She reaches for the door handle, as if to pull it shut in my face. Her hand rests there, poised.

"Do many people apply for counselor positions?"

"There are no openings, if that's what you—"

193

My peal of laughter must sound insolent. "No, no, I'm not looking for work."

"Then why are you taking up this agency's time?"

Faltering at the swift high voltage of this attack, all playfulness gone, I at last remember our respective roles: this woman is Mrs. Lowery's colleague, perhaps even her friend.

"Oh, I'm job hunting, all right, I just meant I hadn't thought of applying *here*. You must find it very satisfying work?" The note of frantic conciliation in my voice disgusts me.

She looks satisfied. "Sure. *Everybody* wants this position. It's the perfect job for handicapped people—the helping professions."

She slams the door closed, but I call out another question, obliging her to roll down the window. "Do they take good care of their employees?"

For the first time she thaws. "Oh, they give me everything I need. They're *very* protective." She pauses before unexpectedly confiding, "I think I'd have looked for a long time out there, if *they* hadn't come along. They really wanted someone handicapped for this job."

I ask how many counselors the Agency employs, and how many are disabled. She says she's the only one, out of twelve. No, none in administration and none in bookkeeping, no. Her irritation has returned. "I really think it's the highest calling," she says, edgily defensive. "Being able to help others who are less fortunate." And she rolls up her window and starts the engine.

Driving home, I imagine with a shudder my Intake Interview being conducted by *her* instead of the complacent Mrs. Lowery. It's not until much later—removing warm bread from the oven, ladling homemade pea soup into a bowl, settling myself with weary pleasure at the yellow wooden table—that I finally take stock of my perversity. I may have sabotaged my new chair. Probably it will be weeks before I hear. If Mrs. Lowery turns me down, will I fight it? Is there any point? Do I really want anything to do with this crew?

By morning I've talked myself out of calling the Agency to cancel my client application.

HE CONCERT HALL lobby is still mostly empty when Kate double parks in front, to assess her situation. It's early yet, an hour to go, plenty of time to deal with parking logistics.

She sits quietly for a moment, watching three musicians leave the building and head down the street together, instrument cases in tow. It's been a dazzling April day, the expressway lined with blooming forsythia. A pair of Baltimore orioles in the back yard woke her this morning with their piercing, clear song, endlessly repeated with only the slightest variation. "Oughta do something about your repertoire," she admonished them over coffee, trying to name their seven-note tune—a Gershwin melody, but which? Sam interrupted, clamoring for breakfast.

Halfway to New York she crowed, "American in Paris!", greatly pleased to be driving to Kevin's chamber recital on so perfect a day. Pleased too with her decision to drive alone, though it would have been easier to ride with Ellen, who'd offered. But Kate wanted to listen to the car radio, sing, talk to herself, insult other drivers. When Kate and Ellen ride together, they talk. No breathless love affair with solitude. No thumping of steering wheel on the upbeat, no tirades over phrasing or wrong tempo. Not that she doesn't like talking to Ellen; but there'll be plenty of time for that later, at Kevin's after-recital party.

Though she first started using a wheelchair on January 3 (the date carved in memory), this is her first solo flight to New York. It'll be fun, she plans to show off to Kevin and Ellen, who haven't yet seen the new lightweight model.

Actually it's not new, in fact it's rather old and not so light, though a vast improvement over its predecessor. Mrs. Lowery arranged it as a stopgap measure until her own brand-new lightweight comes in; Kate picked up this loaner from Reynolds Medical/Surgical last week.

Having spent over a month processing her papers, the Agency finally decided to approve Kate as a client, by which time she'd long since been forced to return the ambulance corps dinosaur. Reduced to crutches for several weeks, she couldn't help recalling Peter's summer in bed with infected stump sores. (*Why didn't he use a wheelchair until he was healed?* she wondered for the first time.) When, in late March, Mrs. Lowery called to say that her application had gone through, Kate was delirious with relief. When she added that it would take three more weeks to "get authorization" for a wheelchair order and that, since the factory in California had many backorders to fill, her chair could take another three to eight months, "if we're lucky," relief gave way to anger, panic, a rising tide of hysteria. No, she could not live through three to eight more months on crutches, *no, no, no.*

Mrs. Lowery, her voice thinly veiling distaste at poor man-

197

ners, promised to see what she could do about a loan chair from Reynolds Medical/Surgical. A *lightweight*, Kate insisted, whereupon Mrs. Lowery suggested that pushing her luck could jeopardize her client status.

Sitting by the curbside, woolgathering, Kate recalls with malice Mrs. Lowery's disapproval. It pays to yell, eh? Peter, listening to her tale, observed that the squeaky wheel got the oil, which prompted a remarkably lewd riposte from Kate, something about not needing more lubrication. *Spring*, she thinks now, embarrassed, remembering her own astonishment. "Glands acting up again?" was Peter's only reply.

Glands, yes. Kate rolls down the window—why not sit here for a moment in the gathering dusk—and drifts, and her drifting glands settle on Carl, with whom she has been lovers for some seven weeks.

Their first meeting—she leans her head against the window frame—was . . . what? Charmed. (Carl agrees.) It was the night of January 10, another graven date and unseasonably warm; Kate and Ellen were out in Ellen's car, traveling backroads in torrential rain. When the car plowed through a deep puddle and then sputtered to a halt, and no amount of coaxing could induce it to start, Kate got out and poked around under the hood. "You've got an electrical problem," she announced to Ellen, her hands black from tinkering with spark plugs. "Cracked distributor cap. There's moisture inside." No cars came to the rescue. No gas stations were near, and not a pay phone within miles. Their friends expected them an hour ago. "Your wires are wet, too," she added. "You should spray 'em with silicone."

At last she gave up and rejoined Ellen inside the car. As they sat debating what to do next, a pair of headlights approached from far off. Without a word Kate leapt out of the car, crossed to the middle of the road, and waved her crutches in the air.

The car slowed to a stop. Rolling down his window, a flat-voiced man asked if there were a problem.

What she liked, telling and retelling herself the story later, was that he never once looked under the hood. Most men—she turns off the radio absently—would have made an obligatory show of trying to fix what was wrong; even those who hate cars, who don't know a spark plug from a muffler, seem ruled by the cultural imperative to fix a woman's car, because that is what Men do. This lean-faced, wiry-haired man didn't pretend to *wish* he could fix it; he simply offered them the use of his phone—he lived nearby—to call a tow truck or the people who were expecting them . . . "whoever you want," he said.

Gratefully they piled into his car, Kate black with grease and drenched to the skin, clutching in one hand what she said was the harness from Ellen's Fairlane. Leading Ellen up the walk to his house, the man unlocked his front door and escorted her to the phone, returning to the car to see if "the other one" would like to come in and use the bathroom. (When she gets to this part of the story, Kate always reverts to Carl's telling of it, swinging back and forth between their two versions like a kid in a funhouse, peering into every trick mirror. She loves these next fifteen minutes as seen through his eyes.)

He found the car empty; she must have followed them into the house and found the bathroom on her own. (Not hard; they'd passed it on the way to the phone.) He headed back indoors then, out of the rain, cocking his ear at the bathroom door (sure enough, sound of running water), continuing to the living room to check on the tall one's progress with her phone calls, wandering finally into the kitchen. (They must be hungry.)

He'd boiled water for instant coffee and set out pretzels, styrofoam cups, and a carton of milk when it occurred to him that "the one on crutches had been in there a helluva long time."

(Kate giggles, stretching her legs on the car seat.) The tall one had by now finished her phone calls and repaired to the kitchen, settling herself at the table with enthusiasm, munching pretzels, not waiting for the others. He left her there and headed back toward the bathroom, feeling like a kindergarten teacher marshaling his wayward charges on a field trip.

Sure enough, the sink water was still running. *She can't possibly be taking this long to wash her hands. Did she go back out to the car and forget to turn off the water? Did she somehow fall? Is she lying unconscious on the floor? Should he knock, call out to her?* (He didn't know her name.) He stood there, uncertain, wondering whether he should ask her voracious friend in the kitchen what to do, when faint thumping sounds suddenly reached his ears. He realized then that the water noise was a steadier, *rainier* sound than sink water. And then he heard her humming.

She's taking a shower!

He was shocked. And utterly charmed.

Could she say of that night, brandishing her crutches, peering into his oncoming headlights, that something about those two points of light telegraphed the information that her life was irrevocably about to change?

He wouldn't dim his brights, the asshole.

Could she say, as he coasted to a stop, rolled down his window, and asked what was wrong, that at that moment she knew?

Flat voice, a voice "without head," her old vocal coach would have said, and brusque, impatient, as if she were a mosquito and he about to swat her.

What, then? Only that when she stepped from the bathroom, damp and steamy from her shower, hair in wet strings framing her face, and found him standing just beyond the door, staring, transfixed, she knew something had happened. The new thing, whatever it was, was in his eyes.

In one hand she clutched his blow dryer. She must have dug

200

it out of the cluttered bathroom closet. *Christ, has she shampooed her hair?*

"Mind if I use this to dry out the harness?" she asked.

It flashes now through her mind, remembering the scene, embroidering on her favorite parts, that in that instant she caught her first glimpse of what she would come to recognize as a cornerstone of Carl's character: unpredictability.

But there's no time for this now. Glancing at her watch, she scrambles back behind the wheel to find a parking space. Circles the block once, twice, then tries adjacent blocks. Nothing, and now it's getting late. She should have come with Ellen, who could have let her off at the door and then parked the car herself. But Ellen had a rehearsal with the quartet; Kate would have had to sit with a book in Kevin's kitchen while the others ran through Schubert in the living room. She didn't want to sit with a book in Kevin's kitchen like some latchkey child, her free time insultingly programmed by watchful adults.

Briefly she'd pondered an alternative: drop Ellen at Kevin's and then borrow her car and take off for a couple hours, sit in her favorite window seat at Giotto's Cafe, nurse a leisurely cappuccino, read *The Times*. But she could not remember whether Giotto's had stairs; she'd only been there on crutches and had not paid attention. And what about parking, and how would she lift the not-so-light lightweight out of her trunk alone, and were there curb cuts in that neighborhood? How would she get from the car to Giotto's without curb cuts? No, it was too daunting. Not on her very first solo excursion in New York.

She passes the concert hall for the sixth time; by now people are breezing into the crowded lobby. *How clever of me*—familiar dry tone barely masking a clot of panic—*to have preserved my dignity by circumventing an hour or two of reading in a nice man's kitchen while my favorite chamber piece is being played in the next room.*

A parking garage, then. This neighborhood has more garages

than buildings. Expensive, but no choice: all the parking spaces she's found on the street are too far away for her to wheel herself alone. She pulls into the nearest garage and starts the long spiral down, following giant black arrows past one after another LOT FULL sign. On level C below ground, she finds some empty spaces. Hauling the chair from her trunk, she hands over her key to the young Hispanic parking attendant who asks what time she expects to return, hands her a ticket stub, points out the elevator, and roars off with her car.

Spirits brightening, Kate zips across the lot. What luck, this garage is practically next door to the concert hall, she'll be on time after all. Skimming along smooth cement, she thinks smugly how cumbersome this trek would be on crutches.

Her first impulse, on spotting the high cement platform surrounding the elevator, is mirth, stagey, shrill: *Whatsamatta, doncha like it?*—Ol' Patty Gumchew, cheerfully derisive—followed by disbelief: There must be some mistake. Elevators are for access. What we have here is a contradiction in terms.

No, Kate. This elevator was installed not for wheelchair access but for the convenience of garage patrons who'd rather not climb three flights of stairs—*can*, but would rather not. They get tired. They're in a hurry.

She glances at her watch: concert starts in three minutes. The garage unfurls on all sides of her like open sea, vast, hollow, salty. The light fixtures buzz.

Sooner or later someone will come and help her up onto the platform. She can hear distant footfalls, screech of brakes, slam of car doors, the sounds seeming to emanate from the walls themselves. Fluorescent hum, smell of exhaust, of damp stone. Gray cement floor, walls, ceiling.

She waits. What if the elevator's not working? No sense sitting here if the elevator's broken. Maneuvering the chair to a parallel position, left wheel hard against the ten-inch step, she leans out across the platform, stretching her arm toward the

202

control panel. It's no use: four inches of air separate her finger-tips from the button.

Gotta get up on the platform, then. She sets her brakes and slides out of the chair on her knees. Crawling across old gum-wads flattened on cement, new skirt bunching, tripping her, she reaches the button, pushes it. Waits for the sweet responding clank of motor: *elevator music,* she smiles, *as defined by a crip.*

Silence. She pushes it again. Pounds the button.

Dead. The elevator is dead.

In the dream (Last night? The night before? Last year?) *she goes to a place to work. She goes there every day and works hard, alone. She gets a little bit of the job done each day. The place is very high up; where she sits she can see out the window to a rocky bluff, a promontory of gray stone. Nothing lives up here. Wind and stone. She does her work. She works hard, alone.*

One day she arrives to find that someone's played a joke, stuck a little twig in a crevice of the rock. A slender, naked stick, barely sixteen inches high. As she works she looks out at it, standing upright in the crevice. A whip, it looks like. Perfect for toasting marshmallows. Who stuck it there?

The joke's not funny, she wants to get out on the ledge and pull it out. But she can't get her wheelchair out there. Every day she sits and does her work and looks at it.

One day something about it catches her eye. She squints hard: there seem to be a few tiny bumps along its surface. They were there all along, of course, she just never noticed.

The next day she spots them more easily, only because now she knows they're there, knows to look for them.

When the bumps appear to be larger, she realizes that it's all too easy to imagine seeing almost anything, alone up here on the rock.

Finally it cannot be denied: the bumps are getting larger. One day when she arrives for work, the bumps have given way to tiny reddish-green leaves.

Every day she looks at the leaves. She can hardly work anymore, she sits and looks out the window. She thinks she can see them growing, unfolding, giving way to more leaves. Squints again: a beech sapling.

Winds whip the baby beech tree. Rains batter it, it has no protection out there on the bluff. No longer able to work, she sits and smiles out at her young green companion, thrusting up out of gray rock. Still it grows. Each day she can count more leaves. Her eyes scan the rock-face: are there any others, tiny seedlings joining their compatriot, now that the trail is blazed? No. Bare granite, wind—and one baby tree.

But now she knows better. If one tree can live up here, others will follow; soon the rock face will be riotously green with moss, wildflowers, trees.

She sits looking out. Suddenly the topmost rungs of a ladder appear at the edge of the promontory. Someone is about to climb up.

She knows it is because she has not been doing enough work. Someone reported her. It's her fault.

She pounds on the window, signaling frantically to the workman who appears at the top of the ladder and steps off onto the rock. "I'll work harder," she screams as he plucks the little beech tree and tosses it over the edge.

Should she climb the stairs? Three flights of stairs, on crutches? What choice does she have, if the elevator's dead?

But the crutches are locked in her car.

Her legs and buttocks hurt from too much sitting all day, muscles worn out, starting to cramp. She'll sit in the car where it's more comfortable and wait for a parking attendant to come and get the elevator working. Probably all he'll have to do is turn a key. She'll stretch out her legs on the front seat and wait. So what if she's a few minutes late for the concert.

Ah. Yes. The car is. Gone.

Crawling back to her wheelchair, she climbs aboard. The ramp, then. The ramp she drove down to get here. It is, of course, impossible—must be a forty-five-degree grade, no wheelchair in the world could make it. And there's no sidewalk, so cars hurtling down its spiral wouldn't see her until they were on top of her.

Kate, don't be ridiculous. Sit by the elevator and wait. Someone's bound to come soon. The owners of these cars will eventually want to go home.

Ah but the night is young, it's only eight-twenty-five, New Yorkers are just sitting down to linen and silver, just sampling their lobster thermidor. New Yorkers are twenty-five minutes into Act One. New Yorkers are nursing their drinks, they won't start dancing till ten. Kevin probably just retuned his cello for the second number. Brief flurry of coughs, riffling programs. The seats are softly cushioned, house lights down (no fluorescent buzz), neighborly squeeze of bodies on every side.

Kate looks up the ramp, a cement banana-curl so steep, so tightly coiled upon itself, it disappears within a few yards.

New Yorkers are raising their glasses: Here's to us, Here's to a memorable evening, Here's to Life, Liberty, The Pursuit Of Happiness. New Yorkers are sliding in each other's arms. New Yorkers' lips are meeting. The quartet has tuned, Ellen has walked onstage with her cello. Settled into her chair, she looks around at the others and smiles. All bows are raised, all eyes meet. (New Yorkers' eyes are meeting.)

The first strains of the Schubert Quintet in C Major seem almost an afterthought, held tensile chord suddenly hanging in air, a consummation of whatever it was that thrummed, anticipatory, among the five players a moment ago, just before bow touched string. As if the piece could end here, now, and we could all go home, filled. Schubert shimmers through the parking garage. New Yorkers are making love.

Kate starts up the ramp.

A car spins past but she cannot flag it down, can't let go of the wheels lest the chair hurtle back down to the bottom. She tries to scream but the car windows are closed tight—or is it that they can't hear her over Schubert? Driver and passenger seem to be looking not at her face but at her body—no not at her body but at a vision, hallucination, rather: a figure in a wheelchair, beetling up a cliff face, alone.

New Yorkers are smiling, slowly waving like seaweed through car windows. New Yorkers are rocking together on hotel room floors, breathing each other's breath. Schubert gives them their pace, their passion, and when, ten yards up the ramp, Kate's arms fall from their sockets and lie on the cement on either side of her chair, it is Schubert who eases her plunge to the bottom, who cushions her spine, cradles her brain when skull cracks on cement.

Or that is what her body thinks. Her arms, her spine think Schubert held her bones together when she fell, but she doesn't fall, does she, in fact she has the good sense to turn the chair sideways and brake it against the grade, freeing up her arms so that when the third car appears she can flag it down. *"Help me!"* she screams, and the nice people do, pushing her up three flights of ramp inch by inch, four strong bodies taking turns, bending their shoulders like oxen to the task. It was Schubert who sent them to her, she knows, and she tells them so, and they look at her. They're kind, they even push her down the street to the concert hall and through the front door. One of the women gives Kate her clean hanky. "Keep it," she says, and the other woman says, over and over, "Are you sure you're going to be all right?" Before they leave they fetch an usher, turning her over to his care.

Intermission is nearly over. Kate asks the usher to push her to the rest room, which has a stall for wheelchair users, equipped with its own sink. She slumps, cheek on porcelain. She's still there, inert, when intermission ends and the rest room empties of women. Dimly she hears a knock followed by the usher's young voice: is everything okay?

She cannot move her arms to wash her hands or slosh water on her face. Cannot scrounge in her purse for the aspirin she knows are there. Stares into the mirror, uncomprehending, dry-eyed, her facial muscles locked.

She washes her hands. She washes her face. She digs out the aspirin, takes two, brushes her hair, sits up straight in her chair, and wheels herself out. Just as Kevin and the group walk onstage, the usher situates her inside the hall.

Kate has no program. She forgot to ask for one, and the

scared usher forgot to proffer one. She could nudge the person next to her. If it mattered.

Opening her eyes a little wider, she focuses just enough to notice Ellen onstage, soberly tuning with the rest. Still it does not register. Not until the fierce, sustained opening note, taut as a high-tension wire, reaches her ears does she realize that Schubert—who held her bones together when she fell—Schubert waited for her.

*I*T'S OVER, BEHIND her. Kate pushes the parking garage into a safe, out-of-the-way storage container. She does not mention it to Ellen or Kevin who, greeting her warmly in the auditorium, inquire with their eyebrows, seeing her face. She thinks she'll spend the night in the city, drive home tomorrow when she has more energy. Kevin quickly offers his guest room—though it could be a little late before she gets any sleep, the party may be kinda noisy . . .

Kate groans inwardly; she forgot about the party. Can't very well not go, not without disappointing Ellen and Kevin, and besides, where else is there to go? She doesn't have the stamina to drive home now. Anyway, if she spends the night in Kevin's guest room, she doesn't have much choice about the party.

Dreading it—their festive spirits, the smiling at strangers, the shaking of hands—she panics: what if they all start to dance?

Her stomach lurches at the thought. Would Kevin mind if she lies down for a while?

By all means! For as long as she likes!

Ah, ever-gracious Kevin. Kate, turning to put on her coat, glimpses the searching look exchanged with Ellen, the anxious shrug.

Ellen drives her to the party, Kate slumped in the front seat, head fallen back against the cushion. "Is anything wrong?"

"Nope, just a little worn out from the drive."

It cannot, Kate knows, escape Ellen's nervous scrutiny that her robust friend, who fools around with cracked distributor caps on her crutches, does not now (arriving at Kevin's apartment building) have the arm strength to wheel herself one inch. She fears equally the asking and the not-asking, how questions spoken or unspoken float menacingly around her well-sealed storage container.

Cheek sunk in Kevin's guest pillow, Kate instantly sleeps.

Laughter pulls her back. Rippling talk, cheerful thump of music: *Come on and let the good time roll—*

Rolling over on her back, she looks around the room: a quiet, companionable space. She likes being in here while the party's out there. *We gon' stay here till we soothe our souls*—turning to glance at the wheelchair by her bed, looking quickly away—*if it take all night long.*

She likes how the party's abrasions are filtered out, giving only the music's backbeat—not the words, she's filling those in herself, out of her Sam Cooke repertoire—and the rise and fall of party talk and occasional strophe of laughter, the voices blessedly indistinguishable, sound without speech. What a pleasant way to take in a party. Sitting up on the edge of the bed, wriggling backward, she rests her spine against the wall, legs stretched out in front of her. The freedom!, delicious, of not having to flirt, smile, make nice.

Last night, curled in bed with her book, she came across a

description of the novel's protagonist curled in bed (beside her husband) with *her* book. Kate wrote the passage down, feeling found out, exposed: "Only when they were home and Leonard had gone to sleep and she lay in bed reading her book did her features once again arrange themselves into the taxed and help-less look, the released strain, particular to the loneliness of those who are natural with no one." The concluding phrase overtakes her now in the form of a question, though in her present languor it doesn't really matter if, as she suspects, her look (in bed with her book) is taxed and helpless, the question seeming more an intellectual exercise than an existential dis-course with self.

There is a small, discreet tap on the door. "Kate?"

Worried voice. Ellen.

"Come on in," she calls, briefly ashamed of her own reluc-tance, clinging tenaciously—shame notwithstanding—to this last solitary split second as the door opens, knowing that every-thing will change, will change forever, the moment her friend enters the room. *What was that?* she'll think later, trying to re-member, to reconstruct how each object in the room—lamp, desk, chair, bed—sat firmly in its place, radiating certainty. How the room seemed to hang suspended in space, its quietude like a blanket pulled over her head.

The dream was of swimming, she suddenly recalls as Ellen steps into the room. *Quicksilver, light as fish, she bucks and dives and tumbles. Smiling, she floats, sun pours in her face. Arching, smiling, she dives back-ward, pulling with her arms, her body tracing a perfect circle underwater, returning to a backfloat, sun in face. A dolphin. She draws a breath and does it again, circling perfectly, breathing again as she surfaces, arching, circling again.*

She's starting to tire, this will be her last dolphin, time to rest. She crests, but instead of straightening and swimming to shore she arches backward again, gulping air at the last minute. After this one, stop, she tells herself,

210

slowly circling underwater, but when the circle closes she arches into another
circle.

Breathe, she orders. Surfacing, she breathes, just in time.

Stop, she orders, on the uppermost curve of the next circle.

But she launches another circle. Her spine feels as if it will snap. She
cannot stop circling.

Kate tells the dream to Ellen, who asks irrelevantly, "Are you
still seeing Carl?"

Kate nods. "Why do you ask?"

"Just curious. How's it going?" Ellen fixes her with huge
brown eyes.

She shrugs: she doesn't know. She only knows him when
they're making love; out of bed he's still opaque, unpredictable,
remote. She cannot tell what he thinks—or *if* he thinks, though
of course he must, since he leaves behind many clues that suggest the activity of thought: arcane scientific terms scribbled on
paper, lists, mathematical computations. Signs of life (if you
want to call it that), like tiny spoor left in the snow. Yes, it
seems clear: he thinks. About what, she has no idea; his static
face, his flat uninflected voice, hold nothing Kate can read.

In bed, though . . . Bed being a separate kingdom. He is not
static in bed . . . But Ellen wasn't asking about bed . . .

How's it going? A good question. Kate opens her mouth to start
again, eager to investigate the matter, urgently wanting to talk
about Carl. But what to say? *He   me.* Fill in the transitive
verb—for it is most certainly not a passive verb, not *Carl is,* but
Carl does. Carl does to Kate.

He . . . fills me, she could say. How corny, how cornily accu-
rate. *He makes me forget that I'm—*

He scares me.

This thought interests her greatly; why should Carl scare her?
Maybe Ellen will know . . .

But Ellen has risen; moving toward the door, her back to

211

Kate, she says, "Ready to party?" She turns toward her friend, twinkling.

Yes, ready. Never been readier, Kate thinks, a little startled by her own sudden zeal. She swings into the wheelchair, and in the time it takes to prod her hair into place and smooth her skirt, it comes to her that these thoughts of Carl—Carl in the Kingdom of Bed, herself in bed with Carl—these thoughts are what just gave her body its instant, wholly unexpected springy grace as she slipped from bed to chair. She reaches for Ellen's hand, squeezes it, smiles.

The party is in high gear when Kate and Ellen make their way out into the living room, carefully steering a path through dancing bodies to a clear space near the windows. Someone appears and introduces herself as Kevin's friend Joan, offering to fetch a plate of snacks to save Kate another trip across the crowded floor; Kate gratefully accepts. When she reappears, Kevin is at her side, greeting Kate with his winning smile, and offering a drink: wine, beer, seltzer?

He takes her order and moves off among the dancers, returning a moment later with a glass of red wine. "Rioja," he announces. "See if you like it." He hovers in front of her, fussily watching as she dips into her glass.

Inspired by her audience, Kate performs on cue, rolling the wine around in her mouth and chewing it as Carl recently chewed, in a demonstration of professional wine-tasting technique, a skill he acquired, he said, in the course of "one of my many former lives." A rare scrap of what Carl would call "hard data," a blip on an otherwise empty screen. Somehow it does not surprise her; she can easily imagine him approaching unmarked wine bottles with all the punctilious accuracy with

which he approaches his owl pellets. It seems to Kate not incon-
sistent that the same man who glues together vole bones and
calls his spindly reconstructed creature a "resurrection" would
subject the lusty musk of red wine to clinical testing procedures.
*(Dear me, where is this wrath coming from? God knows he is familiar with
lusty musk, is lank-limbed Carl.)*

Thinking of Carl's lusty musk, Kate shivers in her thighs,
looking up at Kevin who still stands patiently before her, waiting for her assessment. Lucky thing he's with Joan, she thinks,
remembering the guest room, the night ahead, for once enjoying her wheelchair view of this strapping man's waist.

Having received her wine benediction, Kevin moves off to
attend to other guests, leaving Kate to muse that she has hit
upon the very best way to do a party: hide out in the guest
room till the evening's at full pitch and then dive in. No namby-
pamby toe-testing of the water, no restless enduring of inter-
minable idiotic chat before anyone starts to break loose. Let the
others do the hard work, while Kate reaps the harvest. Already
she's caught a contagious spark from Kevin, Ellen, and Joan, all
of them radiating such pleased well-being that she cannot help
her own responding elation. They know—and she knows it too,
with whatever part of her was conscious at the time—that the
evening was a huge success: sold-out hall, sublime performance,
standing ovation. Even the weather cooperated. No wonder
they glow now, their bodies moving to the music with a particular kind of abandon. They've been unlocked; she recognizes
the visceral tide that pours out of them, through them, rocks
them one against another. Recognizes it as something familiar.

It was not, after all, so very long ago that she, Kate, danced
like that.

Nervously she steps away from the thought, wills herself back
into *their* bodies. It will not do to court her own body's memory
of dance. She chooses safer ground—Carl, in bed, a different
kind of dance—and basks, well pleased with the shrewdness of

213

her choice. Not so different, really, she amends, watching the heated whirl of bodies. Wondering: *Does Carl dance? What does he look like when he dances?*

The image of Carl's wiry boyish frame suddenly floods her. She looks around the room for someone whose movements most closely approximate what her imagination's conjured.

Finding him—a shambling, loose-boned fellow across the room, the quartet's violinist, she recalls, dancing with that sweet-faced Asian violist—Kate bobs along the surface of her fantasy for several minutes, until it occurs to her that if that *were* Carl (Carl *here*, in her music world? The intersection seems stunningly improbable. Though of course Ellen did meet him on that now-legendary January night, still it brings Kate up short every time she hears her friend mention his name—he never mentions hers—as if their encounter had been not so much a meeting as a collision. She cannot imagine him here, in this group, cannot in fact imagine him with any of her friends. Recoils from the thought, agitated, dismayed), if Carl were here, *Kate could not dance with him.*

Ah. So we're back to that. Back in the parking garage. A wave of something repugnant *(Name it, Kate: self-pity)* washes over her. Ugh, her body. Inert.

What about the others, those people she glimpsed at the Agency? When they go to parties, and everyone around them starts to dance . . . ?

She thinks of them as the Experts, herself as amateur. What do *they* do with this heady vortex that transports nondisabled bodies? Where does it take *them?*

Acutely she yearns for the Experts now, that they might guide her. Looking out at a sea of bouncing belt buckles, torsos, groins, she imagines a roomful of people her own height, whose faces she does not have to scrunch her neck to scan.

Peers!

214

Lumpish, purposeful, she transfers herself from wheelchair to sofa as if heaving a drowned body onto a raft.

The sweet-faced violist, having stopped dancing, perches on the arm of the sofa, making conversation. *She feels sorry for me,* Kate flares irritably, wishing to be left alone, longing for the guest room, for home. Woodenly she offers party chat until the violist, a quick study, moves off.

Suddenly Ellen stands in front of her, plops down in the wheelchair for a break. Ellen's dancing is bonelessly fluid, deliriously sexy; for the first half-hour Kate could not take her eyes off her friend. Now, sprawled in Kate's chair, she makes it look like some subtly hip objet d'art.

The loose-limbed Carl-impersonator gets up from a nearby chair and plants himself before Ellen. "Madame?" He bows deeply, extending an arm and pointing toward the dancers.

Ellen looks quickly at Kate, as if asking permission. "Of course," Kate smiles back, annoyed, feeling patronized.

It's not until much later, breathlessly alert in Kevin's guest room, sorting through what followed, turning over each nuance, that Kate identifies that moment—Ellen's look—as the turning point, the dam-burst.

Ellen returns the bow, taking the violinist's arm, but instead of rising from the chair she settles her long black body more securely in the seat, grasps one wheelrim and propels the chair out into the middle of the room.

Kate gasps, glancing furtively around her, expecting someone to shoo them off the floor. As if her friend were leading not the wheelchair but *her*, unclothed, out into the middle of the crowd. She cringes, miserably waiting for reproach.

But propriety is clearly not the thing that matters now; Ellen's face tells her that, and the others', too. (*There is some thing here, now—what?—that matters, that is all that matters.*) Though Ellen's had only one beer or maybe two (her habitual limit)—she

215

doesn't *need* drink, Kate has always maintained—she is loosened, luminous. The violinist, catching her glow, becomes her co-conspirator in the pirating of Kate's chair. His dancing, no longer antic, seems to focus entirely on Ellen, whose movements are more liquid than ever. The chair seems to glide on air. Ellen is looking directly into the eyes of her dancing partner, undistracted, appropriating the chair with authority just as she appropriates her cello when she plays.

Watching, Kate tries to call upon her arms' and legs' memory of making the chair go forward. Having had this so-called lightweight less than two weeks and the Everest & Jennings dinosaur for a previous six, she feels herself still a novice, unschooled. Her arms remember the attitude of pushing, but do their energies produce this effortless arc of motion? She realizes with a start that she has never seen herself in the chair. Her home has no floor-length mirrors; when she rolls past storefronts she avoids her reflection in windows. Nor does she have much occasion to see other people in wheelchairs, which must be why she keeps returning so hungrily to her nameless Experts at the Agency: *I don't know what I'm seeing.*

Ellen sits erect, her hair a nappy, shrubby nest around the dark face that rests on her long neck like the head of some exotic bird. She seems even now to tower over everyone else in the room. No dour staring into belt buckles for her.

Kate is transfixed. As the violinist returns the heat of Ellen's gaze, other dancers eye the pair, their own movements newly alive, smiling, aroused, pleased with the moment and with one another. Pleased with Marvin Gaye, with the wheelchair, with Ellen, all eyes on her, all voices—Ellen's too, and Kate's—joining in on cue: *"I heard it through the grapevine!,"* a thudding sexual wail.

Kevin, who's been dancing with no one in particular, now shifts slightly until it's apparent that he too is dancing with Ellen. The charged air that links Ellen with her dancing partner

216

seems suddenly elastic, stretching to encompass someone new. Bending over her, he stage-whispers to his teacher, "Are you planning to hog that thing all night? Didn't your mother ever teach you to take turns?"

Ellen laughs, holding out her arms; he lifts her out of the chair and seats himself. Instantly the others close ranks around him, turning toward the chair as if in homage. As if warming themselves at a campfire. Someone behind Kevin touches the handgrips, giving the chair a tentative and then a less tentative push, and it occurs to Kate with a peculiar thrill that another dancer has just been added to the group, an equal and respected participant: the chair.

It isn't long before someone else claims the seat, Kevin graciously relinquishing his turn. And now the chair changes occupants with dervishlike intensity, each rider lifted out by the next rider, the lifting itself become a part of the dance. Kate cannot quite keep up, her laughter hiccupping into sobs born of some mingled joy and grief. Later, in the guest room, foggy with amazement, trying to rescue the evening from wine-webs and sleep, sifting through the grief-joy for something she can name, she'll stumble on a slippery new word, one she'll decide to take on faith, not because it makes sense but because it resonates with such authority: *surrender*.

Out of the knot of bodies Ellen once again emerges, this time offering an empty wheelchair. The music has not stopped, nor the dancers, nor Ellen's hips, legs, shoulders. She beckons, arms outstretched, and Kate, frog-become-princess (*no no not frog*), held by Ellen's eyes in dizzying embrace, takes the hands and is borne up and into the enchanted chair.

It is the moment for which the others seem to have been waiting; the room sighs, suddenly released. Dazed, wine-warmed, dazzled by their sweet smiles, she submits.

Kate dances.

April 10, 1981

I KNOW I shouldn't let Lucy climb up on my lap and, standing on tiptoe, reach for things on the top shelf. But it's such fun to watch the consternation of the supermarket manager, who comes rushing up when Lucy dislodges a box or two of crackers, feigning chivalry and puffing, "Here, let me get that for you."

"I hope they all broke," Lucy whispers loudly when his back is turned. "They shouldn't put crackers up that high. It's not fair for wheelchair people."

"Yeah," I say. "Or kids."

Lucy beams.

She's been staying with me for a few days. Having attended the recital to see her aunt perform, she ended up afterward at Kevin's party, her mother in tow. The next day it was agreed she'd ride with me back to Long Island, where she'd stay with Ellen for a week while her mother went off on vacation with her boyfriend. But before we even started the drive she announced her decision to divide her time between me and Ellen, spend half the week with each. Ellen, used to her imperious niece, guessed she had no objection and left it up to me; I was too intimidated to say no.

Halfway home I asked her what she thought of Kevin's party. "It was fun," she said distractedly. Then she got to the point. "You know what I think?"

"No, what?"

"I think Ellen"—I've never heard her call her aunt "Aunt"—"should sit in a wheelchair when she plays her cello."

Intrigued, I asked why.

"So she can dance and play at the same time."

Excitedly she turned to face me. "She could set the cello on those things you put your feet on, so she wouldn't have to use her legs to hold it. That way she could use her arms to play and her legs to make the chair go! She could dance all over the stage!"

I was caught; the idea seemed absolutely brilliant. "Wow," I said. "The quartet could do that, too! They could *all* dance while they play."

"That way you'd never get bored watching a concert, 'cause everyone would be moving around."

"They could move real slow for the slow parts and faster for the fast parts!"

"You could have a whole *orchestra* in wheelchairs, moving around on stage."

"But what about their music stands?"

(Sternly.) "They'd have to *memorize* the music."

"I know! They could have little miniature music stands attached to their instruments, like in parades."

219

"But how would they watch the conductor if they're all watching where they're going so they don't bump into each other?"

"Ummm."

We pondered the matter for a moment before Lucy put in, aggrieved, "The piano player couldn't dance."

Lucy plays piano.

"No, you're right. That's not fair, huh?"

More pondering. She brightened: "But all the other instruments could dance *around* the piano. The piano could be in the middle."

"It'd be like last night," I said.

"No," she corrected, "it'd be the *opposite* of last night. All the wheelchair people would dance around the one who's not in a wheelchair."

The distinction seemed important to us both.

Giddily, thinking what fun it would be having her with me for three days, I said, "Do you think anybody in the audience would really *listen* to the music? Wouldn't they all be having so much fun watching that they'd forget to listen?"

"Nah. They'd have to listen *harder,* 'cause it wouldn't be like they're used to. Ellen says people's ears get into habits. She says when she performs, she tries to break their ear habits. It's like not letting the audience suck their thumbs, she says."

We stopped at the supermarket on the way home to stock up on Lucy food (ice cream, mostly), chose a relatively empty aisle, positioned the chair just right, and Lucy hopped aboard. (Oof, eight years old is getting too big for laps.) Growling, "Okay, let's crank 'er up and see what this baby can do!" I gave a hard push and off we sailed, supermarket wind in our hair, past the toilet paper, past the aspirin, careening into a display of sanitary napkins.

I N THE MIDDLE of the night, waking to her wheelchair's totemic presence by the bed, Kate feels her cheekbones, like a tongue returning to the hole where the tooth was, caressing the pungent fresh crater. Shocked tongue, trying to learn the new terrain. Stares at the wheelchair; what to say to the Agency to explain its condition? Not to mention hers. What to tell Ellen and Peter.

Stay in the house until you're healed, Kate. No one has to know. Fix the chair yourself. By the time your new chair arrives from California, this one will look good as new. Plenty of time: this is only April isn't it, somewhere near the end of the month? Mrs. Lowery said the earliest you can expect the new chair would be mid-July, maybe not till December. Mrs. Lowery might never have to see this chair, maybe you can return it directly to Reynolds Medical/Surgical. Maybe that nice mechanic will help you fix it.

Can't sleep on her side, pillow feels like sharp rocks against

221

her cheek, and the arrangement of her breasts feels as if she's being crushed sideways in a vise. Can breasts break?

Certainly noses break, and cheekbones. Ribs. Is the forehead a single bone? Shouldn't her bones be set, if they're broken? Probably too late by now. You hear that about animals that get hit by cars and lie for days by the side of the road. Too late to set the bones—isn't that what vets say?—shaking their heads.

Head bone connected to the neck bone, shin bone connected to the ankle bone. Eight-year-old Kate used to crow the song at breakneck speed, deliberately scrambling the sequence. *Neck bone connected to the thigh bone, wrist bone connected to the foot bone.*

Eight-year-old Kate *liked* bones. Canned salmon bones especially, you'd come across them in the middle of a bite, sweet little round discs, vertebrae they must have been, that crunched pleasantly, snap, snap, when you bit into them. Kate's family ate canned salmon a lot. It was cheaper than tuna.

Carl could glue my vole bones back together, couldn't he, first arranging me in some cheery, lifelike pose?

She lies on her back, breathing carefully—it's bad when she takes a deep breath—fingering her raw places as the memory movie cranks up. Tattered, this film, from constant reruns, and stuck: these past four days, lying here on her back, she's been unable until just now to summon any image of Carl aside from his role as leading man in one particular scene which plays over and over and which is about to play again. She tries to stop it, to look away but the film rolls and, exhibitionist, forces her to watch.

They've been making love for hours. They stop, doze, drifting toward and away from drowsy desire. They are dazzling together, oh the loveliness of bodies, unbearable, the lightness. Even *hers*. A kind of weightless innocence, all parts perfect, unencumbered. (Her scar: perfect.) Her movements fluid, as if gravity itself had mercifully receded, parking itself outside Carl's bedroom, not to interfere until they're done.

Dawn. Groggily drifting in his arms, she's been reviewing their first encounter, a scene that never fails to make them smile as they tell and retell it to each other, savoring, polishing the story like a stone.

She nudges Carl gently, whispering, would he help her downstairs a little early today?, she's got a date with the dentist. Rummages in her purse beside the bed for her appointment calendar, just to be sure: APRIL 27-DR. LEIGH.

Carl lives in an old two-story frame house. When they spend the night there he carries first her and then her things—purse, overnight bag and, of course, the wheelchair—upstairs to the bedroom.

She hears words, muffled, disappearing into his pillow. Leans closer: "What?" Nuzzling his ear, slipping in her tongue, thinking: *Our bodies have fallen in love.* Wondering, as she often wonders these days, what all the fuss was about.

Odd, how certain kinds of memories have eluded her, ever since the advent of Carl. As if a whole category of events had never happened, or rather, as if they'd happened to someone else, a character in a novel. An unsuccessful novel, full of Sturm und Drang, a novel she's already put down without reading the ending. The parking garage, for instance. Not that she can't remember—it was, after all, only three weeks ago—but when it happens to cross her mind, the image seems curiously bloodless, drained of immediacy. *What was all the fuss about?*

It is as if she's suddenly awakened on a lush green island: tropical fruits, white sand, and no boat in sight to explain how she got here. Not looking for the boat, not looking back to life before. Not caring. Settling comfortably into new life on the charmed island with her guardian angel. He wards off evil spirits, does Carl, denatures them, drawing off the poison so that they seem petty, impotent.

How? "How do you do that," she murmurs sometimes into his ear. She only says this to him when they're in bed, and they are

223

rarely together and *not* in bed. Once they stayed in bed for three days, getting up only to go to the bathroom, to the kitchen for coffee, ordering dinner delivered to the house (Chinese take-out one night, pizza the next), Carl padding naked downstairs to pay the delivery guy through a crack in the door. Three days without clothes, a three-day lovemaking marathon. "Welcome to the Land of Fuck," he smiled to her, borrowing the phrase from Henry Miller, his favorite writer.

Again his voice comes to her (she's sliding her hand along his thigh, oh sweet weightlessness, oh perfect state of grace), and this time she's close enough to catch it: "What a pain."

Here the memory movie becomes, briefly, no longer visual but kinesthetic: something inside her chest cavity twists like a hooked fish. She lies motionless, still poised above the delicate pink shell of his ear. Her mouth is open, silent. Fish-mouth. At length she hears herself echo stupidly, "What a—*what?*"

He turns to look at her, his flat blue eyes opaque. The expression on his face is one she's never seen, but there's no time to read it or to stop the film's action, things start happening too fast. His voice is now clear as lightning, heavy with emphasis: "Kate it's a burden, okay? It's a time-consuming burden and a pain, all this carrying you up and down stairs as if you were a vegetable. If I wanted social work, I would have applied for a job." Seeing her face, he adds, whining, "I'm just being *honest*, you're always saying you want me to be honest—"

And now the memory movie goes haywire, as if her brain's projector suddenly eats the film. *Wait, wait, what just happened, where is the island,* but there's no time, and anyway this is not Carl, Carl is gone, it would not be appropriate to ask such questions of a stranger. (*This is not Kate.*) Images spin by, fast-forward, fast-reverse, freeze-frame, crashing one against another. A naked woman leaps out of a bed, she's throwing clothes into an overnight bag and pulling on her skirt, hair flying. She's at the top of the stairs, huge crash, what, him? She's thrown him down

224

the stairs? No, no, the wheelchair, it lies far down at the bottom, wheels spinning, and where is the man? Behind her, he's followed her and is behind her, his hands seizing her ankle just as she swan dives after the chair so that her head and chest hit hard, once, seven or eight stairs down. She hears the thud, a corny sound effect.

Dangles there, arms flopped uselessly over her head. *I could sleep here, just like this. Quiet, peaceful. I could stay here forever, hold very still, no one will notice me.* Heady vertigo of death on her tongue. Backflashing: an accident, Maine, overturned car, waking on the wrinkled inner surface of its roof in a sea of broken glass. *Like waking up inside a kaleidoscope. It's all done with mirrors, and little pieces of glass.* Four car tires spinning, singing in dark air. Curling then on her side among the shards, chin to knees, drawing glass over her like a blanket, listening to April night wrap itself around her car. *So still.*

Her skirt is bunched up over her waist; she forgot to put anything on underneath it. Her naked breasts against the wooden stairs are already screaming.

He's still gripping her ankle. "Help me, Kate," he rasps, chewing the words, spitting them out. "Help me pull you up."

She does not. She does not help him. Does not even arch her neck protectively back. Her forehead, nose, and cheekbones strike each step in turn, like fingers playing a scale, as he hauls her up by both ankles.

Retrieved, lying flat on the floor face down, head hanging off the top stair, she hears a man's voice, harsh, slightly nasal, tremulous. Very angry. "Jesus Christ Kate you're crazy. I didn't mean it. You know damn well—"

The voice is out of breath. He cannot see the blood on her face or breasts. She lies perfectly still, suspended. Nothing stirs. When the alarm clock in his room suddenly erupts, her body jerks, spasmodic; when the clock runs down, she subsides. It is

225

the screenplay's clever plot device for letting the man know that the woman is alive, is conscious.

He kneels behind her, looking down: bunched skirt bisecting her nakedness. Nothing that he's looking at is damaged: back, buttocks, thighs, calves. All the damage is hidden.

First her back. Strokes it, tentative, light, tender, as if in apology, as if to heal, fingertips gliding from shoulder blade to waist. Again, again. She does not move, and the hand bivouacs down across the tangled island of skirt and finds her nakedness again: twin mounds, the narrowness between. Two hands now, not so light now, purposeful, kneading. She lies as if dead, amazed at the seamless segue, dizzy, can't keep up, his hands now spreading her open. His tongue. His cock.

He doesn't know about the blood. She cannot stop him, cannot move. Itchy rivulets are trickling from forehead to scalp, dripping onto the top stair. *He'll turn me over, see the blood, and then he'll stop.*

He won't stop!

May 7, 1981

*E*LLEN'S BEEN WITH me a week, she sleeps on the living room sofa. Brings in the mail, feeds the cat, puts out the garbage. Mostly, she talks to me. She cooked a big batch of rice and beans, enough to last all week, every night she heats some up. Dirties one pot, two plates. Mushy, not too hard to eat. For the first three days she called in sick, then I persuaded her to go back to work.

Sam curls up with me on the blankets and keeps me company while Ellen's at work. I used to have a rule about no cats on the bed but I changed the rule, now it's no cats *in* bed, I mean I don't let Sam under the covers. He keeps wanting to lie on my chest, but the doctor said the ribs might not knit right if there's pressure on them or if I move around too much.

I feel better when Sam's with me, even if he hurts my ribs.

He's smart, he knows things. Years ago, when I found him on my stoop and brought him to the vet, I was told he'd been hit many days before. The vet didn't expect him to live. He must have been lying somewhere, a little more dead each day, before he decided to find a better place to die and came to me. Little squashed, broken Sam. His bones knit, though. The vet said cat bones heal better than dog, they're smaller, more flexible.

I wonder where he was lying, before he found me. I wonder what he thought about. Did it rain on him? When I think of him out there in the rain I cry, even though he's fine and happy now.

Before Sam, I used to tell myself things happen for a reason. But what reason could there be? Sam out there in the rain. It rained at least once during those days before Sam found my stoop, I'm sure it did.

The emergency room doctor who bandaged my face said my nose will knit nicely, which tickled me, the alliteration. Ellen says now our noses will be twins. One of my eyes is filled with blood, there's no white left, like an egg that's all yolk, but the doctor said the retina's not permanently damaged, the red will go away in four or five weeks. She said the fractured cheekbone will also knit "without significant deformity."

All this knitting, I should open a yarn shop.

No apparent brain injury, she said.

Ellen drove me to the hospital. She says she got worried when she kept calling for days and getting no answer, she knew I was home, my car was parked in the driveway. Finally she picked the lock. Ellen has some funny skills.

At the hospital they wanted to admit me, not for the broken bones and lacerations, which they said didn't require hospitalization. They wanted to admit me to their *other* wing, for my own protection, they said. But I said no, and Ellen said no, and we drove home. She said that when she was eleven, that time her father broke her nose, they wanted to lock her up too, they

228

said she was "excessively traumatized." Typical of justice in this country, she says. Lock up the female with the broken bones and let the man who broke them go scot free.

The next day Ellen called the cops. For a while she spoke to someone at the station, then she covered the phone and asked me if I wanted to press charges.

"What charges," I said.

She looked at me, then told the cops she'd call them back. After she hung up the phone she went over everything with me, same as the day before in the emergency room. The doctor who examined me told her no, the injuries didn't appear to have been inflicted by fists. It looked to her like either I'd fallen down a flight of stairs or someone pushed me, she said, although there were unusual bruises on my ankles. She said the amount and type of damage to my face was also somewhat unusual.

The other thing she said was, I appeared to have been raped.

So I tried to crank up the memory-movie, I wanted Ellen to see for herself what really happened. I'd been trying to play it ever since she found me. But the film was hopelessly chewed up from the projector.

"How can I press charges," I said. "What if he didn't push me down the stairs. What if I fell."

"But he *raped* you," she said.

I shook my head. "If it was Carl, it wasn't rape."

"He *tore* you, Kate. It was the *doctor* who called it rape, not me. And sodomy."

"The doctor's probably jealous. She probably hasn't had any for so long she doesn't know the difference anymore between lovemaking and rape."

"Kate, a man doesn't *make love to*"—she spat out the words—"a woman right after she's fallen down stairs and smashed herself up. *If you fell.*"

"How do you know it was *after?* Maybe we made love *before* I fell."

"Why did he leave you here? It must have happened at his house, he's the one with all the stairs. He must have driven you home in your car, carried you inside, and left you here on your bed, then called a cab to take him home. Why didn't he take you to the hospital? The mailman says he delivered your mail for four days and no one picked it up. Kate. Carl left you here to *rot*. You could have *died*."

"I ate. I went to the bathroom. I didn't rot."

"What did you eat?"

I didn't know. I couldn't remember. I must at least have sipped water, otherwise I would have been dehydrated.

I couldn't remember Carl too well either, except that he glues bones.

"What if it wasn't Carl," I said. "What if it was a stranger."

"If it was a stranger, why hasn't Carl called you?"

"Maybe he has. Maybe he tried to call during the four days before you came. Maybe he's busy. If he doesn't know anything's wrong, why should he call—"

"Okay, I'm gonna tell you," she said. "I went over there. Last evening. I went to his house and waited till he got home from work."

I'd forgotten Ellen knew where he lived. "What did he say?"

"I told him I was gonna put him behind bars for rape and battery. He turned white as a sheet."

"Anyone would turn white as a sheet if you said that. It doesn't prove anything."

"He said you jumped, he didn't push you. He said he saved your life, you should be grateful. He called you a self-destructive, crazy bitch—"

Ellen's voice was shaking. I started to cry, a scream spiraled up out of me, *"Stop, stop,"* but it was too late, the memory-movie started to roll all by itself when she said the word "crazy," the film perfectly intact, not a wrinkle or tear, not even flutter in the voices. *A burden. A pain. If I wanted social work.*

230

I played the whole movie for her, every word. Then I asked how badly was I torn. I couldn't remember the emergency room doctor saying anything about it, and I couldn't bring myself to say, How badly did he tear me?

"Bad enough," Ellen said. Something in her voice made me look up. She was sitting on the edge of my bed, hugging her knees, her eyes focused on a spot on the floor. I wished I'd looked up sooner, wished I hadn't told her the whole story. Selfish Kate. How long had she looked like that?

"Kate," she said, very quietly. "All those years with my father, I didn't know any better. I was too little. I didn't know the word 'rape.' I believed in all the awful things he said would happen if I ever told anyone. And I thought it was my fault, I thought the things he did to me were punishment because I was a bad girl. If I told the secret, then everyone would know how bad I was."

She stopped, staring at the floor. I waited, I couldn't stand the silence. Scratched Sam's belly. Waited.

"I mean," she said. Silence. "If I could take my grown woman's brain and put it into my six-year-old body, I would *never* have let him get away with it. I would have told the whole fucking world what he was doing."

She'd been sitting with her chin on her knees, arms locked around her calves. She looked up at me.

"What happened to you was different," I said. "Incest is different. This was my own damn fault, I should never have gotten involved with him in the first place."

I paused, toying with the cat, afraid to look up. When I finally did, her look was angry, sad, distant. "How can you say that," she said. "*You*. A veteran of how many years in the women's movement."

"It was my wheelchair, wasn't it," I said lamely, pretending not to have heard. "If I weren't in a wheelchair, he would never have—"

It sounded soapy, bathetic, so I stopped.

231

"Bullshit," Ellen said flatly.

Tomorrow I'll see about fixing it. I'm a little too tired right now. Ellen wanted me to put it off until I'm healed, but I don't want to wait. So she made me promise not to fix it unless she's there to make sure I don't move around too much.

She got up from the bed and said she had to go make a phone call. As she left the room she turned and said, "I'll only say it one more time. I want you to think about pressing charges."

I told her I'd already made up my mind. I threw myself down the stairs. All he did was say something mean.

"He raped you," she said coldly.

"No. Not rape. We made love."

July 30, 1981

Dear Mark,

I'm writing this letter in long-belated response to a letter you wrote Ellen back in January, which E. showed me. At the time I wasn't thrilled with her decision to share what was obviously intended for her, since all it caused was a lotta agita. I fumed for months about being patronized, which I gather E. also addressed in her letter to you. The world would be a much simpler place for all of us if those of you who don't have disabilities stopped: (a) tiptoeing around those of us who do, and (b) assuming you know what's best for us.

Since you seemed primarily concerned with my wheelchair, I thought I'd start there. I know E. has already sup-

233

plied you with some answers, but E. is after all not me, nor is she in a chair.

Mark, sit down, stretch your legs: this will be a long one. Maybe I'll break it up into installments. I could as easily say to my journal what I'm going to say to you, but it's more elastic, a letter, there's the tantalizing thought that someone's listening, the heady prospect that some-one—not just anyone but my dear friend Mark, whom I do value, agita notwithstanding—might even respond.

There's another reason, Mark, for speaking these things to you rather than to my journal. This: you've got some thinking to do. That rigorously principled, articulate so-cialism of yours has a few gaps. Since I've been one of the people who've benefited from your values (I still have that letter to *The Times* taped to the wall beside my desk), I now seize the opportunity to return, if I can, the gift.

With the advent of my wheelchair, much has changed. A great deal has happened in the months since your letter arrived, and in the two and a half years between your move to Utah and your letter. Too much to summarize, and anyway, most of that stretch is not worth summariz-ing. What is there to say about years of physical pain and mental darkness? As E.'s sister Michelle—who worked as a screenwriter in Hollywood for two years—used to say: "That's not a *story*, that's *life!*"

The story, then, leaps over those two and a half years of crutches. The story is this, Mark: I've come to view wheel-chairs as conveniences, rather than as portable prisons on wheels or, worse, as badges of moral capitulation. A life-transforming concept that took its time with me, steering a cumbersome path from brain to heart.

The story is this effort of vision, this coming-to-terms.

The story, then, told from the top, with apologies for

length (you can take little breaks, get up, go to the bathroom, eat salami sandwiches while you read):

With the advent of my wheelchair, much has changed. An odd public silence follows my passage now wherever I go, causing me sometimes perversely to yearn for the old innocent nosiness of commiserating strangers. (Remember?) Take men, for instance. (Please.) Many of the men who might have stared when I was using crutches now avert their eyes. Those brassy looks of sexual appraisal—eyes sweeping me from head to foot, sizing me up—happen even less frequently now. I had grown used to those looks (which is not to say I found them acceptable), had come to expect such behavior wherever I went. When I changed from crutches to wheelchair, something happened to men's sexual interest in me.

(Speaking of men's sexual interest in me, shall I tell you what I think of your lurid curiosity about my personal life? No, I did not sleep with Kevin, not that it's any of your business. There was a recent brief liaison, which ended in late April. I've been mending, slowly; the damage was great. But I cannot, or will not, speak of it, not yet. [Soon, maybe.] Except to say that I've come to re-appreciate you.)

I used to have a colleague at school who thought canes enhanced a woman's femininity. You can rest assured he does not think the same of wheelchairs. Women on canes and crutches are still vertical figures, same general size and shape as other women and therefore the same species, more or less. Women seated in wheelchairs are short, our heads no higher than the average adult's chest, which makes us—significantly—the same height as kids. Our bodies are not so easy to appraise, and men rarely get the chance to watch our asses when we walk. The moment men identify my conveyance as a *wheelchair*—not so readily recognizable as most, being a so-called lightweight, quite unlike the clunky chrome tanklike medical models that still dominate the market, the kind of chair Ellen and Kevin first saw me use—their eyes slide away. (The chair I'm using now is a loaner arranged by a local agency until my very own sports model arrives from California.)

Why those monstrosities have had such a stranglehold on the wheelchair industry would be an ideal subject for one of those vitriolic letters to the editor for which you're justly famous. (If only you weren't such a bigot about wheelchairs.) I compare it to the stranglehold exercised for years by misogynist designers on the world of women's fashion. Commercial wheelchairs have started looking attractive and performing efficiently only since their design has begun to be engineered by people who use them or who like and respect others who use them.

Anyhow, it's as if, in that instant of recognition, I cease to exist for men as a sexual being. All their deepest fears and assumptions about *cripples* are summoned forth by the simple visual impact of my wheelchair. Cripples are vegetables. Cripples are basket cases. Cripples have to overcome their handicaps. Cripples have given up on themselves. (Sound familiar?) Cripples belong in institutions.

One would think the change in men's sexual behavior would have come as a relief to me, given how objectionable I found the old role. But it's not entirely consistent. I mean, strange men do still undress me with their eyes, though less frequently, and usually I'm on crutches when it happens. (I still use crutches sometimes, in situations where it's too hard to maneuver the chair.) Because of the inconsistency, and because I'd clearly internalized the old identity to some extent, I can't say I had the pleasure of such relief, certainly not at first. *Au contraire,* I found myself suffering a kind of reflexive *is-my-slip-showing?* anxiety, regressing to the gawky eighth grader at the sock hop in 1959 who never got asked to dance by boys.

This kind of reduction was too silly to last very long; the more I've exchanged notes with other disabled women, the easier it's become to detach myself from old sexual values and to view them and their slavish adherents with a certain calm superiority. Mostly it's been a hard and lonely private struggle, though, since until recently I counted among the people close to me no disabled women who could provide role models, in terms of helping me carve out for myself a new sexual identity. When I found them—my new friend Sheba and others, gay and straight, whose manner and bearing sent a clear message—*I know my own worth, and those who choose not to see it are the losers*—they served as beacons for me. My presence, my personal way of being in the world, underwent a sea change.

It had to do with how they held their heads. How some women in manual chairs jumped curbs, practical, preoccupied with getting from here to there. (It wasn't the wheelies themselves; athleticism per se has no hold on me. It was that *style!*) How they entered rooms full of nondisabled people sitting straight, as if they had a right. How, breathing into fat-ribbed respirator tubes, certain quadriplegic women paused to smile. How respirator breathing could seem suddenly sexy in a way that dragging on Virginia Slims never would, when at the end of that tube there flashed the briefest, most spectacular of smiles.

Mark, it was the Respirator Women who gave me permission to have a disability, whose casual grace finally shamed me into ownership. The Respirator Women, whose heads didn't move, nor their pinky fingers, nor their toes, had minds that did. *Oh the tragedy*, I used to whine inwardly, thinking myself empathetic, until a Respirator

237

Woman grinned. *Imagine*, I would brood, *being trapped inside a body* (standard pop media fare, that; I didn't know better)—until a Respirator Woman winked at me.

What was that wink saying? *What an interesting business*, I decided it said, meaning life. It might even have been saying, *What fun*. Either way it posed problems. How could life be interesting, let alone fun, for trapped people? They must be fooling themselves, or perhaps I was misreading those sassy grins. But how could I be that far off? Clearly they were *not* saying *Poor me*, which is what the media seemed to be saying they were saying, or rather, seemed to feel they *should* be saying.

(Actually, the more I think about it, the more it appears to me that the media wants it both ways. Journalists, TV and film directors, and screenwriters seem to want to do *poor-them* stories ad nauseam about the Respirator Women, but woe unto her who actively solicits this response. Self-pity is unseemly, not to mention tacky, when publicly displayed. It strikes me now as not unlike—you'll appreciate the analogy—our culture's old sexual double standard toward women, i.e., we're attractive only so long as we're "innocent"; if we *try* to be sexy, we deserve whatever we get.)

Sometimes I even thought the wink was saying more: *What's the big goddamn deal*, I thought I read there. But no, it was impossible, a gross irreverence. I kept my puzzle to myself, at least for the time being, and concentrated on the implications of this view of disability (the oh-the-trag-edy-of-being-trapped-inside-a-body-that-doesn't-work syndrome) for those of us who are "trapped."

In the end, though, the irreverence tumbled out without warning. I was speaking at a conference when it happened; by then I had more or less made up my mind that the Respirator Women were right: what *was* the big goddamn

238

deal? Still, I had not meant to risk saying so, feeling un-ready, my gut knowing many things to be true without my brain's yet understanding why. But the words said themselves, and immediately a hand shot up.

It was a nondisabled acquaintance, someone I've known casually for years. I must have come across as glib, to her anyway; she was greatly vexed. "It *is* a tragedy not to be able to do what your body was meant to do. What the hell's wrong with admitting it?"

Well, nothing's wrong with admitting that I can't run track anymore. But then, neither can she—I happen to know—ride horseback. *I* can—gracelessly, of course, but with a certain endearing tenacity. I *do* stay on the horse, which is more than she can boast. Does that make her a "tragic" figure? ("Methinks she doth protest too much," she returned, the little snit, insinuating sour grapes!)

What about that faithful dog, poverty, which we're told is another "human tragedy"? Where have we gotten by calling it that? The distance from "human tragedy" to "human condition" to "the poor will always be with us" is only a stone's throw.

"In sum," I told my audience of social workers, psychologists, health care professionals, etc., "the tragic view of disability makes me break out in hives."

You woulda been proud.

Later, driving home that evening, I expanded my rhetoric, honed my attack. It's the flip side—equally pointless—to nondisabled people's sense of threat in our presence, I soliloquized. It confers upon us stardom; we become Survivors, larger than life. "Anyone who's been through what you've been through can survive anything," went one boozy bar-talk gaucherie addressed to me. As if three hip operations were worse than the Holocaust.

Shall I tell you a little story, Mark? Some time ago, on a

long train ride, I met an awed couple who later confessed that they'd made a point of introducing themselves to me in order to find out if I was "for real." "You don't seem handicapped," they said, thinking themselves complimentary—can you beat it?—going on to explain that while they'd seen lots of TV productions about "courageous people who've overcome their handicaps, who can do anything," they'd "never really met one in person."

"'Till there was youuuu'" I barely stopped myself from crooning. Irrepressible (and unfair, Peter tells me) ridicule foamed like acid in my mouth; I wanted to squash their cheap idolatry and rub it in their placid faces. Nondisabled people seem obsessed with this moral principle that we should "overcome" our disabilities, as if we live our whole lives locked in mortal combat with our bodies. As for me, I'm mostly content with mine, which is not to deny that I live a life of perpetual active combat, but rather to say that my body is the *least* of my adversaries.

People who "can do anything." Well well. My admirers had met their first Supercrip. What exactly had they observed me doing that made them think I could do anything?

Let's see. First of all, I got on the train. Given the inaccessibility of that train (in violation of federal law), getting on meant asking for help. Did that qualify me as Supercrip?

Combat, to be sure . . . But with whom, over what?

Later, stomach growling, I asked the porter about meals. He mentioned the dining car, fourteen cars away. I asked if a meal could be delivered to my seat and he assured me that it could, for an additional fee of only three-fifty. My choices seemed clear: pay the service fee (I didn't have it, and wouldn't have paid it if I had), or refuse to pay on the grounds that it discriminated against people who

240

couldn't get to the dining car. (The train's aisles were too narrow for wheelchairs—not that they could have boarded in the first place—and fourteen jerking, jiggling cars was far too long and hazardous a hike for someone on crutches.)

But taking such a stand on a disability matter was not (yet) my style; besides, nothing on the short take-out list appealed to me. (Many items on the regular menu were not considered take-out foods.) I was seething; though hardly a disability rights crusader at the time, I knew even then that I had a right to order whatever I damned well pleased on that menu.

Leave it to me to be stirred to revolution by matters of food.

My third option, and the one I finally chose, was to find a way down to the dining car. Never having been in or even seen one, I found this choice by far the most appealing, evoking Cary Grant scenes of conviviality, romance. It should be noted that my Pullman car had been booked not for luxury's sake—I was living on welfare at the time, so a friend footed the bill—but out of medical necessity: a Pullman gave me my only chance to elevate the bad leg. Still, I fell in love with that car—its leather seats, its exotic smell of privilege—for the first three hours or so, until I began to feel that oppressive loneliness that too often seems to accompany "medical necessity." Lap of luxury notwithstanding, my Pullman cut me off from everyone else on that train. By dinnertime it had begun to feel like solitary confinement; I was desperate for another human face.

Hence my determination to get to the dining car. And get there I did, carried high above the narrow aisles of fourteen cars by strong and chivalrous passengers. (Transit

241

employees were instructed not to get involved, for liability reasons.)

A set of ordinary impulses—to travel by public transportation, to eat in a public place—were insultingly thwarted, leading me to a set of equally ordinary emotional responses which in turn led me to act. Which so impressed these people that they concluded I could "do anything."

Must wrap this up; Sam's beseeching me for supper. There's more to say, but I want to get this off to you. Another letter, perhaps.

Mark, the fact that you no longer have a "claim" on me—quaint locution, that—does not preclude your writing to me, if the spirit should so move you. Don't be such a chicken.

Love,
Kate

PASSING

You don't seem handicapped,
she said. You seem like an ordinary
person who just happens to be sitting
in a chair with wheels instead of legs.
You look like any minute you'll
get up and walk away from it,
like you just sat down in it
for a moment's leisure in your busy
day. You look like being handicapped
is just one part of you, like being
blonde. You don't look like you've taken
root in that chair, like some fungus
has attached you to the seat. You look
like you have better things to do
with your life than sit around
in a wheelchair feeling sorry
for yourself. You look like someone
who eats eggs and toast in the morning,
not intravenous protein. You look
mainstream, you look cool. Your body
looks whole, and your mind.
You don't drool, jerk,
or twitch. You don't embarrass
us or make us feel guilty.
You don't make our skin crawl.
If you sat in a regular chair,
you could pass.

243

August 7, 1981

Dear Mark,

Thanks for your call last night. It's a relief to know you're not put off by my self-righteous zeal to instruct. Fact is, whatever course I'm charting here is as much for my own navigation as for yours.

About Carl, don't worry that you're "invading my privacy" with all your questions. (And don't worry about my health. As I told you over the phone, I'm back in one piece. There's this fetching little crook in my nose, is all.) If I hadn't wanted you to know, I wouldn't have given Ellen permission to talk to you and Peter. I'd have preferred telling you myself back in April when it happened, but I couldn't bear to talk about it then, or answer questions, or be pushed (as E. at first pushed) to press charges. I suggested to E. that we agree to disagree on the subject and not discuss it further, and she backed off. Actually, she's been wondrously supportive.

She's outside now, weeding my garden. Sam trots along at her feet, eagerly pushing his nose against her hands as she works, as if she were harvesting not zucchini and tomatoes but tasty morsels of fish. You should see him, Mark, his black fur glistening in the sun. Little splinter-boned, highway-casualty Sam. You saw him for the first time only a day after I found him, or rather, he found me. I practically had to scrape him up off my front dooryard, remember?

I look at Sam sometimes to remind myself of change: that it happens. Willy-nilly we move forward; even our falling-back is forward motion.

A new idea has taken root in me, Mark, one that sounds so simplistic I keep it to myself: healing begets healing. Sam's tenacity sent out ripples. And I, healing, eddying in Sam's little tide, create my own current. Of course, that which I've set *my* sights on "healing" is of a somewhat more ambitious order than Sam's cat-sized design for the world.

Did I have the chutzpah to imply, in that last letter, that my being carried through a few train cars amounted to a form of revolution? Oy, the arrogance. It's my guess that if I were to encounter the same set of circumstances now, my response might be quite different. I was in those days far less willing to be abrasive when my freedom was being breached. Still, it seems to me that even then, something had started happening; I entered that train, that dining car, *as if I had a right.*

Supercrip. God knows it's seductive, how the most mundane daily routines of disabled people's lives are transformed into "acts of courage" in the eyes of the foolish. And I admit that for a while, in the beginning, the myth

245

served me well: as a newly disabled person, I now had a kind of personalized yardstick for myself: how would the Courageous Survivor solve this situation? etc. I consulted her freely. She always had answers. She settled problems with style and grace. She never broke dishes. She could get a brimming cup of tea from stove to bedside on her forearm crutches without spilling a drop; she'd honed the daily skills to a fine art. She knew exactly what to say to students who sought her advice, and she said it with panache.

She was my heroic alter ego. I loved having her around, though she often laughed at me.

(I wonder if Peter indulges in such vanities? It was Peter, after all, who told me I could become wise, as if disability automatically bestows wisdom. But no, I'm not being fair. He said I had the chance to become wise, if I played my cards right.)

There are variations on this Survivor theme. "You must have learned a lot about yourself," I hear over and over. Well, okay. I learned, for instance, to spot my own double standard: I at first applied the same mythic dimensions to my new disabled friends, as if they were made of superior thread. They had *come through*. Look at my hospital writings! (Never mind, you can't, I never shared them with you. Take my word for it, then.) "This epic interior voyage I've traveled. . . ."—such self-absorbed bombast embarrasses me now.

As for this word, "courage." It "belongeth neither to me nor to my family" (my disabled comrades), except to the extent that we behave courageously. I mean this: our courage, if we have it, does not inhere in our disabilities. Some of us are wimps. Sam was not courageous to survive. He *lived*, that's all. He did what he had to do.

Am I throwing out baby with bathwater? Is there no such thing, a word without a referent? Harder by far to say what

246

it is than what it is not. Mostly what's clear to me is that it applies, or doesn't, equally to us all, disabled and non-disabled alike. Sometimes, in leaky moments, I think the supreme act of courage is keeping one's eyes—the meta-phorical eyes, through which blind people see—open. Waking up every morning, opening the eyes and then not simply closing them again at the pageantry of pain and injustice that assaults us every day on the streets, on TV, in the papers. Opening the eyes, getting up, pulling ourselves through the day by our fingernails, cleaving to this foolish conceit that what we say, do, believe, will resonate with what others do and say, and that in this resonance, this finding/teaching of one another, will come healing, revolu-tion. Courage is that opening, that staying open, of eyes, that getting-up. As if it mattered. As if we mattered.

Which of course implies *looking*. Courage is active, not a noun at all but a transitive verb. Looking both *in*—"go into yourself and see how deep the place is from which your life flows" (Rilke)—and out. (Rilke again: "the kind of humble yet passionate looking that woos a thing to reveal itself.") Relentlessly, in and out.

I no longer want to hear myself or my people glibly cast as courageous, not by you or anyone. Courage is earned, a rare state of grace.

What do I look at when I look "out?" Lately I've been looking at the physical arrangements of a world I always took for granted, that you still take for granted. I grew up, for instance, riding buses and trains easily and often as a child. My parents both worked, so there was no one to drive me around. I loved it, the hurly-burly of kids and grown-ups getting on and off, blowing noses, quarreling, finding seats. It would have shocked me to be told that I was exercising not a right but a privilege, one that would

247

later be taken away. I thought everyone did it, just as I believed at eight or nine that Love Conquers All.

I remember the moment I discovered, at the age of ten in 1957, watching a TV play about southern black migrant workers, that *not* everyone in America had freedom of choice when it came to such commonplace acts as riding buses and trains. (My parents had just bought their first television set and I, awed, sat glued to the screen for weeks.) I knew that such things were possible, that freedom could be taken away, having pored through Anne Frank's diary. But that was Germany, and history. It seemed unimaginable that some Americans were made to ride separate buses, attend separate schools and churches, sit in separate sections way in the back of movie theaters, and enter through separate doors.

A special kind of anger, a receptivity, was born in me then. Shortly thereafter came my first heartthrob: Sydney, West Indian, an athlete like me who, alone among all the boys in my school, ran barefoot in track meets. I used to tremble, watching his exotic brown feet pound the cinders, thrilled by this small but somehow noble rebellion. My parents invited him for a back yard picnic, in defiance of "what the neighbors would think."

But it was anger I didn't yet own; it stood apart from me, as I continued to take my own range of choices for granted. Even after February 1978, when so much more than mere muscle was quietly cut from my life as I slept, still some part of me went on regarding freedom as a cup always brimming, effortlessly and invisibly refilled just for me. The pain of movement was a temporary inconvenience, that was all, it was the price I should expect to pay for surgery; it would subside and my old life, cocky and bulging with freedom, would return.

For some time I tried to pretend nothing had changed.

The shock of ending up on metal crutches quickly buried itself beneath layers of denial: a little practice and I'd get the hang of it, and then just watch me! Never mind that just as I heaved myself up one clifflike step, the bus driver shifted gears and sent me sprawling shamefully on my knees. Never mind the endless flights of stairs into the bowels of New York subways. It was my own fault that I had to stop fifteen stairs from the top, sit down on those filthy steps and gag with pain. Oh, the indignity! Silly weak creature!

I could not figure it. Kate, my grand courageous Survivor, had abandoned me. Here it was time to renew my driver's license and she was gone, leaving me halfway up the sweeping marble Motor Vehicle Bureau stairs (post office, public library, city hall, my own university), hunched over my crutches, crying in public.

Crying in public. How could she put me through such humiliation? Not to mention the muscle stress pain. Just when I needed her almighty powers most, she vanished and I was left to cope alone, puny, Lilliputian. Had she been sleeping on the job when architects had designed all those stairs? Surely her splendid presence should have reminded them not to create streets, buildings, whole transit systems that excluded not only her but all the special mythic people they so adored.

After all, everyone went to great lengths to call us "special." Special Education. Special Children. Special Olympics. How nice to be so special. And how odd that such special people could be so easily forgotten when those who sang our praises sat down at their drafting tables or in their city council chambers.

It took me some time to sort these things out. I was unprepared; no rehab counselor took me firmly by the hand before I left the hospital and said, "You are about to reenter a world made for people with two working legs, ears, eyes, a sturdy brain. You are a pariah. Get ready." On the contrary, I was wooed with my "specialness," or advised, in the words of one seemingly well-intentioned social worker: "Whatever you do when you leave here, don't join any *handicapped groups*. As long as you don't see yourself as handicapped, you won't *be* handicapped."

At the time I understood only that I was once again being exhorted to "think positive," this time by a member of the hospital team. Once again, handicaps were "all in the mind." It's possible that I could have spared myself years of anguish if I'd been less ambivalent on this point.

(The ambivalence went deeper than conscious thought. Certainly my intellect was outraged; but oh, how my heart longed to believe her! leaping from one precipice to another, flapping its arms in a mighty rush of faith . . .)

There was another element, too, in her admonition, recognized by me (then) only dimly and without understanding: *she seemed to be trying to keep us apart*. The "us" was for me a brand-new and exciting use of my favorite pronoun. It was not until I began to meet other "special" people and hear their stories that the full significance of my new status came clear to me: *If we're so special, why ain't we rich?*

It startles and shames me now to acknowledge how unaware I've been of people with disabilities, throughout most of my life. Where on earth was I? (Well, and where were *they* when I was young? Closeted in institutions and in their homes, most of them.) I think that as a small child I simply didn't know disabled people existed. Occasional glimpses on the streets eventually taught me otherwise, though so far as I could tell they didn't seem to *do* anything, didn't contribute to the world. Some begged.

These were not conscious notions, of course; I acquired them through cultural osmosis, just as you and Kevin ac-

250

quired your attitudes about wheelchairs. I remember my response to one child who attended my school. Her twisted body was covered with open sores, her painful one-foot-in-front-of-the-other gait a kind of miracle of locomotion. At six or seven, other kids were not impressed with this achievement. Why did she never look up as she passed? Why didn't she joke around or smile or say hi but only looked at the ground, her small solemn face drawn into itself? A snob, the kids concluded, hilariously mimicking her gait.

Though I was one of them, never did I mock her openly, and something in me hated my schoolmates for their treatment of her, and hated myself each time my cousin and I indulged in our private ridicule. (We had her walk down pat. We performed it at home, for the entertainment of my parents.)

Why then did I do it? Where did it come from, that stunning cruelty? (*Ah, forgive me, Barbara. And be angry. Cherish that anger. Let it guide you, like certain dreams. Courage is anger, its just, pure, molten core. Owning it, and acting.*) For I don't think any of us really wanted to torment her; the wellspring of compassion that sprang up in my throat when I watched her silently moving through her world ran in all of us, I am convinced. There was a nervous urgency about the mockery, as if it went against our own grains, as if we were doing what we knew was expected of us and we wanted to be done with it. Weren't we after all simply mirroring, in our grand theatrical style, what we saw grown-ups do every day, in their gossip, their furtive stares, their embarrassment? I encountered people with disabilities only as aberrations. How many deaf kids were featured in the Dick and Jane trash we labored through at school? How many of our favorite stars were disabled? Did Doris Day use a wheelchair? Did Elvis?

Small wonder that my childhood worldview didn't encompass such people I believe the message we (non-disabled American kids, including you, Mark) all absorbed at some level was that "they" were not in the mainstream *because they didn't deserve to be. They were flawed.*

Later, having started to outgrow my mute acceptance of such bigotry, I befriended a high school girl who had cerebral palsy. Her gratitude was puppylike. We had nothing in common other than our status as outsiders. (Mine was thoroughly cemented by my friendship with her, though its origins had nothing to do with her. I was a plain, thoughtful, solitary girl, disdainful of teased hair and football rallies. My best friends were grown-ups: the orchestra conductor, a few janitors whose dignity I liked and who treated me with respect.) I could not stand to see Sue's loneliness; like Barbara in grade school, she was the butt of an elaborate repertoire of jokes. Though I couldn't have articulated it, I think I felt personally answerable for the meanness of my peers, for hadn't I colluded in that same behavior as a child? My kindness toward Sue was an act of contrition, of reparation. "The quality of mercy"—it was my favorite Shakespeare text, I murmured it to myself often, caressingly—"is not strained, but droppeth as the gentle rain from Heaven upon the place beneath."

Fourteen more years would pass before I'd contemplate the fine line where "mercy" ends and condescension begins . . .

Ah, here comes Ellen, in from the garden, a basketful of zucchini and tomatoes under her arm. We're about to cook up some ratatouille and have a picnic in the yard. My friend Sheba, whom I met in mid-June, will be joining us. Wish you could be here, Mark.

Think I'll send this off as is, though I haven't yet quite gotten where I'm going with you. One more letter should do it.

Love,
Kate

Kate dreams of Carl, her first Carl dream in twelve days.
Throughout May and half of June they were nightly visitations.
Sometimes it was screams that woke her, sometimes grunts, or
her body pedaling the sheets. Or sweat, buckets of sweat. After
that she began to disengage herself mid-dream, staring watch-
fully into the black room till morning. Toward the end of July
the dreams disappeared. This time she lets the whole dream
unfold without interruption, waking at her accustomed hour.

Carl is standing by the work table in his study. Kate sits in front of him.
On the table are his tools and the set of fine brass metric weights he uses to
weigh his owl pellets. In real life, Kate admired these tiny golden
weights; they were like minutely perfect toys, she wished she
could steal them for Lucy. Once Carl showed her how the

scales worked by weighing her earring, first demonstrating how to calibrate before placing the shiny weights one by one on the left pan, opposite her earring on the right.

He picks up a tiny brass weight with his watchmaker's tweezers. "Open up," he instructs. Kate obeys, and tenderly, carefully he places the weight on her tongue. She submits, sitting quietly as he adds another, and another, until the surface of her tongue is filled. He works quickly, gently, skillful as a surgeon.

"How will I talk?" Kate manages to ask.

"You won't!" he chides her solemnly. "These are very important, to counterbalance the other weight."

Kate sits, mouth open, the weights squatting sturdily on her tongue. Will they slip and fall down her throat, choking her? Will they tumble out of her mouth, freeing her?

They do neither. They stay in their place, as if glued. She feels their heaviness. She cannot speak.

Waking, she slides her tongue around inside her mouth: *A dream, Kate, it was a dream.* Calls out to Sam, to hear her voice.

In the shower she feels unaccountably buoyant. August sun splashes through the window by the tub, her skin looks ivory-gold. Slowly soaping her thighs, smiling, she thinks: *Something's changed. Something's good.*

Sheba will be here soon. They're working on a project together—drafting some press releases and a newspaper article.

Sheba. Ah. The smile stretches. Is that what it is, the good thing? Kate wants to linger, soap herself slowly, think about Sheba. But there's no time, she's due in half an hour, gotta make coffee.

When Sheba arrives, characteristically late, the coffee pot and mugs are set out on the kitchen table; Kate is at her desk in the living room. She's been sitting for some minutes, vaguely thumbing through the telephone directory, unsure why she's there, but the instant the doorbell rings ("Come on in, the door's open, I'll be with you in a minute"), her fingers find the number they're looking for. Her hand picks up the receiver. Sheba's battery hums as she wheels herself into the kitchen, followed by the footfall of her attendant. It is the thin, high hum of Sheba's chair that galvanizes Kate, nudging speech from her throat. As if just this moment emerging from her dream, she hears herself say: "Hello. I'd like to report a rape."

August 20, 1981

Dearest Mark,

First, an update on Carl. Since your last phone call two days ago, I've heard from my lawyer. Interestingly enough, though I like her much better than the dreadful D. A. they assigned me, and though I'm far more willing to trust her judgment, her conclusions about the case were not so different from his. She called this morning to say that if my purpose is to put Carl behind bars, I may or may not succeed and that, whatever the ruling, it would be an ugly, drawn-out business. She cited a number of nuggets she guaranteed would be used against me: that I waited over three months before reporting it to police; that Carl was my "boyfriend"; that he "saved" my life; that I have a history of suicide attempts and "emotional instability"; that before Carl I'd "had affairs with married men," namely you. And so on. She cautioned me to think hard about whether or not I want to spend the next two years or more being dragged—and possibly dragging others—through the mud. She said she's willing to represent me if I decide to pursue it, but . . .

I *am* thinking hard, and I think my decision may be to close that door and move on. My new life is very full; it seems the only way I could pursue the case would be by giving up something else, or at best stealing time from it. But what to steal from? Certainly not Sheba and my other new friends, or the work I'm doing with them (about which I'll tell you when the time comes), or even my swimming. (I'll be using an indoor pool when it gets too cold for the beach.) Doesn't it follow, then, that the thing to give up, let go of, is Carl?

Ellen says I owe it to other women to pursue the case, to the women Carl hasn't yet hurt. And I know she's right. And I owe it to *her*, to the child she was, who couldn't defend herself against her father. (I remember her telling you the story, though she may not have shared all the grisly details.)

But I can't undo what happened to Ellen, can't make it right. It happened, and the man who did it is long dead. (Though not for Ellen, whose nights are still occasionally stalked by him, who slugs it out with her demons, alone.)

The dilemma is this: I know I'm needed elsewhere. My energy, my skills must not be depleted. The lawyer says it will be painful; actually what she said was, it may be agony. Mark, I've had enough of pain.

Is this cowardice? I don't know.

But I want to get back to my ongoing exploration, which seems to be nearing a conclusion of sorts. I'm not sure why it matters so much that I get these things said. A kind of closure, maybe.

I did finally grasp what had happened to me. It took nearly three years of living with disability for the process really to begin. Once the seed was sown, there was no stopping it.

In retrospect it seems worth looking at that three-year lag. After all, I spent most of my life since age ten examining and embracing struggles against injustice. Usually they were other people's battles, like the union work in Maine, calling upon my gift of empathy. In 1969 the women's movement landed on my doorstep, demanding a skill very different from empathy: self-identification. By the time I'd become disabled, I'd put in some nine years fighting the good fight and forging a role for myself in *my* movement, sometimes on the barricades, more often at my typewriter.

Don't you wonder, Mark, why it took me so long to comprehend that I had joined, involuntarily, perhaps the most harshly oppressed minority in this country? Here were the separate schools and separate transportation, the separate entrances, the "public" buildings that were not public for us, the books and movies and TV shows that did not feature us at all, as if we didn't exist, and the books and movies and TV shows that portrayed us as insulting caricatures, pathetic "vegetables"—one of the nondisabled world's more charming bits of nomenclature—no better than the Aunt Jemimas and picaninnies of the fifties and before. Here was oppression so vivid it burnt the eyes to look at, and I spent my first three years doing—what?

The textbooks say the newly disabled person experiences first rage (*Why me?*), then denial. Does whatever comes next depend on how "healthfully" one completes these two crucial stages? I try to look back now at my first few months of reckoning, but they're a blur. The only real record I have is my journal, which tells me that yes, there was one pure moment of rage (turned, as is my habit, against myself) the day I bought the forearm crutches. I'm sure you recall, since you colluded with Ellen and Peter in the hiding of my pills. There were also, at E.'s, moments of seething ill-humor. But it was not until I'd moved out of E.'s and was on my own, away from the protective, kindly, suffocating care of friends, that my rage had its first real chance to spread its dark wings and fly. As long as I was sheltered, rage had a way of deferring to gratitude and guilt. (Is that why I speak of suffocating? Didn't I comprehend even then that my healthy, necessary anger was being swallowed up, that it must be given its rope?)

But the trail ends there. The journal stopped shortly after I moved into my own place and didn't resume for two and a half years. I rummage among memories and come up with a chapter of living so intensely felt, an emotional tumult so searing, that nothing emerges to pull the pieces into some sensible whole. *Was there rage? If not, where did it go?*

Certainly there was grief (the flip side of rage), a stunning sense of abandonment. And dizzying pain in the muscles that remained in my leg. The pain tended to convert itself into more grief, and later into denial, resignation, depression, and yes anger, righteous anger, though its sources were still only vaguely perceived. But as for *rage,* that bone-grinding egotistical frenzy—*How can this be happening to me, I'll kill whoever made this happen*—I scour the past in vain, thinking to re-create it. Even my body seems to have pushed its memories out of reach, except for slicing flashes that pass almost before the brain can apprehend what's happened. A certain high school snapshot sometimes used to have that effect, a photo of me running in a track meet, winning, yards ahead of the rest, a grin of savage joy pleating my face. The cells of my leg muscles would suddenly remember how it was, the glory, but before the brain could catch up, process it, convert it into some useful lesson it was gone, sunk below the surface with hardly a ripple of déjà vu. That hot gymsuit smell, the *whump whump* of sneakers pounding track—gone.

(*Don't give up, Kate. Keep worrying your rumpled little bonebag of grief. Late 1977, try that. Christmas celebration, Bulgarian and Macedonian music and dance, one of your favorite events of the year. Somehow you danced that night, though you had no gluteus medius left. They'd cut it out in April of that year. Somehow you walked in those days with only a cane, somehow you danced. You danced with Neil, remember? Full-bearded, soft-voiced Neil, most graceful dancer in all New York. He was dying of cancer, remember? You knew. Neil knew, everyone knew. When Neil crossed the floor and asked you to dance, you smiled your determined, pleased, grateful smile, stood up, lay down your cane and danced with him. Neil's dancing was so light, so subtle and courtly that your own unpracticed body started to match his movements, found itself dancing with a grace it had never known, until the fire in your leg—muscles screaming out against the abuse, and tumor pain too, for by December the tumor was back, shooting molten needles through the hollow where they'd cut it out before . . . And you knew that, too—until the fire made you wobble with pain, and Neil helped you off the floor.*

It was your last dance on two legs. Soon you were back in a hospital bed. By the time you were up and walking on aluminum crutches, Neil was dead.

Remember that? Remember that?)

It's no use. Whatever happened to the rage, it won't be summoned by sheer will. For nearly three years it seems to have crawled off into a hiding place, accompanied by its stepchild, political clarity. (My vision of us as a minority. My vision of *us*. My willingness to trade in first person singular for first person plural.)

260

Perhaps it would have happened sooner—that leap of faith from *I* to *we*—if I'd earlier encountered other disabled people who'd already leapt. But they were not there in my daily life, or rather, I didn't know to look for them. Or was not ready to look. I went to work—as Anne the German from Liberty Memorial would say—and came home, went to work, came home. All my energies were bent toward denial, toward forcing my muscles to do what they had always done, regardless of the cost.

It shocks me now to recall how I brutalized both body and soul during those years. I made myself climb the two long flights of stairs to my office, sometimes four times in one day—some of my classes being scheduled for the first floor, some for the second—and only when the pain so twisted my face that a nervous student or colleague offered help would I consent to being carried. And never once did I request to be transferred to a first-floor office or to have my classes rescheduled for first-floor rooms, even though it could have been arranged with relative ease, certainly with far less effort than was required of me each time I climbed the stairs. As for suggesting to administration that an elevator be installed, it would be years before this solution would strike me as anything other than a personal pipedream. Nor did it occur to me that the school's facile solution to its library access problem—I was issued a key to the ground-floor delivery entrance, to circumvent a long flight of stairs leading to the main entrance—effectively bought me off, silenced me, while doing nothing to address access for disabled *students*, who were not permitted keys. The indignity of back doors did not escape me, but I said nothing.

The self-abuse took subtler forms, too. There was the colleague who advised me, back when I walked with a cane, to stop introducing the English Department's

261

monthly chamber music concerts, turn the honors over to someone else, someone who doesn't use a cane. "People will be embarrassed," she said. "They'll think you're looking for pity."

That concert series was my brainchild. I'd conceived it, got authorization from the department head, designed it, booked the musicians, made arrangements for the room, publicized it—and I introduced each concert, with considerable pride. Did I say to her, *Sorry, Jane, but just because you feel threatened by my disability doesn't mean the audience will?* No, I did not. I drew back, stunned. I could think of nothing to say.

Reviewing these things, I shake my head: *denial.* Isn't that what the textbooks call it? But is that really all there is to say? Where was my righteous indignation? Nearly all the "catastrophically disabled" people I know put themselves through similar misery, both physical and mental, before they "adjusted." What on earth is going on here? I clanked around on crutches for almost three years in intolerable daily pain, before it dawned on me that: (1) crutches were the wrong apparatus for me; (2) life didn't have to consist of nothing but pain; and (3) I deserved better. I deserved a wheelchair! Sweet freedom!, if not from architectural barriers, at least from physical hurt. *My disability was not my fault, and did not merit punishment.*

Certainly people with disabilities have no corner on the self-abuse trade. What oppressed minority has a cheerier history? That social worker who warned me to stay away from "handicapped groups" knew perfectly well what she was doing, if not the implications of her advice. My instincts were right: she was indeed trying to keep us apart, by convincing each of us that our disabilities were our own personal problems. We were offered "adjustment counseling" to help us "adapt" to our disabilities (read, to help us

262

accept our place), but no one counseled us in ways to adapt society to us. We were apprised of the multiplicity of "special" programs and services—door-to-door library book delivery for "the homebound," door-to-door van transportation, the absentee ballot—but no one talked about how to get us out of our homes and into "public" libraries and buses and polling places. No one spoke of the civil rights those library and university administrators and transit authorities and boards of elections were violating with all their stairs. And no one, nope, *no one*, in my world anyway, tried to name the problem: whose fault was it we were "homebound?" *Who bound us?*

The real wonder is that any of us troublemakers find one another at all, given the forces that stand in our way . . . But I'm suddenly terribly worn out by all these letters. For now I have to stop; Sam's importuning, I think he wants to go out, and anyway it's time for my swim.

Love,
Kate

P.S.: You asked, two days ago, what I'm doing for work. I never answered, did I? Somehow the conversation kept circling back to Carl. Briefly, I work with my friend Sheba and some other people I met through her. It's unpaid labor, but right now that strikes me as the best kind of all, since it's undertaken out of pure choice. As for paying the bills, I cadge a living from free-lance copyediting and occasional journalism gigs. Though marginal at best, for now it's what I want. But I'll tell you more on the phone, when we speak again. Better swim now; if I wait too long the tide will be out.

*I*T'S SIMPLE," PETER, who knows nothing's simple, is saying. "You put down your pen and push the last page away from you."

It's an old theme. He waves off Kate's protestations. ("You don't just *finish* a journal, any more than you finish a life.")

The moment seems to Kate to embody a fundamental and defining difference between them. She sees herself as harboring a passion for closure, a quest so urgent as to propel her from one day to the next. The journal is kept open, its final page unwritten, because surely closure's just around the corner.

Throughout Kate's life, others have disparaged as childish naivete this faith that unfinished business can, *will*, be finished— the unread books read at last, the unspoken, unspeakable words spoken. Thanks, forgiveness, reparation, justice, all rendered where due.

It's not—she inwardly corrects, trying to get it right—that the final page remains untouched, but that it's always in the act of being written, a never-quite-completed gesture.

Peter, on the other hand (it seems to Kate)—world traveler, vessel for music so wrenching it singes the bones, veteran of how many hospital stays throughout his first ten years—shares with Ellen a refusal to clutter his life with the apparatus of expectation. He *finishes* in order to *start*, arbitrarily inscribing one page THE END and the next, PAGE ONE. It is, Kate thinks, what gives both Peter and Ellen their endearing breeziness; unlike Kate, they are not burdened by the compulsion to weigh everything they say and do, feeling its heft as if this very word or act might be the key that will set things right—a sometimes paralyzing encumbrance, though she suspects it is what fuels her political work. Still, she envies them their jaunty cynicism.

Peter has a point, she concedes; it's time to stop. Anyway her life seems already to have catapulted itself into new country; she might as well mark, retrospectively, the passage.

Peter, bored by easy victory, at once leaps to the defense of Kate's too readily abandoned position: "'Course, there are a couple things you need to add, before you wrap it up."

"What things?"

Well, first of all, he wants Kate to tell the journal of her swimming. He is impressed with it. Smug Peter! self-vaunted president of the Seen-It-All Club. (He reckons her a Member in Good Standing. "So to speak," he adds.) He of course never joins her; he says beaches are decadent. "Besides," he says, "my bald spot gets burnt."

Which is why he's wearing his cowboy hat right now. He pokes one wooden toe in the direction of Ellen (laboring among the tomatoes), upbraiding Kate: "You could do your own weeding if you weren't so lazy. You don't need Ellen's help."

It's true, she could do it herself, with some effort. (Sit in the dirt and slide along the rows on her rear.) But she likes to watch

265

Ellen, whose long, aristocratic black body in grubby corduroys, bent at the waist to pluck a glossy purple eggplant, reminds her incongruously of Van Gogh's stocky somber peasants. And Ellen likes it too, she says weeding makes her calm.

Anyway it's just as well that Peter hates beaches; Kate doesn't want his or anyone else's company when she swims. She swims alone, at the same Greek beach where, four years ago, she lay down in the sun. The souvlaki stand across the street still features lamb slowly turning on a vertical spit. The fishermen still fish with nets.

Kate, having left Peter and Ellen in her yard, apologetically explaining that beach season is almost over now, gotta swim while she can, promising to be back in a couple of hours for their cookout, lies down now in the sun.

Peter's right, she thinks, I ought to write about swimming. Shouldn't be too hard: A daily, excruciating pleasure.

As for the other thing he wants her to record, Kate told him not to hold his breath. So many layers and textures, so much light and dark. Joy, vertiginous. She hoards it, savoring, slowly sucking out the juicy pulp. Methodically wrapping her brain around it piece by piece, she as yet has told the story to no one from her old life: not her journal, nor Peter nor Ellen nor Mark.

Not that it's a secret; certainly those who populate her new life know. Anyway, she meant to talk with Ellen and Peter sooner . . . But happy preoccupations have rerouted her attention for several weeks.

Time to break silence, she thinks, deciding to rehearse it first, here on the languorous beach. Yes. Time to metabolize this memory, now over two months old.

Kate closes her eyes. Sun nudging her toes, she sorts the warm sand as if sifting for gold.

Everyone kept saying it wasn't the heat that was so bad, it was the humidity. The festival producers didn't mind; having forecast rain, they were counting their blessings. You had to expect hot days in mid-June. As for Kate, she minded both heat and humidity, but having come alone, she had no one to complain to. At least it was sunny, she told herself, remembering a previous year when this same music festival had gotten rained out, or rather rained on, for they'd gone ahead with it anyway. A sodden mess, that. Heat and humidity, Kate thought, are better than mud.

What year was that, the mud? Kate can't recall. She'd attended this event for many (mostly sunny, mostly nondisabled) years, though she'd missed a couple. Her memories of dragging herself around the huge festival site on forearm crutches three years ago, collapsing in pain and exhaustion at each stage, deciding to forego certain performances because she knew she hadn't the strength to make it to the stages where they were scheduled—these memories were potent enough to have kept her away for the next two years.

Taking the matter finally in hand, Kate had decided that *this* year would be different; this year not only would she attend but she'd *have fun*, dammit. Not because of her wheelchair, for she knew she didn't have the arm strength to wheel herself around that giant grassy field, and all the friends she might have enlisted to help push the chair were otherwise engaged that day. Nope: no wheelchair and no crutches. Clever, resourceful Kate had rented an electric golf cart for the occasion.

It was late afternoon. She was hovering at the head of a dirt road that led down to the festival's most remote stage, eager to

267

see a performance by one of her favorite musicians. Preening herself on her ingenuity, she prepared to launch her cart down the steep hill when a figure approached in a wheelchair, battery-powered, trailing a second person, nondisabled. Both women regarded her sourly. If wheelchairs could be said to totter, this one did, seeming barely to make it to where Kate sat coolly astride her golf cart, surveying the scene. She was about to sail down the hill when the two planted themselves in front of her.

Kate found herself staring at the largest wheelchair she'd ever seen. It had a way of bearing down like a tank, so that even though *she* was the one on top of the hill and therefore plainly in command, she felt somehow disarmed. Its occupant was similarly large and imposing, and breathed with a respirator. The fat tube protruding from her mouth was disconcerting, though Kate could not have said why.

The other woman lingered behind the first, subordinate, respectful. It was the Respirator Woman who spoke. "You people," she accused, her voice pointing a finger, nothing moving but her lips, the animation of her face, "should stop using that site for a staging area. We've been after you for years to pick another site. Someplace *flat*."

Kate gasped. It was not the first time that day she'd been mistaken for festival staff, many of whom rode around on golf carts just like hers. Nor was it so unusual to be mistaken for a nondisabled person; able-bodied people—"ABs," as Kate would later learn to call them—had done that throughout her crutch years, whenever she sat down in a regular chair and stowed her sticks out of sight. But to be misidentified by another disabled person was a different matter. Kate shifted, squirming, in her seat.

Underneath the squirm, though, a sly voyeur thrilled inwardly, for when others mistake us for people we are not, don't they sometimes reveal themselves to us in ways they would not dream of otherwise? Knowing she should disabuse the woman of her error, Kate was silent. She could not speak. And something in the words sent an unexpected tremor through her heart.

"Why, what happens when you go down there?" she murmured finally. "I should think it would be easy for you . . . Isn't that electric?"

Aghast at her own temerity, she suddenly understood the tremor. It came to her as she heard herself say "you." Something in the sound of the word—appropriating it as she had, for purposes of her disguise—brought to Kate the other woman's pronoun, "we." Exotic, glorious two letters, in unfamiliar context.

"Sure it's electric. But what about all the people in manual chairs? And anyhow, batteries don't last forever. I just ran out of juice coming back up that mountain."

She glared. She was grand. Later, driving back from the festival, golf cart bouncing behind her on its trailer rig, Kate would think about that grandeur, turning it over and over, clutching it like a charm against the long drive. At the moment, though, she could only stammer, horrified, "But what . . . will you *do* now? Are you stuck here?"

The woman looked at her curiously.

"How will you get home?" Kate shrilled, oblivious. "Won't they recharge you, or something?"

"That's for *you* to tell *me*," she said shortly, staring.

Clearly, an explanation was in order. "I'm not staff." Kate picked up her forearm crutches—stowed on the floor of the cart, out of sight—and waved them in the air. "I rented this cart to get around the festival."

A quick smile darted across the woman's face, her eyes flickering something Kate could not read.

"What will you *do*?" Kate persisted.

"Get a charge." She said it the way a smoker speaks of getting a light. "Just enough to get me to my van in the parking lot."

"But don't you want to see more of the festival? Could you be lifted onto my cart? Could I drive you around for a while?" Then she noticed the head support built onto the woman's chair to keep her neck in place, and looked again at the respirator tube perched in front of her face. *Kate, you are an ignorant fool—*

The woman was gracious. "No, it wouldn't work," she said gently, declining to explain the obvious. "I'm pretty much done with this festival anyway. It's too damn hard." She smiled again, a kind of twinkle creasing her eyes. What a face. Surrounded by a mop of dark curls, it had an amplitude, that twinkle seeming perpetually to hover behind her facial muscles.

"*That* was a clever idea," she said and then, as Kate was not yet accustomed to her habit of pointing with her eyes, added, "renting the cart."

Kate brushed her comment aside. She did not feel clever at the moment. On the contrary, she felt as if she'd been asleep for three years and was only just now noticing the webs in her eyes. "Clever ideas *work*," she retorted, and she found herself telling the saga of her misadventures with the rented cart. How expensive it had been. How many phone calls she'd made to track down a rental place that had any golf carts left (the festival producers having apparently rented every golf cart within a hundred miles for their staff), only to end up with a dealer in Yonkers, of all places. How, in order to get the cart from Yonkers to the site and back, she'd had to borrow a friend's boat trailer rig. How she'd borrowed another friend's station wagon to tow the rig, her own car being too small and having no trailer hitch. How the unfamiliar car had broken down. How, no garages being open, the day being Sunday, Kate had finally crumpled by the side of the road, swooning in the heat until a kindly passing driver took pity, pulled over and repaired the car himself. How, as soon as she'd started up again, she'd gotten lost in Yonkers. And how, turning into the festival parking lot, glancing at her watch, she knew that nearly every musician she'd set out to see had already performed.

270

Her listener's generous features darkened as she heard this tale. "Not exactly a clever idea," Kate concluded, whereupon the woman burst out, righteously indignant,

"You shouldn't have to go through all that! No one should! They have no business making it this hard for us!" She paused, then added, "And it certainly makes no sense for you to blame yourself!"

Kate stared, dumfounded. What a novel idea. She was blaming herself. Suddenly she tripped over the pronoun, "us," and just as suddenly it came to her that this time *she was included.*

What happened next Kate would later—for weeks, months afterward—liken to a series of small explosions occurring separately and simultaneously in both her brain cells and heart, explosions that suddenly ignited one with another, roaring finally through her like a prairie fire, permanently altering the landscape. Her first thought was that she had not planned to talk to anyone about the day's disasters. The moment she'd arrived at the festival, she'd buried the nightmare away in a corner, a place to which she'd fled so often over the past three years that by now it was littered with an accretion of hurts and private battles. All the bloodied fingers were stuffed in that corner, crushed by doors that had closed too quickly for her to get through; all the bruises on her forearms where poorly designed crutch hinges had caught her flesh; all the supermarket and shopping mall struggles, before she'd switched to a chair; the three-month search for a pair of good, sturdy shoes that would support her legs without looking like hell, and a friend's casual remark that they were "the ugliest, most orthopedic-looking" shoes he'd ever seen.

And stairs, millions of stairs, towering staircases, stairs that seemed to sprout, fungal, just in front of her wherever she went. Stairs to be climbed on crutches, one at a time. Stairs to be carried up, like a package. Stairs to hurtle down, head first. Stairs to bleed on: brown oak, red blood.

271

Carl's words were there, neatly folded and put away, perfectly intact. *Burden. Pain. Vegetable.* His tone of voice. And the sound she made hitting the stairs, a nauseating thud.

Carl himself was there, Carl breaking and entering, not even bothering to hold her down. Not needing to.

The parking garage was there too, floating eerily behind all the rest: fluorescent-lit elevator on a ten-inch platform, its power switched off by one turn of a key. Curling gray cement ribbon of ramp.

Three years' daily living, packed into a storage space so small that by the time the Respirator Woman made her entrance with her simple pronoun that reached out and cradled Kate in its arms, there was no room left to cram even one more artifact, and all those stuffed-away demons started tumbling out, eager for the light of day, the moment the door cracked open.

And then it came to Kate why that strident note of panic crept into her voice when the woman said she'd run out of juice. Kate suddenly envisioned her sitting in her wheelchair, alone on a darkened festival field, unable to move either the chair or herself. Unable to go home. And the crowded ghosts, clamoring out of their hiding place into the unaccustomed daylight, swept in to take the place of this image, so that Kate found herself seeing not the Respirator Woman, abandoned in her wheelchair, but herself, Kate, alone in the parking garage, unable to go home.

They were interchangeable—or almost. The difference was, Kate had hidden her demons away, believing they were a private matter, vaguely ashamed that ordinary living had become so difficult. The Respirator Woman, on the other hand, had not; her ghosts had been transmuted, through her own gift of vision, into the public domain, where they acquired the properties of a common historic legacy with a name: *discrimination.* To which the only appropriate response was a just, pure anger, coupled with the will to change that which, as anyone could plainly

272

see, was the cause of her pain, far more than having a body that "didn't work."

Kate, flattened by sun, limply held in place on warm sand, stretches and recalls, out of nowhere, Peter's stump sores, those solitary bedridden months in his apartment after the Agency turned down his request for legs. For the first time it enters her mind to wonder why neither Ellen nor Peter, each having survived a childhood chamber of horrors, each carrying the scars, has apparently ever sought out other survivors, peers who could have offered sustenance, comfort, mutual support. Could have brought clarity, by naming the pain, the anger, the moving-beyond-anger. Could have brought *motion*, the possibility of change.

The Respirator Woman's name was Sheba. She was active, she said, in the "disability rights movement." Kate bombarded her with questions: Did she belong to a particular group? Who were its members, where did they live, when and where did they meet? Were they all in wheelchairs, or did some have other disabilities? What kinds of issues did they work on? What were their tactics? Had they gained any ground, or was their movement still in its infancy? Would they characterize themselves as reformist in approach or did they, like Kate, perceive a need to overhaul the system as a whole? Had they all been born to disability or had some, like Kate, come to it lately? Did they work with any other civil rights movements?

Sheba responded patiently, pleased and amused by Kate's zeal. Her answers, and the meetings Kate began to attend and then to lead, the hearings at which she's lately testified, the press conferences she's planning with Sheba, the civil disobedience she helps to organize, the life she's carved out for herself within this movement she claims as her own—these things belong, she knows—Peter's advice notwithstanding—in her next journal. (Page one.)

For now, lying in the sun, watching two dark-eyed Greek

273

kids chase each other down the beach, Kate ponders Sheba, the startling pathways of her mind. It seems entirely right and appropriate to have devoured, ravenous, what she heard that day from gentle, feisty Sheba's lips. Any prisoner who's lived in solitary on bread and water for three years would have done the same. It was a heady draught, the sweetest wine she'd ever drunk.

She knew she had come home.

Better swim now. It's getting late, she's due home in half an hour.

Getting into the water is usually easy, except at low tide. Crutching her way out to knee-level, Kate turns and hurls the crutches back up onto dry land. By now, crusted over with minerals and rust, they look like detritus chipped from a sunken ship.

At low tide it's trickier; her arms aren't strong enough to throw the sticks that far, once she's walked out to a swimmable depth. This means she has to scramble on her hands and belly out to deeper water, legs dragging behind, having first disposed of the crutches at the limit of her hurling distance.

For a long while this indignity was also her only way *out* of the water after swimming, until she began to ask for strangers' help. Odd: they've never volunteered it, in all her months of daily swimming. They simply stare, nonplussed, at her scrabbling crawl to shore, as if witnessing a prehistoric sea beast's first journey onto dry land.

Ellen, who accompanied Kate only once, refuses to go back (which is fine with Kate), having sat on the beach and watched her friend swim straight out toward the horizon, her head a receding speck on the glittery waves. For a few weeks she harangued Kate about the undertow, sharks, jellyfish, and lack of lifeguards (private beach). Eventually she gave up all attempts at domestication.

It was Kate's swimming story that defeated Ellen, a little set piece that quickly acquired the cachet of legend. Kate delivered it with giddy pride, honing the accent, timing, pause before denouement:

She was swimming out toward open sea one day when she came upon a small fishing boat. In it sat a lone Greek who stared down, open-mouthed. He turned and peered in all directions, looking for her boat, but his was the only one in sight. At last recovering speech, careful not to offend; he ventured, polite, his voice thickly Greek: "Are you . . . drowning?"

Kate smiled up at him. "No. I'm swimming," she said.

WHAT THE FISH FEELS

It's different, out there.
Water lifts, bounces me
like a kite. Head empties, fills
with water   fishy
slap slap
water in my armpits
water surrounding each toe
water under the roots
of my teeth. Gone the stares
the niggling pull of gravity
I can do anything
I will swim forever, holding
the water between my strong thighs
water slides past my belly
anxious muscles
lap at it like dogs
This is what the fish feels
this rippling arc
this ecstasy
the slippery sun on my back
water
water
I can do anything

Quality paperback fiction titles from St. Martin's Press

B-Four by Sam Hodges
The adventures of a young Southern newspaperman. "What a
funny book, what a spirit lifter.... A simple, unalloyed delight."
—*The Atlanta Journal-Constitution*
$10.95, ISBN 0-312-09246-6

The Body's Memory by Jean Stewart
A woman's journey through disability to triumph. "Suffused
with grace, exuberance, and imaginative power."
—*San Francisco Chronicle*
$10.95, ISBN 0-312-09253-9

Brighten the Corner Where You Are by Fred Chappell
A magical day in the life of an Appalachian schoolteacher.
"A wonderful tale, one full of wild humor and humanity."
—*Los Angeles Times*
$8.95, ISBN 0-312-05057-7

The Fred Chappell Reader by Fred Chappell
Fiction and poetry by one of the South's—and the country's—
best writers. "A fine celebration of an immensely gifted, exuber-
ant, versatile writer." —William Styron
$13.95, ISBN 0-312-05092-5

More Shapes Than One by Fred Chappell
Thirteen unusual tales: "As circular as Borges, as richly symbolic
as Kafka, and as zany as Woody Allen." —*Kirkus Reviews*
$8.95, ISBN 0-312-08265-7

The Run of the Country by Shane Connaughton
An acclaimed first novel of Ireland, by the author of the screen-
play for *My Left Foot*. "The language is beautifully rich."
—*The Washington Post Book World*
$10.95, ISBN 0-312-08883-3

All of these titles are available through booksellers. If you cannot
locate a given book at your local bookstore, you can order it by
calling St. Martin's Press, 1-800-288-2131. Have a credit card
ready.